Who is Francesca Oliver?

Joyce Myerson

AOS Publishing, 2025
Copyright © 2025 Joyce Myerson

ISBN: 978-1-998662-80-7

Cover Design: Meredith Lindsay

Visit AOS Publishing's website:
www.aospublishing.com

This book is dedicated to my own psychotherapist, who is nothing like the analyst/protagonist in this novel, but who, in her own inimitable way, made the writing of it possible.

Chapter One

<u>In Munich</u>

<u>Francesca in the Office I</u>

"That couch is only a metaphor for being vulnerable." Francesca turned and pointed her arm behind her at the couch in question. "I wouldn't lie down on it at the beginning, and I probably never will." Francesca took a deep breath. "It probably does not seem that logical to you. I know you are not a man. And I know you would never hurt me...beat me—"

"—Your father beat you? When your mother was home?"

"Not when my mother was home. She often worked the night shift in the hospital, and sometimes my *nonna* would call and say that my *nonno* was impossibly miserable, and my mother would leave to spend the night there doing whatever she could. I used to beg her to take me with her, but she wouldn't hear of it. She just told me to go to bed."

"You never told me that your father hit you."

"I don't deliberately hide things from you." The tears began to well up in Francesca's eyes. "I tell you so much sometimes...I'm sorry. I think everything will come out in the end. I do tell you the most embarrassing things," she wailed, "even how I feel about *you*. It's not easy to speak of everything."

"I am not admonishing you, Francesca. I understand."

"And...and despite the fact that I don't lie down, I am completely vulnerable to you. I say things not knowing how you will respond or...or react, but they come out anyway. I entrust myself to you. I enfold myself into this room. I...I...I surrender to you. I abandon myself to you." By now the tears were copiously falling down her face.

Dr. Paul moved slightly forward in her chair. "Francesca, look at me."

Her patient raised her head.

Dr. Paul spoke slowly, enunciating her words carefully: "I fully believe that it is not necessary for you to lie on the couch. You do give yourself up to me. You enfold yourself, as you say, into this room, and lay yourself open to me. I believe that. And the couch *is* a metaphor. And you do not need it." Dr. Paul moved her body back and straightened her spine. She smiled. Francesca returned the smile.

Chapter Two

"Wow! She certainly is an attractive woman!"

"Were you undressing her?"

"Yes, but that is not what I meant. She reminds me of you. And I think that she could actually be your spiritual mother."

"Explain."

"Well, remember when we were in Montreal?"

"How could I forget?"

Birgitte started the car and began to ease it out of the parking spot. As soon as they were on the road, she began to explain.

"So, I remember the kindness emanating from your eyes—the kindness, the gentleness, the concern. And that is why those high school students loved you. There is absolutely no cruelty in you."

"You're never cruel either."

"But I have hurt you, Francesca. And I hope I never do so again. I am not like you. But your psychoanalyst, she has that kind vibe, too. When she came out of her office and only the receptionist and I were in her waiting room, she asked me where you were, and I told her that on the way, we were forced to stop the car because you had to vomit. I told her you were in the bathroom, probably brushing your teeth. When you came out and walked towards us, pale as pale could be, that kindness and concern started pouring from her eyes. You were probably looking down. And it was at that moment that I sensed she was your spiritual mother."

"You know that what you are saying is really neither here nor there. Just because I would like her to be my mother... She is kind and gentle, yes, but so are many others. It doesn't make them my spiritual mothers."

"But she plays a role in your life akin to that of a mother."

"She's not supposed to."

"But we have already established that your analyst, unlike mine, is not orthodox. And as you have so clearly explained, mine has to be, because if we both emoted in her room, it would explode."

Francesca chuckled. "I can just see it."

"But you emote, too, Ollie."

"I do, but at the same time, I am always, always trying—no, struggling—to find the exact words for what I am feeling. That is probably the most important thing that I do in that room. You, on the other hand, express so much without words. That is why you are the greatest conductor. You emote what you want from the musicians. It's written on your face, in your body. How do you think Magda and I, when we play with you, know exactly how to play the music, how we are always in sync with you? We listen to your violin, and we know what to do."

"Do you always do what I want?"

"Inevitably. And I am a better musician for it. Magda as well."

Birgitte sighed. "You've never told me that before."

"I thought you knew. You're the genius, Ghita."

Birgitte said nothing. She was deep in thought. They were almost home. When they arrived at their short driveway, she pushed the button that made the garage door open.

"We're going inside?" Francesca asked.

"Yes. I don't want anyone to see what I am going to do to you next."

Chapter Three

<u>Francesca in the Office II</u>

"Well, look who's at my door," Dr. Paul said as she exited the elevator. She was wearing running clothes, a green T-shirt that said UBC, and a pair of black leggings. Francesca was startled. Dr. Paul's light brown hair was tied back in a ponytail and there was a sheen of moisture on her face. Her slimness and muscularity were visible beneath her tight-fitting running gear. She looked healthy and fit.

"I didn't think I was late, but I was running a bit more slowly than usual."

"I may be five minutes early."

They entered the reception area and Marisa, the receptionist, gave them a smile.

"Am I late, Marisa?" asked Dr. Paul.

"I don't think so. Francesca is five minutes early."

Dr. Paul moved quickly towards her office. "Give me a few minutes to take a shower and change."

"It's okay if you want to hold the session in your running outfit," responded Francesca.

"Not going to happen." Dr. Paul shut her office door behind her.

"Does she always run to work, Marisa?" asked Francesca.

"About three times a week she comes in around seven-thirty, goes for a run, and always comes back before her nine o'clock appointment. But this isn't your usual time, so you wouldn't know that. Actually, no one knows, since she is always back before her patient arrives. Don't worry. She'll see you on time and be in good form."

"I'm not worried. I'm impressed."

"Well, you just ran the Munich marathon, and *I'm* impressed," responded Marisa.

"It's not that meaningful. I like running, and where I run is beautiful, but marathons I could live without."

Marisa laughed. "Do you want to take care of this month's bill while I have you here, Francesca?" asked Marisa.

"Sure." Francesca handed her a card, waited, took it back along with a receipt, and sat down. Within around five minutes, Dr. Paul's door opened, and she beckoned to Francesca.

As Francesca sat down, she looked up at her therapist with a rapt expression on her face. Her very astute doctor picked up on it immediately.

"So, what are you trying to tell me, Francesca?"

"I...I..." Francesca hesitated. "I'm not really trying to tell you anything."

"M-m-m, I think that look means something."

Francesca seemed uncomfortable. "Do I have to tell you? It's...it's embarrassing."

Dr. Paul looked straight at her without responding.

Francesca sighed. "Okay. I'll tell you. You...you...look so beautiful right now." Francesca dropped her head down and held her hands together on her lap.

"Is that important to you?" her therapist asked.

Francesca raised her head a little, stunned. "What? Is it important to me that my therapist is...is...beautiful? Am I so...so...superficial as to think that your appearance is more important than your beautiful mind? Is that what you're asking me?"

"Well, what if I were—"

"—Unfit, sloppy, unkempt? Would I be unable to talk to you? How should I know?" Francesca opened her arms wide in front of her. "I'm sorry. I'm sorry." She shook her head. "That came out all wrong. I feel so..."

"Did my question hurt you, Francesca?"

"I don't know. Maybe. I have only known you, and I don't want to know anyone else, either. I have never talked to another analyst before. I can't make any kind of comparison. But I do like that you're beautiful. Beauty is important to me. Okay, call me superficial. It pleases me to look at you."

"I'm going to ask you another question now, Francesca. Okay?"

Francesca nodded. "Is it going to hurt?"

"I don't think so."

Francesca took a deep breath.

"Okay. Let's say you're at home or in your office at work and your internet stops working. You call a technician from your internet provider and tell him the problem. He checks everything on his end and then asks you to do certain things, which you do. And the procedure succeeds. You are relieved. What would you say to him?"

"Uh...I would tell him that he did great—no, that he *was* great—and that I appreciated his efforts. Then I would thank him. What are you getting at?"

"Francesca, do you really believe that you are a superficial person because you appreciate beauty, or something well done?"

"What are you saying?"

"Francesca, you are one of the most ingenious and intelligent humans that I know. What am I saying?"

"You're saying that I am not superficial? That actually my appreciation of beauty or a job well done is profound?"

"Francesca, it *is* profound to love beauty, to search for it—no, just to see it wherever it may be, to notice it, and to say it. You see it. You hear it. It is what you do, who you are. It doesn't matter if you are a musician one day, an art historian the next. And you don't have to choose. You can be both—you are both—because for you what is important is the recognition of beauty. And now I have said too much." Dr. Paul chuckled as Francesca looked at her, open-mouthed. "Listen, you have to understand that anything you utter in this office will have consequences."

Chapter Four

<u>Francesca in the Office III</u>

"Hello.... Francesca?"

"No, Dr. Paul. It's Birgitte. I'm sorry for disturbing you. I didn't know what else to do."

"Did something happen to Francesca?"

"Well, yes. And...and...I'm not the one who can help her now."

"What happened?"

"We were practicing together, and her phone rang. It was her father. She picked it up and put it on speaker. I told her to record it."

"Good."

"He just laid into her, calling her an ungrateful bitch after all he'd done for her."

"Why?"

"Because she never told him about her concert in Paris."

"I see."

"It was awful. He's a monster. He's evil. But she held her own. She gave him an answer I will never forget. He ended the conversation, and she went from a spectacular adult to a whimpering child in seconds. Then she jumped up and said she had to go upstairs to take a shower. I don't know what to do."

"Birgitte, go upstairs, tell her to get out of the shower immediately."

"But, but what if...she doesn't—"

"—You tell her in no uncertain terms that she is *not* dirty, and she has an appointment with me. It's five-thirty now. Can you be here by six-fifteen? I will have to give my present patient a few extra minutes."

"Yes, I will do my best."

"No, you will be here at six-fifteen. I will tell the receptionist to wait for you. Do you understand?"

"Perfectly."

"Bring the recording. I want to hear it. I have to go now. Good-bye."

"Thank you. Bye."

Dr. Paul exited her private room off her office. She immediately went out of her office to speak to her receptionist and then returned to her chair beside the couch, upon which her patient was lying. "It *was* an emergency, as I said, Adam, but I have taken care of it." She sat down. "Completely. You have my undivided attention. I am here. Okay? Are you prepared to stay a bit later today?"

"Yes, of course. Actually...it was kind of nice to have a bit of a break from you."

"Oh, really? Am I that overbearing?"

"Well, not exactly. But I do feel pressure sometimes in your silence. However, I was thinking of something as you were taking care of your emergency."

"Oh, good. Tell me."

*** * * * * * ***

When Adam left, the first thing Astrid did was call Emma to tell her what was happening. After Birgitte had told her that Francesca was washing up, because on the way she had vomited, she waited for Francesca to emerge from the bathroom. When she did, Francesca looked wan and pale. Astrid was practically moved to tears. Francesca made her way towards her. Side-by-side they both turned and headed towards her office. She opened the door wider, and Francesca walked into the embrace of the room. She couldn't very well do the embracing herself.

As they sat down, Dr. Paul asked, "Did you bring your phone?"

Francesca nodded.

"Can I hear the conversation?"

"Yes."

"Did you listen to it before coming here?"

Francesca shook her head.

As the man's voice bellowed out of the tiny contraption, Astrid found herself nodding in agreement with Birgitte. He *was* a monster, pure evil. Then, finally, Francesca's voice rang out, clear and bell-like.

"You sound, Dad, just like a regular father berating his daughter for being an ungrateful bitch. But you forget that you are not a regular father. A regular father does not fuck his daughter on her fourteenth birthday. A regular father doesn't tell his daughter that she gives head better than her mother and then proceed to teach her a new trick. A regular father does not steal his daughter's childhood out from under her. And no matter how much money you spent on my education...no amount of money is ever going to be equal to what you took from me."

The line went dead. Obviously, this was when Francesca's father had ended the conversation. Francesca's elbows were on her knees, and her head was in her hands. Her body was heaving. Astrid felt like doing the same thing. *His daughter gave head better than her mother! He had actually said that. Francesca had never told her.*

When her patient lifted up her tear-stained face, Astrid handed her the box of tissues from her desk. Francesca took several and started wiping her face and nose. She was finding it hard to breathe.

"Take deep breaths, Francesca. Slow your breathing down." She would have liked to move her chair closer to her patient but thought better of it. A little distance between them, physically and metaphorically, was necessary.

Finally, Francesca spoke. It was an apology. "I never told you that before. I know. About my apparent prowess at oral sex. I know. I know. I'm sorry."

Astrid had the terribly disgusting thought that her "apparent prowess" would be something her present partner might appreciate. She groaned aloud. *What is wrong with me?*

"Remember when I told you about what he said about my breasts, that they were like two small, round blobs of flesh stuck on my chest?"

Astrid nodded but said nothing.

"Well, I was going to tell you then, but somehow the entire session evolved into a discussion about my self-image, my body image...and it never happened."

Astrid sighed audibly and placed her hands over her eyes and face. "I remember it well, Francesca." She removed her hands and placed them very consciously on the armrests of her chair. *I can't reveal so much of my feelings now. Hang on, Astrid. Be her psychoanalyst.*

"The last time my father called me and was angry about me not telling him of my various concerts I told my mother, and she phoned him and told him never to call me again. I can't tell her about this conversation, obviously."

Astrid shook her head. "That would be horrible. Not that you have to mention that comment about oral sex. My God, what a frightful thing to say to a child. How old were you?"

"About ten maybe. He didn't penetrate me until I was fourteen. He was saving that for when I was older. But it all stopped when I was sixteen and I brought Colin, my boyfriend, home. I was at boarding school by then. Colin was a perfect foil. I was sleeping with him already and before we left to go back to Ontario, I threatened my father. I said that if he ever came into my room again, I would tell my mother. He never did. But it may also have been because he wasn't so interested in me anymore. I was too old for him by then. I stayed with Colin practically all the way through university in Toronto. My mother thought that we would eventually get married. Of course, I didn't love him, but he was good—a good boy, and then a good man." Francesca looked thoughtful. Astrid remained silent.

"I think. I really think that something is wrong with my father."

"You *think* that something is wrong with your father?"

"I don't mean because of what he did to me as a child. I mean now. Now that he is berating me like a regular guy. It's as if...as if he has forgotten or has buried that past. He's not pretending. He really thinks I owe him something, that I have to tell him about my concert career so that he can reap the rewards of what he gave me in financial terms. Is that possible?"

Astrid nodded. "Yes, it's very possible, even likely."

"Do you know what he said when my mother first confronted him about what he did to me? This was just two years ago, when she came to Munich for the first time and I told her everything, or almost everything."

"What did he say?"

"He said that I was lying. Just trying to get attention."

"How did your mother respond?"

"She said that at thirty I was not trying to get attention."

"Was he surprised that it took so long to come out?"

"I think so. It's hard to believe."

"What exactly is hard to believe?"

"Who could possibly tell a story like that for attention? Why would anyone want to be like me? Have a past like that? Who could want to be me?" Francesca wailed. The tears were falling again. "And now...and now...the shower is never going to help me anymore."

"Did it ever really help?"

"Well, what I mean is, Birgitte is never going to let me wallow in self-pity under the shower. As she said, I am not dirty."

"I told her to say that, Francesca."

"But she believes it even if I feel contaminated." The tears kept falling. "The first time I came to see you..."

"Yes?"

"And I told you as much as I could get out about my father..." Francesca was finding it hard to go on.

"Yes?"

Francesca took a deep breath. "Well, when I got home, I ran upstairs to take a shower. I curled up into a ball and allowed the water to fall on me. When Ghita got home and I wasn't downstairs playing the piano, she took off her shoes at the door, as she usually does, and ran upstairs. She knew that I had had my first session with you." Francesca stopped abruptly and put her face in her hands.

"Go on, Francesca. Tell me."

Francesca raised her head. "She heard the shower going, and when she saw me like that, she walked into the shower immediately."

"In her clothes?"

"Yes, in her clothes, and wrapped herself around me until I stopped crying. Then she shut off the shower, pulled me out, removed her own clothes, took me to the bedroom, and continued to hold me on the bed. She just waited until I was ready to speak."

Astrid sighed and leaned back in her chair. "Are you afraid that she will never hold you like that again?"

"No. She told me that whenever I wanted her to make me feel whole again, I could call her, and she would come running. She would take off her clothes, and skin-to-skin, she would wrap her body around mine—not just her arms, her legs, too. She does that as often as I need her to...when I feel as if I am disintegrating. But I know the shower thing is over. She will never let me feel that I am contaminated in some way."

"Because you're not dirty."

Francesca nodded. "Right."

"And today she called *me* because she absolutely knew that her holding you in any way wasn't going to work."

"It's always worked."

"But not after that conversation with your father. She felt that she did not have the tools to help you."

"Dr. Paul?"

"Yes."

"I am so glad she called you."

"It took a lot of courage."

"Ghita has plenty of that."

"And when she holds you, skin-to-skin as you call it, does anything happen?"

"What do you mean?"

"You know what I mean."

"Oh, God. We're going to have a sex conversation again, aren't we?"

"Does that bother you?"

"Well, I know that you do not judge me for my sexual proclivities."

"My dear Francesca, let us give credit here to your friend, Jordan, and call them your emotional proclivities."

"Okay. Okay—my emotional proclivities. But nonetheless, we are going to talk about sex now."

"Yes, we are."

"You know something?"

"What?"

"Ghita doesn't really believe me, or fully believe me, when I tell her that it is actually her body that I need. Before I fall asleep at night and I look at her body, I thank Jordan for forcing me to call Ghita and tell her that I loved her. And when I wake up in the morning and that precious body is still there beside me, I thank her again."

"Every day?"

"Yes, every day and every night."

"What doesn't your wife understand?"

"She thinks that it is her being that keeps me together, not her physical being. But her physical being is so precious to me. It is essential. You know how people separate technique from music or musicality? You practice your technique, play scales and arpeggios and *études* in the various keys. And then you play music. Musical interpretation for these people, and many teachers—I've had a few—is separate from the technique. They talk about technique as an aspect of learning to play your instrument."

"So, you're saying that technique and music are one and the same?"

"Yes. I would never play anything unmusically. An *étude* is music and should be respected. It *is* possible to play a scale musically."

"And the body and the spirit, for want of a better word—"

"—Are inextricably linked. Ghita's body keeps me from disintegrating. That's why it has to be skin-to-skin. I have to feel her body touching my skin, enveloping my body. I have to sense her through my pores. Do you understand?"

"I do."

Francesca breathed a sigh of relief.

"And after she holds you like that for a certain amount of time, does it stimulate you sexually as well?"

"Well, I feel that I want to touch every part of her with my hands, my fingertips, and...and...my mouth."

"Does that bother her that you aren't acknowledging her 'spirit'?"

"No, I don't think so. She has never rejected my...my advances."

"Is it always you who initiates after she holds you like that?"

"No. Sometimes she expresses her need for me before I express my need for her."

"And that's alright?"

"You bet it is."

"And even after some horrible incident, for example, like the one with that French conductor who came on to you, it is still possible to...to...enjoy a sexual moment, or several moments, with Birgitte."

"It is. I have no trouble responding to her touch."

"And you always have an orgasm?"

"Always. Always. I can practically come when she just starts speaking Danish to me—"

"—Your language of love...." Astrid paused for a moment and then continued.

"And when you were a child living at home, how did you emotionally deal the next day after what your father did to you the night before?"

"I went to school and thought exclusively about coming home and playing the piano in the afternoon—all afternoon and into the night. Except for the time that I had to prepare the dinner."

"Right. You did all the cooking from the age of thirteen."

"My *nonna* taught me how to cook. It wasn't hard. My father, or both my parents, bought lots and lots of food—for the week—and I cooked. But only if I knew my mother was coming home. If she wasn't, I didn't cook for my father. I couldn't have cared less about what *he* ate. And when I was playing the piano, he left me undisturbed. He never touched me when I was at the piano. Playing the piano saved me."

"And now?"

"Of course—and Birgitte, her love. And you, I might add."

"But if you played the piano all afternoon and until, I don't know, midnight, what about the neighbours? Were there any complaints?"

"No, because we lived in a big brick house in an area called Westmount in Montreal—a very wealthy neighbourhood. My father was making tons of money. He still is, although he lives in Toronto now. We had a yard in the back, a huge yard with loads of trees. Then there was green space on either side of the house, and it was far from the front curb with a huge lawn in front of the house. There were trees everywhere."

"I know Westmount." Astrid felt extremely uncomfortable admitting that. *What would Em say? Would she be furious?*

"What? You've been to Montreal? To Westmount?"

Astrid swallowed and nodded.

"How...how is that possible?"

"Well, after high school here in Munich, I went with several friends to hike on Vancouver Island. When I realized how much I liked Canada, I called my parents and said that I wanted to enroll at the University of British Columbia in Vancouver. And I did. I got my B.A. in psychology there."

"But...but how did you get to Westmount?"

"Well, I didn't always come back here to Munich during holidays. I met a Canadian at UBC—she was from Westmount—and I often went with her to visit her family in Westmount." *Not to mention the fact that she was my first lover.*

"My God, all this time and I never knew of your connection to Canada?"

"Not exactly something you need to know." *And something I might get into deep trouble for when I get home to my beloved wife.*

"Why are you telling me, then?" Francesca looked at her therapist, and then it was as if a light went on in her head. "Oh, I get it. I'm feeling normal now, not like I did when I came in here. I really am feeling normal because we just had a very normal conversation, although I can also tell that you really didn't enjoy telling me those things. You did it for *my* benefit."

Astrid slowly exhaled. "When I finished my undergraduate degree, I applied to do a Master's degree in Seattle, and spent two years there, but knew that I wanted to return to Canada. I did my PhD at the University of Victoria."

"Wow! Really?"

"Really. And then when I knew that I wanted to be a psychoanalyst, I went to London—"

"—To the Tavistock Institute."

"How did you know that?"

"I didn't know. That's a place where people study to become psychoanalysts, as well as the British Psychoanalytic Institute."

"I studied in both those places." *And I met my wife, who is going to kill me, there.*

"I am thinking that there are several psychoanalysts of old, like Melanie Klein, for instance, who would not approve in the least of these revelations. She would have had you going back into psychoanalysis immediately."

They both laughed.

"I'm sure she would have," said Astrid. *Not to mention my wife.*

"But you did it for me. Does that count? That you were thinking of me and what I needed?"

"Francesca, you had a horrible experience today, but you survived it."

"And everything you did helped, including telling me of your studies in Canada. And I do feel normal now. It worked."

There was silence between them for a minute. Then Astrid stood up.

"Thank you, Dr. Paul, for seeing me today."

"There is someone in my waiting room out there whom you really need to thank."

Francesca nodded. "I am so lucky to have both of you."

Chapter Five

<u>Astrid and Emma on the Phone</u>

After Francesca and Birgitte left, Astrid locked the front door and went into her office. She decided to lay down on her own couch and call her wife.

"Hello Asti. Did you handle the emergency?"

"I did...Em?"

"What, my love?"

"It was painful. I barely kept it together. I had to talk to myself in your voice."

"Good."

"But I did do something in the end, something which you may not approve of."

"You didn't touch her or stroke her arm or anything?"

"No. No. I would never do *that*. I'll tell you when I get home. I just wanted to talk about Francesca and Birgitte as a couple. They are beautiful."

"Is Birgitte a Scandinavian beauty?"

"Individual beauty aside, I am just thinking about the way they are together."

"Okay. Go ahead."

"When Francesca was leaving my office, I opened the door, and her wife stood up and gave her the most exquisite smile of total acceptance and love. I was mesmerized. I got my keys because Marisa had locked the outside door. I unlocked the door and the two of them went towards the elevator. Birgitte turned around, put her hand on her heart, and mouthed a thank you to me. I was so moved by her gesture. As I was closing the door, I saw Birgitte put her arm around Francesca and hold her shoulder. Francesca turned her head towards her, and they looked into each other's eyes. And then their heads moved together, and their lips just touched."

"Nothing sexual."

"They are not very affectionate in public, so Francesca has told me. She is not excited about people, especially her students, finding out about her. I mean, they have friends that know, but few. I think it's mostly Francesca who wishes to be careful."

"You are not that different."

"But she, like you, is a teacher, not a therapist."

"Right. Right. There is a difference. So, you fell in love with them as a couple?"

"No, not exactly. But I felt like crying. And here I am lying on my couch talking to you."

"You are so emotional, my love. Maybe you shouldn't be a psychoanalyst."

"Shut up, Em. What happened to me being the best psychoanalyst you know?"

"You are. But it is very hard for you to keep your emotions in check."

"That's true. Especially now."

"What do you mean?"

"Em, we haven't made love in a week. I go to bed and you're working on your book. You don't even come into the bedroom to kiss me goodnight. I wake up in the morning and you've already gone to work to write some more. I don't even get a morning kiss. I miss you."

"I've been an idiot. Come home now!"

"Can I make mad, passionate love to you?"

"Every day from now on."

Chapter Six

<u>Professor Green (Emma) and Francesca</u>

"Professor Green, do you know me? Or at least do you remember me and our correspondence from about five or six years ago?"

Francesca had headed over to the head of the psychology department as soon as she entered the hall where the professors from the various faculties were meeting each other, some for the very first time. She had spotted Bradley almost immediately, but had decided that she wasn't here to converse with someone she knew quite well.

The illustrious professor was taken aback and did not at first answer. She stared penetratingly at Francesca with her large brown eyes. She scratched her dark short hair and finally dropped her arm down the side of her angular body. She gave an impression of considerable strength.

"I guess that's a 'no'. Hard to remember some Italian student from Siena wanting to read one of your papers in the original. We—that is, my boyfriend at the time and myself—had the article in Italian translation."

"Oh my God! Yes! Francesca! I remember your first name. But I thought you were a psychology student yourself. You seemed to know so much about the subject matter."

Francesca smiled. "Unfortunately, I did. You see, Massimiliano needed my help with anything English, and his work demanded a lot of my attention. He discussed everything with me. I don't think he could have written his dissertation without me." Francesca sighed. "And I'm not boasting here. I did learn many things—especially from you."

Professor Green looked at her interlocutor intently. "Is that why you left him? Too dependent? You were his unpaid research assistant?"

They laughed at Massimiliano's expense.

"I did read your entire essay, though."

"And you wrote to me of your impressions as well. That's why I never would have thought that you were the same Francesca, seeing as you are an art historian...and a concert pianist, I might add."

"You know that, too?"

"Everyone at this university knows that. And because you could easily up and leave to pursue your music career full-time, you just might be the first faculty member to get tenure at such a young age."

"Are you telling me that I am going to be offered tenure in the near future?"

"I am."

"How do you know?"

"I'm on the committee."

"Ah-ha..." Francesca reflected on what she had just been told.

"Will you accept?"

"Of course."

"And why is that?"

"That's a very long story."

"I can imagine."

"I wanted to tell you that Massimiliano, probably for covert reasons, although to me they were overt, gave me your book as a present, the one about the three analysts and their different views on countertransference."

Professor Green looked surprised. "Did you read it?"

"I did. It was very meaningful for me. I actually have the book here in Munich."

"Don't tell me you are studying it?"

Francesca laughed. "Of course not. I just liked it too much to leave it in Montreal. I tend to tell others to read it, too. Maybe it's also because I never really studied psychology and just got it second-hand from my boyfriend, but my understanding of some things comes directly from you. I've noticed you've written more books since then. I think I will read them."

"My God, Francesca, I don't have students that are as intent on learning from me as you are."

"You have a great mind, Professor Green."

"Well, thank you. And while I have you here, let me pick *your* brain. Have you ever thought of the possibility of psychoanalyzing Renaissance subjects in portraiture?"

"You mean like Bronzino, Sustermans, and their portraits of the Medici, for example?"

"Yeah, like that. Bronzino was so psychologically adept. Do you think it is a valid pursuit?"

"I wrote a paper last year about the pitfalls of such analysis."

"Really?"

"Yeah, really. You see, artists, no matter how astute, do not work within a psychoanalytic framework with guidelines about how to interpret, let's say, expressions and the like. You..." Francesca pointed her finger at Professor Green. "Spend years studying things like that and being aware of your own reactions."

"Countertransference."

"Yes. You know it best of all. But artists pour themselves into these portraits and we can't really separate the artist from the subject. We say that Bronzino was an amazing psychologist, but what we don't know about is *his* countertransference, how much he is reading his own self into his subjects." Francesca stopped and smiled. "However... I do it all the time—privately. I wonder to myself or to someone I am with, standing in front of a painting, if the person I see before me is sad or angry, or feels insignificant, hates her husband. You know."

Professor Green nodded. "Me, too. But I can see your point. There is no way that we can make a serious judgement about the subject's demeanour. And then, of course, we put our own emotions into the painting."

"But that's what I love about some artists. They make us *feel* so much. I am all for intensity in art, in literature, in music. It's what I live for."

"And then we psychoanalysts come along and break everything down, breaking up the intensity."

"Oh, but you are so valuable, nonetheless, at least from my point of view. Do you practice as well as teach?"

"I am a training analyst at one of the institutes here in Munich, but many of my psychoanalysts-in-training come from all over—the U.S. England, Canada..."

"Really? And you work with them remotely?"

"Yes. Sometimes they ask me to be their personal analyst, but I never consent, because their reasons for wanting me come from their knowing me and what I believe. It wouldn't work."

"I understand their motivation, though. It's comforting knowing how your analyst may react to an emotional outpouring...."

Professor Green nodded and smiled benevolently at Francesca. "However, for psychoanalysis to really work, there has to be that unknown, that discomfort, that fear of exposure."

"But why? Why can't the patient have some confidence about the analyst's possible response? Why can't we lessen the fear to some extent?"

"Francesca, if you are presently in analysis, maybe intellectual questions such as these are not the best thing for you. Just live your psychoanalysis. Just be in it however it is happening. How long have you been in analysis?"

"About two years. How could you tell?"

The professor laughed amicably. "It's my job to know. But if you have already been in analysis for two years, then you must obviously trust your analyst."

"I do." Francesca swallowed hard and seemed to be on the verge of self-revelation, but then thought better of it. "You're right. Too much thinking doesn't help. I am in very good hands."

"I am sure you are, Francesca. I am so glad we had this chat. My other books are all in the library, should you wish to read them. I'm actually on the verge of finishing a new one. I see there is a young man who wishes to speak to you now."

Francesca noticed Bradley making his way towards her.

"I will leave you to him."

"Thank you for talking to me, Professor Green."

Chapter Seven

<u>Astrid and Emma</u>

"Asti, I have something difficult to tell you. You are not going to be happy with me."

The two women were sitting at their kitchen table after having finished dinner. Astrid looked worried. "How bad is it?" she asked.

"Pretty bad, but it couldn't be helped. There was nothing I could do but have that conversation with her."

"With whom?"

"With your patient, Francesca. And by the way, I can easily see why you love her."

Astrid put her face in her hands and groaned. "I'm not giving her up, Em. I have so much to do with her yet. Please tell me I can still keep seeing her." Astrid raised her head and pleaded with her partner.

"Okay, it's not that bad, but it had to happen sometime. We teach in the same university, after all."

"Just tell me what happened."

"Well, at this sort of get-together for faculty members, she walked right up to me and asked if I knew her. I almost had a heart attack. I thought she somehow had found out about us, about our twenty-year marriage. But that wasn't the case at all. She then asked if I remembered her. Do you remember about five or six years ago I was contacted by a student from Siena about a paper I had written? That person, a Francesca, needed my original paper in English because she and her boyfriend had only read the Italian translation."

"But you told me that particular Francesca was also a psychology student."

"Well, I thought so, because she was so articulate about the paper. She really understood it, and after I sent her the link for the

English version, she actually wrote back to me to tell me her thoughts about it."

"Yes, I remember you being very impressed." Astrid took a deep breath. "You don't mean to tell me that 'psychology student Francesca' and *my* Francesca are one and the same?"

"She's never studied psychology. She was studying art history and music, as you well know, but that boyfriend of hers needed her so badly that, as she told me, he would never have written his thesis without her."

"It's funny, but I can sort of believe that. Her powers of comprehension are significant."

Emma was nodding her head. "And apparently this Massimiliano gave her my book on countertransference as a gift."

"Did she read it?"

"In fact, the book has been very important for her. I tell you, Asti, she knows more about the subject, or wants to, than most of my students who are already psychotherapists."

"She can't find out about me and you, Em. I need to be more anonymous with her. I want to be her analyst."

Emma stretched her hand over the table and placed it on top of Astrid's. "I know, my love. I know. But how could she possibly ever find out? Not a single one of my colleagues or our friends know that she is a patient of yours. I don't think you have to worry."

"That's why she made that funny comment about Melanie Klein the other day."

"She got that one right. Melanie Klein would certainly have you going into analysis again after what you told her."

"But we did decide that I did the right thing. *She* even understood why I told her about my strong connection to Canada. She needed to feel normal after that horrible conversation with her father, and I told her a very normal thing about me, about where I studied. She was even aware of how loath I must have been to tell her, but that I was only thinking of her and her well-being. I still believe it was okay to reveal those facts about me. And the levity afterwards was necessary. She was laughing about how Melanie Klein would not have been pleased with me. It was good for her. I don't think our relationship has suffered because she now knows that I studied in Vancouver and then in Victoria."

"I agree, my love. I agree. And this little blip could not be helped. I couldn't lie to her. I did remember our correspondence. I had to tell her."

Chapter Eight

<u>Francesca in the office IV</u>

"There's something I've been thinking about—well, not really thinking. It's sort of floating around my head, but I haven't wanted to say it to myself." Francesca swallowed and took a deep breath.

"Do you think you are ready to say it out loud?"

Francesca shook her head, and then said very quietly, "No."

"Why is that?"

"Because you'll never leave it alone. We will have to talk about it. I will have to say how it makes me feel. And it feels terrible."

"So, you *have* already said it to yourself."

"Just recently. Like today. After I gave my last class of the day, which was pretty good, mind you. The students really responded well. They had so much to say about Donatello's *David*, I was surprised. And they all want to go to Florence with me this summer to see it in the flesh, so to speak. And I'm looking forward to taking them. But all of a sudden, out of the blue, this thought hit me, as we were exiting the classroom. I didn't have much chance to think about it because, before coming here, I had to talk to several students in my office. My encounter with the students kept it inside me uncontemplated...unreflected upon...pristine...and without emotion. But as soon as I tell you, all hell is going to break loose, and I am going to fall apart." Francesca looked down at her hands. She was holding them together on her lap.

"Are you holding yourself together now?"

"Barely."

"I can't make you tell me what you don't want to tell me. I won't force anything on you, Francesca. I haven't done that yet. Although you may think that a question I might ask is already a type of pressure. I am sorry if you feel that way. But you seem to always answer my questions even if you tell me that what you say to me can be terribly embarrassing. I have a feeling that this is of a different category. It's not embarrassing. Am I right?"

"The most embarrassing things I tell you have to do with you and with sex. Usually when I talk about music or about my work at the university, I...I...I don't know. Everything is hard to say, especially stuff about my father or my mother, but not always embarrassing. You're right. This would not be embarrassing."

"Do you want to talk about something else?"

"I don't think I can."

Dr. Paul remained silent. She began to write something down in the notebook on her lap.

"What are you writing?"

"Would you like to read what I have written? I can always show you what I write. I don't mind."

"What do you usually write about?"

"Actually, I write mostly about what your body is expressing, so I can remember. What you *say* is hard to forget."

"Really? You always remember what I say?"

"Francesca, when you learn a concerto, do you need the sheet music when you play it in a concert with the orchestra?"

"No, not if I have really practiced it. Sometimes I remember whole concertos that I played with the student orchestra at the Accademia Chigiana in Siena. I played Rachmaninoff's second piano concerto with that orchestra, maybe six years ago, and when our conductor here asked if I would like to play it with the Munich Symphony Orchestra under Birgitte as conductor, I was quite thrilled. It was just sitting in my head, ready to come out. Of course, I play it differently now. And that's important." Francesca stopped speaking and seemed to be concentrating very hard. "Are you saying that you have a memory similar to mine? Perhaps musicians and psychoanalysts have that in common? That sounds crazy. Birgitte has told me that her therapist writes almost everything down, or a great deal, anyway. She writes about what Birgitte says. But you say that you write about what my body says."

"It's just that what you say 'floats around my head'. Those are your words." Dr. Paul smiled. "I contemplate your words and so they stick. Sometimes I say them back to you at the end of a session. But body language, Francesca, is just as important for me. Alas, I don't always remember how you move or look. I write it down, and then I can contemplate your physical movements when re-reading my notes. Who knows? Maybe I have a memory like yours, a very good aural memory."

"I like that."

"Why?"

"I guess I like to know that I have something in common with you. Now *that* was embarrassing to say."

"And you said it anyway."

Francesca laughed. She paused and then said: "What I have been thinking about has to do with my father." Francesca brought her hands up to her face and covered her eyes. She took an audible breath. "Can I tell you without looking at you?" She dropped her elbows to her knees and leaned forward.

"You can do anything you want, Francesca. I am listening. Whenever you're ready."

"You know how I always get that question: how come I stopped studying music and switched into art history when I was considered a child prodigy?"

"Yes. And what do you answer?"

"I answer that..." Francesca started rubbing her face with her palms. "Oh, God, maybe I'm not yet ready."

"I think you are."

"Okay. Okay. I say that my brain doesn't work like that. I play the piano all the time, every day in fact, unless I am away on holiday and there is no piano in sight. I say that all that applause and adulation from the audience is not something I crave. I prefer the attention from my art history students who want to learn about the beauties of medieval and Renaissance art. I love music *and* art history. I am not the kind of person who does one thing exclusively just because I am good at it. I...I..." Francesca stopped.

"Take your time, Francesca. Consider your words carefully. Make me understand."

"You always understand. Even when I am totally inarticulate." And then Francesca sat up and removed her hands from her face. She drew her long black hair away from her face and behind her ears. Then she placed her hands on the armrests of her chair.

"Okay. Okay. Maybe, all that crap about my brain is a lie."

"Do you really think that is a lie? Perhaps not the whole picture, but a lie?"

"You're right, as usual, Dr. Paul. It is partially true. But what about the other part? The dirty screwy other part. The part that shows just what a mess I am. Because I am a mess, although I give a pretty good imitation of a good art historian, teacher, and musician. That's probably what I am best at. Maybe I'm a fake if not a liar."

"Do you really believe that—that you're a fake?"

"I don't know. Maybe?"

"Francesca, I'm not a psychiatrist or a neurologist, but I do think you have a very unique brain. Trust me."

Francesca sighed and in a very cracked voice said, "I do trust you."

"Good."

"So, this thing about my father...it has to do with him desperately wanting me to be a concert pianist. He always wanted me to enroll in competitions." Francesca was crying. Dr. Paul passed her the box of tissues, and she took a few.

"Did you?"

"Never."

"Okay. Why not?"

"Please stop," Francesca wailed.

"Okay, let's stop."

Francesca was sobbing now. Dr. Paul tried to be as still as possible.

"There is no need to continue, Francesca."

"You already know what I am going to say anyway, don't you?"

Dr. Paul did not answer. Then she took a deep breath and exhaled slowly. "It's just that I think you really want to tell me. You're safe here. Your father can't retaliate. He can't hurt you. I won't let him."

"It's just that I've never wanted to give him the satisfaction. I don't want to give him what he wants. He's already taken everything he wanted from me. Why should I give him this, too?" Francesca continued to sob. Her breathing became ragged.

"Take deep, slow breaths, Francesca. You've just done a remarkably brave thing. You've admitted to me a very long-held secret. I don't have to tell you what a really important moment this is in your development."

"But what am I going to do with this knowledge now?"

"What you are already doing. You *are* a concert pianist. You *are* an art historian and a great teacher. You are in a loving relationship. You deeply love music, art, and Birgitte. You are not making a mess of your life."

"You mean that?"

"Of course I do. Can I ask you a question now, one seemingly off-topic?"

Francesca nodded, the tears flowing down her cheeks unrelentingly.

"Is your wife home now?"

"Uh, I think so. I'm not sure."

"Would you please call her? I feel that it would be a good thing, if she were home. Or you could at least know when she was coming home."

"You don't want me to be alone?"

"How do you feel about being alone right now?"

For answer, Francesca pulled her phone out of her bag and rang her wife. "Birgitte, are you home? Okay, good. Dr. Paul just wanted to make sure I wouldn't be alone after what just happened here." Francesca listened and then said, "You're prejudiced." Some more listening. "Okay. See you soon."

"And?" asked Dr. Paul.

"She said that it's pouring outside, and she is coming to pick me up. She'll be here in fifteen minutes. I'll meet her out front."

"She tells you she is picking you up and you tell her she's prejudiced?"

"Do I have to tell you what she said? It's so embarrassing."

Dr. Paul smiled and stood up. Francesca also stood up and headed towards the door. She turned towards her therapist.

"Okay. Okay. She said: 'The woman loves you. How could she not?'"

"And you said, 'You're prejudiced.'"

Francesca was blushing. Dr. Paul turned the handle of the door and opened it slightly.

"Dr. Paul, I have no idea if what Birgitte said is true. Somehow, I doubt it. But the fact of the matter is, I love *you*." Francesca rushed away as fast as possible.

****

As soon as Francesca left, Astrid shut the door and sat down. Thankfully she had no other patients that day. She began to cry. She took her phone and lay down on the couch that her patient had always rejected. She heard a knock at the door. It was Marisa. "I'm leaving now, Dr. Paul. See you tomorrow." And she was gone.

"Hello, Asti. Finished for the day? I will be leaving the university shortly."

"Em, wait." Astrid was sniffling.

"Oh my God. You're crying. What happened?"

"I'm not sure. But I held it together through the entire session."

"Who was your last patient?"

"Francesca."

"And she made you cry?"

"It was heartbreaking. You would have been proud of me. However, before she left, since it was a truly momentous session and she had been sobbing, I asked her to phone her wife to see if she would be home. I didn't want her to be alone. You understand.

"Uh-huh, sort of. You're not her mother, Astrid."

"But I care."

"Okay. Go on."

"I couldn't hear her conversation, but then Francesca said something kind of inexplicable. She said, 'You're prejudiced.' Then she told me that her wife was picking her up. And I couldn't resist. I wanted to know what that comment referred to. She said it was embarrassing but she told me anyway. Her wife had said: 'The woman loves you. How could she not?'"

"And it made you cry?"

"Well, I was on the verge of tears anyway. But what really made me cry was when she told me that somehow, she doubted what Birgitte had said was true, but then she actually told me that *she* loved *me.* Then she disappeared."

"Of course, she loves you. How could you doubt it? All your patients love you."

"But no one has ever told me that before. Has a patient of yours ever said it?"

"No, you're right. It's pretty amazing. I would be in tears, too."

Chapter Nine

<u>Francesca in the Office V</u>

"Do you know what Birgitte asked me after I told her about what went on in here last time? I think I should tell you, Dr. Paul."

"Why do you think you should tell me?"

"Because...because...I found it so hard to answer her question and I think I need you to help me answer it."

"Okay. What's the question?"

"She asked me if I loved my mother."

"Good question. Very fitting."

"Why, because my mother neglected me, never defended me, didn't seem to care about me at all? She was never at home when I needed her. I didn't care about making all the dinners. Cooking is a useful skill, and I am very good at it. Also, I got to choose what I wanted to eat, and since I didn't—and don't—care for eating animals, my parents, through no choice of their own, became vegetarians. At least, at home they were. Or is it a fitting question because of what I said to you at the end?"

"About loving me, Francesca?"

"Did you have to say it? I'm embarrassed enough just thinking about it. It just came out...But I m-m-meant it. Oh, God, now I'm stuttering. I don't know if I loved my mother then. I don't know if I love her now. She says she loves me."

"Do you believe her?"

"She said that when I was a kid, she thought I was the most self-reliant human being she knew. She was proud of my ability to take care of myself. But did she have to take advantage of it? I was still a kid, and I needed my mother to be home sometimes."

"And to protect you from your father."

Francesca gasped. Astrid could tell that she hadn't expected that remark. *Did Francesca not think that was her mother's job? Should I ask her?*

"But if I never told her, then how could she even know that she had to protect me? So, are you now going to ask me the most obvious question?"

"And what would that be?"

"Why didn't I tell her?"

"Can you answer it?"

"Yes. I can. But I don't know if I want to. I've never said it out loud."

"Is there someone else you would like to say it to?"

"You mean like Birgitte? Or my mother?" Francesca stopped and looked lost in thought.

The room was filled with their silence. Francesca moved around in her chair as if she were feeling uncomfortable. At a certain point she broke the silence. "No, there is no one else I would rather tell. I would like to tell you if you want to hear it."

"Of course, I want to hear it. I want to hear anything you wish to say to me."

"It didn't bother you that I said what I said about you? About how I feel about you? It's one thing to say that you think your therapist is beautiful. It's another thing to say that you l-l-love her. To her."

"Are you trying to get me to tell you how it made me feel?"

"I guess so. But I'm not so sure. It's scary. I have never laid myself open to someone like that before."

"You did call Birgitte up on the telephone from Montreal and tell her that you loved her heart, body, and soul."

Francesca sighed. "I guess I did. It was terrifying."

"But look how well that worked out."

"Yeah, that worked out well. Anyway, so far you are not rejecting me, and that's good." Francesca took a deep breath. "Okay. I never told my mother because I didn't want to hurt her. I knew it would hurt her even if I didn't tell her about my abilities, according to my father, in the area of oral sex."

"Hurt her sense of self-esteem, as a lover, as a wife?"

"Exactly."

"But not hurt her because you are her daughter, and you were being hurt by your father."

"Uh…I don't know. I didn't know if she cared about me that much. Anyway, she is trying desperately to make it up to me now. She talks to me as much as possible. She flies over to Europe to come to my concerts, but also to see Stefano. They come together. I've never seen her so happy before. She is making a great effort…Dr. Paul?"

"Yes, Francesca."

"I have a theory about my mother. Do you want to hear it?"

"Yes."

"I think she stayed away from home so much, neglecting me all the while, because she was trying to stay away from my father. Maybe she didn't want to admit it to herself when she was younger. Maybe she hated him. That's the only emotion *I* have for him. I don't think she was that different, but not being a terribly introspective person, she pushed her feelings away and avoided the whole issue, as well as him…and, more importantly, me."

Astrid remained silent. *How astute of you, Francesca.*

The silence lingered for a while. Then Francesca spoke. "Okay so I know what we are avoiding in this room. I am going to say it. You are not my mother. First of all, you are too young to be my mother. My mother is almost sixty. You are my therapist. And I have to learn to deal with my mother, because she is my mother. And I will try to. With your help, hopefully."

"Yes, with my help. I will not abandon you in your effort to come to terms with her inadequacies."

"But, Dr. Paul, are they just inadequacies? If they were just inadequacies, maybe I could accept her. But somehow, I can't. I can't get over her being absent and blind, her willful withdrawal from me. Sometimes I hated her. I still do, sometimes…" Francesca sighed. "I didn't want to cry today. But I think it's going to happen whether I want to or not."

"Why does it matter if you cry? This is a place where your feelings are very raw. Things that we say here can be very painful."

"But I'm scared of you now."

"Why?"

"Because of what I told you at the end of the last session."

"You cannot imagine all the things that have been said to me and about me in this room. Good. Bad. Very bad. Horrible. I've heard it all. A lot of 'I hate you.'"

"Really? I can't imagine. How many have said what I said?"

Can I answer that, Em? What do I say? I know we have to talk about this. What do I say? Tell the truth, Astrid.

Astrid took a deep breath. "The fact is that no one has ever said that, although I have known they felt that."

"Oh...I know...I know...somewhere inside of me I want you to be my mother. But I didn't say that I love you because I wanted to...I only said it because it's true. I don't think I had an ulterior motive."

"And I believe you, Francesca."

"Really?"

"Yes, really."

"And you accept it—my love, I mean."

"Of course, I accept it. Why wouldn't I?"

"I don't know. Because it's inappropriate?"

"Love is never inappropriate, unless it's not really love."

"And my love is real."

Astrid smiled, a real smile, full of acceptance.

Chapter Ten

<u>In Montreal, two years earlier</u>
<u>Francesca and Jordan</u>

"I have bombshell news," pronounced Jordan with a big smile on her face. She placed coffees for her friend, Francesca, already seated, and herself, onto their regular table at their regular coffeehouse.

In response to Jordan's announcement, Francesca's intensely green eyes opened wide. "Should I feel overjoyed or worried?"

"You are such a pessimist!"

"No, Jordan, I am not...only where you are concerned. I am never sure about the terminology you use. 'Bombshell' can mean anything," Francesca retorted, defending herself from her friend's assessment of her. Francesca was well aware of Jordan's tendency to engage in extreme activities. She often admired Jordan for her courage and her originality. She genuinely loved the woman's enthusiasm, but sometimes her exploits were dangerous and scary. She eyed her friend's body as it slithered beautifully into the seat in front of her. There was just something so enticing about the woman's physical confidence. And she had an equally acute mind to go with that striking body.

The two of them had known each other since graduate school. They had been inseparable at first as students, but now that they were each working in their respective professions, they had much fewer opportunities to see each other, something they both regretted. Jordan was a high school psychologist, a job she loved, and Francesca was a high school history teacher, a job she did not truly love, but thought of as a stepping-stone to a possible position in a university now that she had completed her doctorate in art history, something she would much rather be teaching.

Francesca felt she needed to be around Jordan's fieriness, and she suspected that Jordan might feel that a restraining hand from her less restless companion could be useful once in a while. She wasn't actually sure what Jordan wanted from her. But whatever it was, Jordan must have been feeling that she was getting it from her, for she sought her out as much as or even more than Francesca pursued her. It was also true that she herself was less available lately, since she had become involved with Peter, her boyfriend of four months, with whom she was almost exclusively spending her weekends.

Jordan was playing with her spoon as Francesca stopped talking. She seemed to be preparing her speech about her bombshell news. Francesca was definitely curious.

"Okay, out with it. I'm ready. I've fortified myself with coffee and various defensive mechanisms."

Jordan undid the elastic keeping her long hair in a ponytail and let it spread across her back and shoulders. "I'm experimenting with my sexuality."

"You what?!"

"I said I'm experimenting with my sexuality. I've decided to make a foray into the joys of same- sex lovemaking." Jordan beamed at Francesca. Her smile was a mile wide.

Francesca pulled away from the table, leaning her back against the chair. Jordan had certainly caught her off-guard. What did all this mean?

"Actually...I...I...am not sure how much I really liked it, Francesca. I mean I enjoyed the ardour of my chosen partner and her willingness to pleasure me so passionately. From the point of view of my gratification, it was a success, but I suppose I was less enthusiastic when I had to return the favour. That sounds awful, doesn't it? Selfish, perhaps. But I cannot say I found...Never mind."

Francesca sighed. She realized that Jordan was speaking about a co-worker at her school, the newly-arrived American woman, about ten years her senior, making the woman in her early forties. "Are you talking about Candace from Maine, the librarian?"

"As a matter of fact, I—"

"—Jordan, how could you? How could you be so insensitive?"

"What do you mean? I made no promises. I told you I'm experimenting. Maybe, it will get better. I think I may keep at it another while, see if I can perform better or more willingly."

"Jordan, you are impossible. You have to stop this."

"Why?"

"You know very well why. It's grotesque, what you're doing. She's a serious and loving individual and you...you're playing with her. If a man were doing this sort of thing, you would call him a pig."

Jordan looked uncomfortable. Francesca figured she was possibly getting through to her. How could Jordan do such a thing to another human being? Francesca felt sick about it. She liked Candace. Of course, that didn't matter. To do that to anyone was unthinkable. "Couldn't you just seduce someone less vulnerable, someone who didn't actually care?" Now Francesca leaned in towards the culprit in front of her and barked an order, "Just stop, Jordan. I mean it." Then she took a deep breath. "Please."

Jordan moved backwards as her preferred confidante moved forwards. She cocked her head to the side and squeezed her eyes almost shut, as if she were trying to see a distant object more clearly. Then she started slowly nodding. "Okay, so you're saying I'm being a bitch, but that was not...I mean..." Jordan shook her head. "I just wanted to be good to her, you know...give her something she just seemed to want so badly. I mean...I didn't think it would matter that I didn't do it out of love, but just out of like. Is that so terrible?"

"You may be giving her the wrong message, since you seemed to enjoy it, at least her loving you, and that would be very harmful. Especially if you go back and do it again and again, which I think is likely; that is, if you don't listen to me. Were you really thinking of her? Be honest with yourself."

Jordan looked down at her hands resting on the table. "I don't know." She shrugged. "I felt good doing it...and...it was kind of exhilarating. It was new." She drew one hand through her hair. "You're always telling me that doing things because they're new may not always necessarily be right." She looked at her friend and smiled. "Maybe you're a better psychologist than I am."

"I doubt it. I'm just more moral, and a pain in the ass as well." Francesca smiled, too. Jordan, in fact, was way more perceptive and insightful than she was. She just didn't always consider the consequences of her actions if something seemed exciting. Exciting was just her friend's brand of morality. "So...will you call Candace, and tell her that you don't feel comfortable continuing to explore your sexuality with her?"

Jordan eyed her carefully. "Well, as long as we're being honest with ourselves—and I guess I should probably admit that I was thinking more about me than her—what about you and your relationship with Peter, and all men, past and present?"

"What are you talking about?"

"You know exactly what I am talking about. Every time you get involved with a man and he gets serious...starts mentioning the l-word, you back away so quickly, you're out the door before the guy in question has a chance to close his mouth."

"What is that supposed to mean?"

"Francesca, you're twenty-nine years old, but have you ever been in love with any of the men you date? Even the ones, like Peter, whom you seem to like, and who definitely will be asking if you'd like to move in with him, since he has this great big beautiful house, and you live in a rented one-bedroom apartment? Do you actually think you might love him?"

"I don't understand at all what you are getting at. I haven't met the right man yet, but he's out there. Maybe even Peter—"

"—Give me a break, Francesca, you'll never settle down with Peter. *You're* not being honest with yourself."

Francesca felt the tears well up in her eyes. Why was this conversation hurting so much now? Why was Jordan pounding her with these types of questions? Did Jordan think that she was being cruel to Peter by giving him a chance? He deserved a chance, even though she was already beginning to feel that she was indeed feeling very little. He seemed like the right kind of guy for her long-term, but there was no intensity there, coming from her, anyway. Though, truth be told, he appeared to be very happy with her. And he *was* dropping hints about living together. He would love it if she just moved in with him, and they could begin to live the life of a *real* couple, one with other couples as friends. He had even begun talking about having babies. But Jordan was right. She would never settle down with him, and if she left him tomorrow, she would not miss him. Was she behaving as badly as Jordan? It reminded her of the previous men in her life, whom she knew she had used because she felt she needed them. Especially Colin, her first boyfriend, from the age of sixteen to twenty-one. He still troubled her. Jordan was a great friend, but she, Francesca, had never told her anything about her sick childhood.

She took her eyes off her coffee cup, where she had been staring as Jordan pummelled her with her question about men and Peter, and looked up into her companion's face. "I guess I should call it off sooner than later. Peter does not deserve my lukewarm participation." She sighed deeply. "I will miss his body, and his bed, and his beautiful bathroom. He's a very satisfying lover, you know. I love the feel of his skin..." She smiled sadly.

"Just not him."

"I guess not, but...but...how did you know?"

"Oh, Francesca, you're so obtuse."

"Am I really?"

"Yeah, really. Let me ask you something. You know your friend from last year, your Danish—or was she German?—friend Birgitte. Remember her?"

"Remember her? How could I forget her? I've missed her so much since she left our school and went back to Munich."

"Have you talked to her recently?"

"I talk to her at least twice a week. We compare boyfriends. Günter, her boyfriend, lives and works in another town and only drives into Munich on the weekends to see her, an arrangement that suits her because she likes to be by herself during the week. She likes to be alone, she says. She prefers her solitude to the sameness of having a man around all the time. It gives her more time to play the violin."

"Are you trying to tell me that she's not a very passionate person or something?"

"No, definitely not. She's a very passionate and intense person. She's full of life. And the things she loves, like playing the violin and teaching music at the conservatory in Munich, like listening to music for hours and hours every day...when she talks about that, she just glows. It's incredible to see her face. She gets so animated." Francesca was talking with her hands and her body now. She was making Jordan smile. "She's a brilliant musician. She studied at Julliard. I love it when she plays the violin. We were just starting to play music together. I accompanied her on the piano. But then her one-year contract to start the orchestra in the school ended, and she had to leave."

"It's time to go, Francesca."

"Go where?"

"To Munich. To see her. School is ending in less than two weeks. You could finish marking papers and exams by the end of June. Don't wait a minute longer. Get rid of this Günter, and Peter, of course, and find your real love."

"What?"

"Come on, Francesca, wake up. You've been in love with Birgitte for more than a year, two years, in fact, and you let her slip through your fingers."

"Wait a second. Are you saying that I'm not heterosexual? I just finished telling you how much I loved, and still love, sex with Peter. Weren't you listening?"

"Of course, I was listening," Jordan said impatiently. "It has nothing to do with sex."

"Heterosexuality or homosexuality has nothing to do with sex? What are you getting at, Jordan? You're making no sense."

"I'm talking about emotions. You don't get emotionally involved with men. You don't fall in love with men, because you fall in love with women, and there's a great one out there now, who, I am sure, would give up music to have you all to herself."

Francesca listened in shock. "Are you being my psychologist now? I hate when you do that, you know."

"Francesca, I will never be your psychologist. I am only your friend. Why do you think I haven't brought this subject up before? I should have brought it up before Birgitte got on that plane bound for Munich, but I couldn't. *Because I am not your psychologist.* But it killed me not to tell you that you were being blind, wilfully so, in fact, that you couldn't see what was right in front of you. And...I reiterate...it has nothing to do with sex. I mean, I am sure you are bisexual, but you are not bi-emotional. You are emotionally gay. Just like I am emotionally straight. I fall in love with men. I may not be with Lawrence anymore, but I loved him deeply, and I will never love Candace, that wonderful, kind, and sweet woman whom I have no right to deceive anymore, because I will never be in love with her. You're right about that. But you're not right about Birgitte. She's also emotionally gay. Like you—since, when it comes to sex, she is perfectly happy mingling fluids with Günter—she hasn't a clue that it is about emotions and not sex."

"I always thought sexuality had to do with sex," wailed Francesca.

"Maybe it does, but not in your case. You feel more deeply about women. When you talk about Birgitte, your eyes light up. I've never seen you talk about any man like that...ever."

"And you're just telling me about this now?" Again, Francesca expressed this question with a wail. "Even if you're not my psychologist, didn't you owe it to me as a friend, *my best friend*, to inform me of your opinion before?"

"You're actually taking my bombshell analysis of your situation...your predicament...quite well, aren't you? I suppose I could've told you years ago. I'm sorry. Perhaps I thought you'd just figure it out. Are you really okay with this new self-knowledge, though? Because it *is* okay to love women, or to be in love with women. The sky is not going to fall down on you. Make yourself happy. Give in to those powerful feelings and get the hell out of here."

Francesca stared at the room around her. She hoped the other patrons hadn't heard anything of what they had been discussing. But did she really care if they did? Was this all true? Was waiting around for the right man an illusion to make her feel more comfortable with herself, feel more "normal", just like everyone else, when she wasn't, not with her familial history? She rested her elbows on the table and then dropped her head into her hands. What was happening to her? She felt like crying, because...because...she knew Jordan was right. Whenever she heard Birgitte's voice on the phone and then saw her face on the screen, she felt warm inside, a feeling no orgasm with any man, Peter included, had ever given her. She craved that warmth. Birgitte was her sunshine, and she longed to be near her. But what if Birgitte didn't feel that way? Admitting it would then surely turn the woman off. But Jordan, the only psychologist she knew, said that Birgitte was the same, just like her. What was she to do?

"Okay, maybe you're not taking it so well. Are you going to start crying now? Francesca, my dear, tell me what you're feeling. I can handle it. Anything. Really. Yell at me if you want."

Francesca lifted her head up, and Jordan stared into her eyes. "But what if...what if Birgitte doesn't feel the same way about me? What if I tell her I want to come, and let whatever will happen to happen, and she rejects me, tells me that I'm crazy? What then, Jordan?"

"It won't happen. Trust me. I've watched you two together. You're climbing inside each other with your eyes, with your souls. You guys are desperate to declare yourselves." Jordan picked up her friend's phone from the table. "Call her, Francesca. Call her now."

Francesca looked at her watch. "It's ten P.M. in Germany."

"So what? She'll still be awake."

"But what if Günter will be there? I can't call her at night."

"It's Thursday, not Friday night. He only comes on weekends. Tell the woman you want to see her. No, tell her you need to see her. Tell her you love her."

"I don't know if I can. I've never told anyone that before. I can't just say it."

"You've never told anyone you loved them before because you didn't love anyone before. But this woman you do love. Give her your unadulterated truth. Make her know she's worth it."

"How can you be so sure? Anyway, maybe I should call Peter first."

"Don't back down on me now, Francesca. Be brave. Do the bravest thing you've ever done. It doesn't matter that you don't know the outcome beforehand. You'll find out soon enough. You call Birgitte and I'll call Candace. We'll both tell the truth." Jordan took Francesca's hands in hers and squeezed them. "I'm right here. Your best friend is right here."

Chapter Eleven

<u>In Munich</u>

<u>Francesca and Cora</u>

Francesca was sitting with her student Cora in her office, going over Cora's outline and proposal for the paper she was writing about the Sienese trecento. The door was slightly ajar. Francesca seldom shut the door. She wanted her students to know that they were welcome.

"Well, this is a very detailed outline. I doubt you will have to do much to fill it in. A couple of 'The's' and a few adjectives, a few more verbs, etc. Good work. I am anxious to see the paper in its entirety." Francesca smiled at this very hard-working student, who was actually a final-year history student of Bradley's and not an art history student at all, except for the fact that she had been one of Francesca's students in Florence the spring before and had seemed to really enjoy the trip. At that moment, another student, an Engineering student, and roommate of Cora's in the students' quarters, and who had also been in Florence, opened her door wider and crossed the threshold.

"Oh, I am so sorry to disturb you guys. Are you finished? If not, I will wait outside."

Francesca looked up at Melanie. She liked the look of this girl. It had pleased her to think that a student of body mechanics, who wanted to invent new ways to keep human body parts functioning, thought that looking at Renaissance paintings and sculptures of rather beautiful—perhaps idealized, although organically correct—bodies, would be of use to her in her future profession. She liked both these twenty-something-year-old young women very much. They were a decade younger than her and well on their way to making good educational choices. They had both discussed with her their desire to stay on at this American University in Munich and do graduate work.

"Uh, Melanie, I think I want to talk to Professor Oliver, if she has the time and agrees, about graduate school."

"I am ready to discuss anything like that, Cora, but I am not in the same department as you."

"I really think you can help."

"Okay, then."

Then there was another eruption into her office. A very tall and lanky basketball player type of a youth stepped in, bent over, and kissed Melanie on the mouth. *What is going on,* Francesca thought. She stared up at him.

"Let's go, Melanie. I'm very busy."

"But I...wanted to talk to Cora for a moment," said Melanie.

"You can talk to her later," her boyfriend urged her. "Come on."

"Alright. See you later, Cora," Melanie said to her friend. The two of them filed out of the office. Francesca glanced at Cora, could see the girl's distress, and so got up to shut the door. *A closed door is called for once in a while.*

"What just happened, Cora?"

"The guy's an asshole and he's going to hurt my friend. I hate him. He pushes her around as if she belongs to him."

"Somehow I think he is already hurting her."

"I know. I can't stand it. I think she's enthralled. How could anyone stand that kind of behaviour?"

Cora looked really upset, as if she were going to cry. *Asshole aside, something more is going on here.*

"I know you really care about her. Do you want to talk about it? I'm a good listener. And I have ten years on you of experiences with assholes."

Cora managed a smile. "It's too complicated. My problems aren't...aren't anything you want to hear about." Cora sighed and passed a hand over her eyes. Francesca saw that those eyes were glistening. She was also an expert on tears, being someone who cried copious amounts about twice a week.

"Come on, Cora. I know that you are about to shed tears. This is serious. I'm on your side. I have time and I care about you."

Then the tears started to fall. *What does Dr. Paul do right now? She hands me the box of tissues.* Francesca got up and took her box of tissues from the shelf on the other side of the office, came towards Cora, and put it beside her on the desk to her right. Cora raised her hand and took a handful.

"Thank you."

"Something's going on here, Cora, and it's not just about that asshole."

Cora leaned back in her chair and sighed. "How could you tell?"

Francesca waited. *Is this woman in love with her roommate? Oh, dear, what a dilemma.*

"Cora, just say it. You won't surprise me."

"It won't surprise you if I tell you that I'm in love with the person I have been sharing a room with for the last three and a half years? It's just so hard, Professor Oliver. She's around me all the time. She's completely uninhibited about her body. She undresses in front of me as if it were nothing. She slips into bed with me like a sister when she wants to talk about intimate things. At least she's wearing pyjamas when she does that. She has no idea that I feel this way about her. She can't even imagine that I could love her not like a sister but like a lover. My situation is hopeless. And she is hopeless about that idiot, Jeremy. Why can't she see that he is just using her? He needs a pretty woman on his arm, and that is all she represents to him."

"While you love her and want to hold her in your arms."

Cora started to sob. Francesca moved her chair on wheels closer to her student. She touched her head, just slightly. "Cora, tell me more."

Cora wiped her face and then threw the tissues into the waste-paper basket. "Why do you want to know? What's the point of telling you? There's nothing I can do but suffer."

Francesca moved back and Cora finally lifted her head.

"On a scale of one to ten, how bad do you think you are feeling now?"

"At least ten, Professor Oliver."

"Okay, here's a thought. Why don't you tell her how you feel?"

"What? What if she completely rejects me? I don't want her to walk out of my life forever."

"Listen, Cora. Could you feel worse than you do now? Is it possible?"

"No, I don't think so."

"So, do it. First confront her with her ridiculous relationship with Jeremy and then land that bomb on her. It's the twenty-first century. Homosexuality abounds. If she doesn't take you seriously or return your affection, at least you can start to think about other possible partners.

"But I love her."

"Tell her you love her. She's not a superficial person. It's kind of nice when someone says, 'I love you,' even if you don't return the feeling. If she doesn't return the feeling, I don't think she will hurt you deliberately. She will try to let you down gently. And as you said, you couldn't feel any worse than you do now."

"Really? That's what I should do? But she is obviously heterosexual."

"How do you know?"

"Well, she's only been with men."

"So?" Francesca thought for a moment before continuing. "When did *you* know, Cora?"

"About my feelings for girls and not for boys?" Francesca nodded. "When I was a young adolescent, about fourteen or so." Francesca kept on nodding. "What, Professor Oliver? What are you asking me?"

"But is it possible that someone could figure it out later in life? Maybe it depends on upbringing. What kind of family does she come from? A very progressive, liberal-minded New York family?"

"Oh, God, no. A very conservative, religious family from the midwest."

"So, is it possible she is afraid of them? Afraid of admitting to herself that she is not 'normal', not like everybody else?"

"I don't know. We have never talked about it. She just assumes that I am also a straight heterosexual American female. Otherwise, she wouldn't get into bed with me like a cozy normal teenage sister."

"What do you do when she does that?"

"I grit my teeth, and desperately hold onto the book I am reading. But I do love looking at her naked body. It feels really good to talk to you like this. You're really cool, Professor Oliver."

"Call me Francesca."

"Really?"

"Why not?"

"Well, I'm supposed to show respect."

"And if you call me Francesca, do you respect me less?"

"No! I respect you so much, enough to ask you to be my thesis advisor when I'm doing my Master's degree."

"But I'm an art historian and you study history."

"I've already spoken to Professor Lavigne, and he says you know more about the Renaissance than most historians, so why not?"

"But Bradley is not the head of your department."

"I have an appointment with him tomorrow. I've already been accepted into the program. I was going to ask him as long as you accept."

"But I'm new here. I'm not tenured yet."

"Professor Lavigne said that Professor Putnam will want to meet you, and you could charm the pants off anyone."

"He said that? And charm is not what's needed, anyway."

"Well, you're a genius, and in two seconds he's going to figure that out. Will you be my thesis advisor?"

"I will be your thesis advisor if Professor Putnam agrees without twisting his arm."

Cora smiled broadly. "Thanks."

"Will you tell me what happens with Melanie?"

"Of course. And by the way, is anything going on between you and Professor Lavigne?"

"What? Get out of here, Cora."

Cora laughed and went over to the door.

"And by the way, absolutely nothing is going on between Bradley and me."

Cora turned around and looked at her with a 'Yeah, sure' kind of look. *Is that what my students think?*

Chapter Twelve

"Francesca, I will now take you in the limousine to the Hong Kong airport."

The two of them had been breakfasting in their hotel. The Ravel concert had been a success and Francesca was heading home before the others, the members of the Swiss orchestra, because she was flying directly to Rome, and then two hours later on to Munich. They were going a different way back to Geneva. It had been a harrowing, exhausting experience. She did not know if she would do this, go so far away from home, again. It had been hard to be without Birgitte. Physically. She had managed musically. And she had played the Ravel concerto before in Paris with this same orchestra and conductor.

This French conductor was supposed to have been the guest conductor in Munich when she had played her first concerto, the Brahms, with that orchestra, with Birgitte as concertmaster. But in the end, he had not conducted, because the Munich Orchestra had rebelled against him during the rehearsal. He had made a snide comment to her: "You don't worry your pretty little head over matters such as *tempi*..." It had been humiliating, especially since she had spoken to him in French about the *tempi*. She had gone up to him and spoken softly to him, telling him how she preferred to play the particular movement. She hadn't wanted anyone else to hear or understand. But as she walked back to the piano, in a loud voice—in English, no less, so everyone could hear—he had made that comment. Immediately, Magda, the first cellist and Birgitte's oldest friend, who had studied with her at Julliard, stood up and said, "Sir, Ms. Oliver is the soloist, and if you don't apologize to her for that sexist remark, I will walk out of here." The entire orchestra then stood up in unison with her. The conductor, whom she still did not like much, threw down his stick, turned to Goldschmidt, their regular conductor, who was sitting in the hall, and yelled at him to take back his orchestra. He no longer wished to conduct them.

When Goldschmidt took over the baton, he profusely apologized to Francesca, and they began the concerto from the beginning. Goldschmidt completely respected her choice of tempo. Since then, Goldschmidt had become a great supporter of both her and Birgitte. They had a wonderful relationship.

As it happened, the French conductor did not leave during that rehearsal and he listened to the entire concerto, and when Francesca left the stage when the orchestra began rehearsing the symphony that they would be playing in the second half of the concert, he came up to her, startled her, and asked her to accept his apologies. He had thoroughly enjoyed her interpretation of the Brahms and asked her if she would play the Ravel concerto in Paris the following month with the Orchestre de la Suisse Romande. She hesitated. "Okay, take my card, or better yet, do you have an agent?"

"No, I don't."

"Okay, call this agent. He's the best. He's in Paris. Tell him I sent you to him." He gave her the agent's card. "And give *him* your answer." He then took his leave of her.

She had discussed this with Birgitte, and since Paris was close by, and Birgitte could come and at least listen to her, she called the agent, who had since become her own agent. He was pretty disappointed, however, in the fact that she didn't always say yes to him when an orchestra wanted her to perform with them. But often enough, she acquiesced. The concert in Paris had gone well, and so upon the urging of the agent, she had consented to play again with that orchestra in Hong Kong.

But she was glad that she was going home. She needed to get back to her normal life, to her students, to Birgitte, especially.

In the car, however, the conductor, a man twice her age, started to come on to her. He touched her arm, her hair, her face, and she was disgusted.

"Come on, Francesca, you've always known of my interest in you. We have a special relationship."

"Stop touching me. I have no such relationship with you."

He was worse in the airport. As soon as she could, Francesca walked towards security and away from the importunate man. He went ahead of her and stopped her in her tracks.

"Don't you understand? You are the type of woman—no, the only woman that I could be faithful to. I want you. Why don't you want me?"

"Get out of my way. You are older than my father and I never want to see you again. Don't call me. And I certainly don't ever want to play another concerto with you. Goodbye." She sped off. What she wanted was to be completely unconscious for the next fifteen or so hours on the plane. She felt in no condition to even ponder what had just occurred or her reactions. She felt sick. While still in the airport, she phoned Birgitte, having no idea what time it was in Munich. Birgitte was happy to hear from her. She almost cried when telling her what had happened. "Don't think about him. Think about me, that you are coming home to me and my love. I love you. Call me from Rome." Francesca promised.

Fortunately, since she was the soloist, she always got a seat in business class. Magda had sent her to a doctor who she said would provide her with a magic sleeping pill for long-haul voyages. Armed with one of those, she told the flight attendant as soon as the plane took off that she did not want to be disturbed for anything, that she was going to sleep. She took the pill and plunged into oblivion. She woke up about four hours before the arrival in Rome. She went to the bathroom. She was able to wash her face, and with some bottled water, brushed her teeth. She sat down and noticed that the man next to her, a man of about her own age, was reading a book in Italian, a novel that she, too, had read. When he looked up, she smiled at him. He asked her in Italian if she was Italian, too.

In Italian, she responded, "I am of Italian origin, but I was born in Canada; in fact, I am an Italian or European citizen. I live in Munich. I've read that novel. It's pretty special."

He smiled at her, and they began a very pleasant conversation. He told her that he worked in Brussels for the European government as a legal consultant in international law, and had been at a conference in Hong Kong. "I also teach at the university in Rome, and it is terrible, for me anyway, to have two professions."

"Actually, I also have two professions." As she talked to this pleasant enough man, she almost began to feel normal, although the experience with the conductor continued to play out inside her head.

"My God, you are impressive. But you, unlike me, are happy with your two professions. I think I just may return to live in Rome and forget about Brussels."

"Really?"

"Well, I was involved with a Belgian woman, and as long as we were together, I really didn't mind going back and forth between Brussels and Rome. I was even considering settling down permanently in Brussels, but she left me two months ago, and Brussels no longer has any magnetism for me."

"I'm sorry to hear that," said Francesca.

"And you are settled in a permanent relationship in Munich?"

"I am."

"You are happy with this man?"

Francesca had no desire to explain her situation. "My partner and I are very happy."

The young man nodded his head. Francesca began to feel uncomfortable again, and told him that since they had a few more hours in the air, she wanted to sleep again.

"In about an hour they will serve some breakfast. Should I wake you, then, since you had no dinner to speak of?"

"Alright. Thank you." She put on her eye mask and pulled the blanket over her head. She fell asleep again. That pill, still in her bloodstream, was potent. Then she felt Paolo shake her arm. The flight attendant was coming with breakfast. They were going to land in about an hour and a half in Rome. Finally in a familiar place where people spoke a familiar language.

Paolo told her that he had googled her while she was sleeping and had learned that she was a concert pianist of some renown. He especially liked the article about her performance of the Brahms second piano concerto in Munich, the one called 'Who is Francesca Oliver?'

"Why don't people know you well? Why were you out of the limelight for so long?"

"I wanted to study art history, and I did. I am happy teaching art history in Munich. And then I slipped back into music."

"I don't know if I really understand how that can happen. I am amazed that you were a child prodigy. Perhaps one day soon, you will play in Rome or Brussels, and I can come and hear you. I'd love that."

Now that made Francesca really uncomfortable. He was becoming a little too enthusiastic for her taste. They busied themselves with breakfast. And then the descent began.

When the plane landed and they went through customs together, since she carried a European passport, he started making overtures to her of a romantic nature. Hadn't she just told him she had a partner in Munich?

"I will give you my e-mail address, and when you come to Italy, perhaps we can meet up. I would really like that."

"Well, I hope you find someone to fill the void that your last girlfriend left."

"And maybe you could do that. Is it possible?"

It was her turn to see the customs agent. After she did that, she practically ran towards the gate for Munich. Why didn't men leave her alone? Why didn't they ever listen? And then this Paolo was following her and wanting to press upon her his e-mail address. "Please don't do this. I can't see you. I am in love with someone. It was nice talking to you. Goodbye."

When she arrived at her gate, the plane was slightly delayed by about a half hour. She sat down and called Birgitte again. Thankfully it was a Saturday. "I miss you so much. I miss your arms around me. I feel like crying." Birgitte did her best to calm her down. But she felt almost worse than before her long sleep. Birgitte told her to go and get an Italian coffee in the airport before she came back to Germany.

"You need some pleasure. A cappuccino and a brioche. Go, my love. I will be waiting for you." So, Francesca did just that. She felt a little better. She just wanted the nightmare to be over.

In the Munich airport, Birgitte did not hug her, knowing that she hated displays of affection in public places. But Birgitte understood just how awful she felt. She took her by the arm and directed them to the parking lot. Inside the car, Francesca closed her eyes.

"Can I hug you now? Or not yet?" Birgitte asked.

"Not yet. At home. Park in the garage. I'm not feeling well. But I am so glad to have your familiar self beside me now. I don't think I can go away from you again."

Birgitte started the car and maneuvered out of the parking garage. "You spent three weeks in Florence with your students in May last year. We only talked once a day. You seemed to survive."

"I didn't have a choice. And I didn't have men touching me when I didn't want to be touched."

"But I am sure your male students were..."

"Could we not talk about this? Just tell me you love me, please."

"I love you. I love you. Can I touch you? Can I kiss your hand?" Francesca opened her eyes. "I love you, too. I think I love you more than ever before. Your face is the greatest reward of this entire ordeal. You won't ever leave me, Birgitte?"

"I will never leave you."

Francesca put her hand on her lover's thigh. "Drive me home as fast as you can."

When they got home, Francesca knew she was going to vomit. She leapt out of the car and ran up the few stairs from the garage to the powder room off the entryway. Birgitte was close behind her. Inside the bathroom, she knelt down beside Francesca, pulled her lover's hair back, and held her head in both hands. Francesca heaved and heaved.

"Are you finished, my love?"

"Uh...maybe. Oh, no, here it comes again."

Finally, it was over, and they both sat on the floor. Francesca looked exhausted.

"I know what you want now," said Birgitte.

"Besides brushing my teeth?"

"You want a bath—"

"—With you in it."

"Of course. Shall we go?"

Birgitte held on to Francesca and they climbed the stairs together. Their heads were close together and Birgitte's long blonde locks mingled with Francesca's dark ones. While Francesca brushed her teeth, she ran a bath and helped Francesca to undress. Francesca put her long hair up and got into the bath while Birgitte undressed. Finally, they were in the bath together, facing each other. Francesca's eyes were closed.

"Are you going to fall asleep, *meine Liebe*?"

"Oh, Ghita, you are going to give me an orgasm just saying those words in German."

"I don't mind. Do you want me to speak Danish to you?'

"Yes. Yes. Please speak Danish to me. When you do, it feels as if you are touching me in all the most special places."

"I could just touch you in all those special places, too."

"Let's just stay here for a few minutes and you talk lovingly to me in your lovely language."

Chapter Thirteen

<u>Francesca in the Office VI</u>

"It was a horrible ordeal. Not the music. I love that concerto and especially the second movement when I get to play with all the winds. You know what I'm talking about?"

"Yes, I do."

"I am so glad you love music and go to the orchestral concerts here in Munich. I am glad that you have heard me play the piano. I mean, you are my therapist, and I have to talk to you, but playing the piano is also a kind of talking. I am still telling you who I am but through the music."

Astrid smiled. *I love hearing you play the piano. I especially loved hearing you and Birgitte playing Vocalise by Rachmaninoff as an encore after the concerto. It was a surprise, a great surprise when she came out with her violin after conducting the orchestra. I would love to go with Em, but alas, I have been going with my sister for a lifetime. But when you are playing, I make sure Em comes, too.*

"Why was it such an ordeal?"

"Well, first of all, I was away from Birgitte for four days. It sounds like nothing, and I did spend all that time in Florence with my students, last spring. Three weeks to be exact. But I just felt she was closer. Geographically speaking. And Italy is like home. And my mother was there—thankfully. She saved my student's life knowing immediately what he was suffering from. And then she met Stefano Frattini, the Florentine surgeon in Emergency, and actually assisted him in the surgery, because he wanted her there. My students loved my mother, and so did the parents of the boy in question. That helped me a lot. And anyway, if I needed Ghita, she was an hour away. Hong Kong is so far away. So foreign. In another time zone. But that was not the worst part. The worst part was that conductor. I never liked him."

"The one that insulted you and 'your pretty little head'?"

"Yeah, that one. I don't understand why I continued to perform with him. He's horrible. Different from my father, but horrible, nonetheless. I've blocked his number now. He had been texting me for days, so I cut him off."

"I am sure it will not influence your career. He isn't the only conductor in the world."

"And anyway, he gave me that Parisian agent, and I don't need him at all now."

They sat in silence for many minutes.

"Francesca?"

"Yes?"

"Are you avoiding telling me what happened?"

"Sort of. Maybe. I'm just enjoying being here with you. When I start talking, I know it's not going to be so pleasant."

"Start talking."

"Okay. Okay. You know, when I got home, I vomited and vomited."

"It was that bad. Vomiting, however, can be healthy. It's like sweating. Sweating cools the body down. Vomiting got the toxicity of that horrible man out of your system."

"It wasn't just him."

"Oh?"

"I'll go in order. You better have the box of tissues handy."

"For you or for me?" *Did I really just make that joke? What is wrong with you, Astrid? Please forgive me, Em. I am showing how emotional I am.*

"I don't think you're going to cry." Francesca sighed. "I know that was a joke, but...but...emotions aside, I really feel that...I really feel that...I don't even know if I can talk today."

"Are you afraid you may vomit again? Here in my office? There's a bathroom behind that door, so you don't have to worry. If you feel sick, we're prepared."

"It could happen."

"Did you often vomit after your father returned to the marriage bed and left you alone?"

"I did. After some time, I got used to him. But not entirely. The fact is, when I was a child, I only vomited for psychological reasons. I never had stomach flu, or digestive problems."

Oh, Francesca, I could cry now. Where was your super nurse mother then? Running off to help her depressed father? When her daughter was right there in front of her, vomiting her husband's sperm.

"Francesca, I don't want you to feel that I am pushing you to reveal what happened, but you should know that I think you want to tell me, you want the feeling that it is all over. It's not pretty to say, but it is a little like vomiting. Did you tell Birgitte?"

"Yes, and I cried and cried and cried. But we really didn't try to figure out what was going on with me. I vomited. We took a bath together. She spoke to me in Danish because it really makes me feel loved. Then we went into the bedroom. I told her. I cried. She comforted...and then...and then..." Francesca stopped.

"And then what?"

"And then, we were touching each other and the inevitable happened. So, we didn't discuss it like I know you will make me do. I know when I tell you it will be different. I will say other things."

"Other things?"

"Yeah, other things."

"What other things?"

"I have to tell you first."

"Okay. No more questions from me. I am not impatient. In fact, you are the last patient of the day. You will get it out. Okay?"

Francesca nodded her head. And so, she began to recount the story of the conductor and herself, about how it made her feel to be touched by him, of how it made her remember her father.

"He's older than you, this Frenchman?"

"He's even older than my father. He's probably older than sixty. My father isn't sixty yet." Francesca had a very difficult time telling Dr. Paul about him, saying that she was the only woman who could make him be faithful and that they had a special relationship.

"Do you think he meant it or was it just a line?"

"I think he thought he meant it and he was just fooling himself. All I wanted was to get as far away as I could from him and fall into a deep sleep and not come out of it until I was in Ghita's arms."

"But that didn't happen."

"I was so uncomfortable for all those hours. It was an endless journey."

"But the sleeping pill worked."

"The sleeping pill worked, but the Italian man, Paolo, who was sitting beside me, came on to me, too, even though I explicitly told him that I had a partner and was happy. He thought it was a man. Who cares? I wasn't going to tell him the truth. But why don't these men ever listen? He didn't touch me, though. He just kept saying that when I come to Rome we should get together. And when I said I hoped that another woman could fill the void of his ex, he suggested that it could be me. Was he even listening? Sometimes I think that it must be written on my forehead."

Astrid looked at her questioningly. Francesca touched her forehead several times.

"It must say, 'you can take advantage of this woman. She's been molested before, so go right ahead. She's used to it. She can handle it'. Except she can't." And then Francesca started crying. *So that's what she meant by other things. She thinks her past is visible. That people can see that she has been a victim.*

"Francesca, do you really believe that people see your past, like a film being played in front of them? Do you really think that people are so astute as to divine what is so well-hidden?"

"Well, I've been victimized. I exhibit certain behaviours, don't I?"

"Like what? What are you talking about?"

Astrid handed her the box of tissues. Francesca wiped her face. "I don't know. Why don't men leave me alone?"

"They don't leave you alone not because you've been a victim but simply because you are attractive to them. You do know I presume that you are an attractive young woman."

Francesca slowly nodded. "You mean it's just that simple?"

"For them it is."

"But not for me."

"I'm afraid not, Francesca. And that is why you are in analysis. Because the trauma of your past has seeped into your present."

"Can I ever get better?"

"What do you think?"

"Well, I have you."

"Yes, you do."

"I have Birgitte."

"Yes, you do."

"I have art and music and the life I've built here."

"Yes, you do."

Chapter Fourteen

<u>Francesca in the Office VII</u>
"Remember when we talked about whether I loved my mother?"
"I do."
"Well, there was something else Birgitte and I talked about that I failed to mention. Mostly because I didn't agree with her. But now I am feeling guilty about not mentioning it, about that and several other things that I left out. And since I am so used to crying in your office, and if I cry when I tell you, what difference would it make, anyway? It's all embarrassing, because when I talk either about you or about sex, I have the most trouble. Eventually, we tend to get there anyway. So, why should I avoid certain topics?"
Astrid smiled. *You are so right, Francesca. Why avoid anything? But we all do because psychoanalysis is a hard thing to do.*
"Do you want to ask me anything, Dr. Paul?"
"No."
"You are going to make it even harder, aren't you?"
Astrid kept silent. *Go for it, Francesca. Take a deep breath and go for it.*
Francesca took a deep breath. "This was just after the session with the recording and definitely after the 'love' session. You know what I am talking about."
"I do."
"I don't have to repeat all those embarrassing things, do I?"
"Not yet anyway. I remember both sessions well."
"Okay, well, Birgitte started talking about when we first met in Montreal. What she noticed immediately about me was that I have no cruelty in me, that I have kindness and gentleness in me, and that is why my high school students loved me. And what she noticed about you in those brief moments when I came out of the bathroom, and you were waiting for me, was that you...you also had that 'kindness vibe', as she calls it." Francesca swallowed.

Why thank you, Birgitte.

"She said that the kindness, the gentleness, and the concern were pouring out of your eyes. Her words. And then, then, she noticed that when we walked towards your office, you walked beside me, not in front of me or behind me. She...she...thought that was very important." Francesca breathed deeply again.

Birgitte, how observant of you. I couldn't exactly have put my arms around your wife. That is your job.

"Do you want to comment at all?"

"No."

"Well, now comes the harder part. Several hard parts. The first one is that she...she...felt that you certainly couldn't be my mother. After all, I have a mother."

Astrid nodded. *This is getting interesting. Don't get emotional, Astrid. Be like Em, calm, cool, and collected. Some chance if my feelings pour out of my eyes. Will I never learn? I guess not. I am who I am.*

"But she said that because we exhibited those emotions so readily that perhaps you were my spiritual mother." Francesca covered her face and looked down. "This is so embarrassing. Please don't be angry with me. Please. Please. I didn't agree with her. Lots of people are kind. It doesn't make any of them my spiritual mother."

"Why would I be angry with you?"

"Because...because...maybe you think I am trying to get you to actually *be* my mother."

"I see." *Don't worry, Francesca, Em would never allow me to be so unorthodox. Even if I have tendencies in that direction. We should have had children, Em and me. Then I would never get into trouble like this. She didn't want children, despite my maternal instincts. Am I angry with her because of this deprivation? I don't know. Something to talk about with her. We have talked about it endlessly, but maybe it's time to return to it.*

"Francesca, I am not angry. I will never be angry over any feelings you express here. They are genuine feelings, and I respect them."

"Really?"

"Of course. Now, I know you are not finished. I think you have more embarrassing things to say, whether about me or about sex, I am not sure. I am here to listen."

"Okay. Okay. When she said that about me having no cruelty in me, I responded by saying that she was never cruel either. But she reminded me that she had hurt me and hoped never to do it again, and that made her different from me." Tears were welling up in Francesca's eyes. Her breathing became ragged. "I have to tell you about the incident, don't I? I'd rather forget it. I hold no grudges against her. I still think it was my fault for being so obtuse."

Astrid passed the box of tissues to her. *Tell me, Francesca. I am sure it was not your fault. I believe in your kindness. I am sure you are never cruel.*

"This happened early on in our co-habitation, maybe three months after I got here. This is so hard. Why? It was stupid. Why can't I just say it to you?"

"Maybe because it still hurts?"

Francesca gasped. "I know she never meant to hurt me. She just got frustrated with my 'innocence', as she calls it. And she raised her voice slightly. It was over in seconds, and her arms were around me, and she was telling me how much she loved me."

"Well, you tell me what happened, and then we'll work out why you still feel hurt. Alright?"

Francesca nodded and wiped the tears from her face. "It was the middle of the afternoon, on a day when we only worked in the morning. And we were...in the bedroom...just starting to...you know...undress each other. We were happy, happy to be together, after a year apart, after she left Montreal. It felt like we were making up for that wasted year. We are still making up for that year. I am not sure if we can ever make up for that year. The bell rang. Birgitte had an inkling that it was the mail carrier because she had ordered an Italian book for me, but she didn't say. She just threw some clothes on, jogging pants and a T-shirt, without a bra. She would have been the one to go down and answer the door, because my German wasn't that good yet. But I...I was so disturbed by how exposed she looked. You see, she is so-o-o beautiful. And I couldn't bear it that some man was going to see, you know...the shape of her breasts, when they are exclusively for my pleasure and no one else's. And I said it. I said that I was being stupid but that I couldn't handle it. I apologized because I don't own her body. But I begged her to put something else on top of the T-shirt. She said nothing but threw a sweatshirt over her T-shirt, looked at me, and I nodded. When she finally closed the front door, I came down, not much more clothed than she had been. We stood in the hall and looked at each other. I was on the verge of tears, because I knew that I had behaved abominably. I don't own her body. I repeated it again. I apologized over and over. She told me to stop." Francesca began to sob.

"Is this when she raised her voice?"

Francesca nodded. "I can't forget it. But she wasn't angry about me feeling possessive of her body. She just wanted to make me understand that she felt the same way about *my* body. And why couldn't I see that? She said...she said...in a slightly louder tone than usual...she said, 'How do you think I feel when Bjorn or Bradley stare at *your*...chest?' She didn't use that word. Do I have to say the word she used? Anyway, she made me know in no uncertain terms that she felt just as possessive. And me, being me, being naïve and innocent—she used both those words—couldn't understand because I see her as the beautiful one, and I'm the one, as my father says, with those two blobs stuck onto my chest. And I wailed that I never tried to look provocative, and I would be more careful in the future. I begged her to forgive me. And then she, too, started to cry. She held me in her arms and said that she loved my innocence, my being guileless, but that sometimes it frustrated her. Then she said in German *'meine Liebe'* over and over again and I melted. She threw in some Danish, and I was helpless in her arms. Finally, she said that it was time to play some Bach together. And we did, the sonata that we recently recorded for Deutsche Grammophon, and...and...do I have to go on?"

"Only if you want to. Did something happen after you played Bach?"

"Something did. Something different. She made love to me in a way that...trying to show me that my father was wrong. I have to tell you that I have always felt that I have very little sensation in my breasts. Birgitte, on the other hand, is tremendously sensitive in that area. So, she rarely emphasized, let's say, that area of my body in our lovemaking. But after our 'fight', which to this day she denies was a fight—it was the day she hurt me—she basically took no notice of this declaration of mine about my lack of sensitivity and pursued her own course." Francesca stopped momentarily.

"And?"

"It was an awakening for me."

"She woke up a part of your body that for you was almost dead after your father so damagingly described it to you."

 "Yes. I had never experienced anything like that before. And she was not gentle. *I* have to be really gentle with her. She was like a tiger. It scared *her*. She kept asking me if she was hurting me. And when it was over, she remarked that my pleasure centres were so close to my pain centres. And I guess she is right. Because my first experiences of sex were so painful." Francesca stopped suddenly, unable to go on. "I don't want to cry, Dr. Paul. I don't want to give my father the satisfaction of having hurt me, of having changed me, of having made me feel pain as pleasure. But he has."

"But you *did* feel pleasure, didn't you?"

"Like never before."

"And Birgitte continues to make love to you like that?"

"Yes, but she still asks if she is hurting me."

"But you love it. And you let her know that you love it."

"Well, I don't want her to feel guilty. It's just the way I am. And I do love it. We are still continuing to learn things about each other. A few weeks ago, I started to do something to her that she had thought she would never like. And now she asks for it."

Astrid was nodding. *My, my, I had no idea we would end up here today. What will Em say? I hope she tells me that I am the best psychoanalyst she knows.*

"Francesca, have you ever done stretch classes?"

"All the time. I work out in the gym, but stretch classes are just as important."

"And you have felt that pain when you are stretching a specific muscle?" Francesca nodded. "But then slowly, as you try to release the tension, you begin to relax, and it doesn't hurt so much?"

"If I can relax, sometimes the pain goes away, or at least, it diminishes. What are you trying to tell me?"

"Yes, Francesca, what am I trying to tell you?"

"You want me to answer my own question."

Come on. Francesca, I know you can figure this one out.

"So, you are trying to tell me that there may come a time when pain and pleasure may not be so close together because I will be more and more awake to the pleasure that I receive from Birgitte, since my father's voice will become more and more diminished, less and less predominant in my memory, in my mind. I will be released from his grip on me."

Good girl. I love your brain. Em would say that I actually love you. Because I do. Astrid smiled. So did her patient.

Chapter Fifteen

<u>Astrid and Emma</u>

"That...that was just what I needed, Em."

They were lying in bed after a strenuous round of lovemaking.

"Glad I could pleasure you, my love."

Astrid turned towards her partner and took her hand. "I love you so much. It was really hard a few weeks ago when you were ignoring me. I...I can't live like that."

"Live like what?

"You know. Live without knowing."

"Live without knowing what?"

"Oh, come on, Em."

"You're going to need to say it. I want to hear what you feel that you don't know."

"When we don't make love, I feel that you don't love me. There, I said it."

"Oh, my God, Asti, where did that come from? How could you doubt my love?"

"Well, it felt like that. I felt unloved."

"Oh, Asti, I am such a terrible, selfish person. I get so caught up in what I am doing. But there is no excuse for my behaviour. I know I do that—get lost—and you are always there, and I don't value it. I have always been the selfish one in this relationship. There are things you want, and if I don't want them, too, I deprive you of them, because I know you would never go against my wishes." Emma stroked Astrid's face. "There is malice in me and none in you."

"Like when I wanted a baby?"

"Yes, like when you wanted a baby. I denied you that desire."

"Do you regret it now?"

"I regret hurting you. I regret taking advantage of your devotion to my wishes."

Astrid began to cry. Emma put her arms around her. "Oh, Asti, Asti, Asti, Asti. Do you still want to have a child now, at forty-seven?"

Astrid shook her head. "No, but I think it has had an effect on me."

"What kind of effect?" Emma continued to stroke Astrid's head, her hair, her neck. "Can you tell me?"

Astrid tried to stop crying. She pulled away from Emma and stared up at the ceiling.

"Tell me, my love. Please tell me."

"Well, I was wondering today if my maternal instinct with my patients—"

"—With Francesca in particular—someone who has not had a good mother, whereas you would have been a great mother—"

"—Would actually be less pronounced had I had my own child."

"You actually wondered that?"

"It seems to me like a logical question."

Emma sat up and drew her knees towards her chest. "Asti, you *are* maternal. You care so much about your patients. You find it really difficult to turn off those feelings of concern for the good of your patient sometimes. It is who you are. You could have had ten children, and you would still be maternal, and caring, and sensitive, and kind. No, my dear, there is no way that you could ever shut off your maternal instinct. I know I reprimand you sometimes for crossing the line, but I love you for it. I would not have you any other way. And in the end, despite my attempts to rein you in, you always succeed. Your instincts turn out to be right. You know your patients because you feel their pain so deeply. But I know you suffer. I just want to lessen your suffering. When you call me in the evening from your office, I know you are lying on your couch, feeling all the sadness that has been expressed in that room. You chose an impossible profession for yourself. But, at the same time, the right profession for you. No one could do it better."

"You really believe that, Em?"

"I do, and I'm the expert. I teach others how to be analysts, but I happen to live with the best of the best, no matter how much I admonish you."

Chapter Sixteen

<u>Astrid and Emma</u>

Astrid's parents were getting ready for bed in their guest bedroom, and Astrid and Emma were getting undressed in their own. Astrid's parents, after retiring, had moved to her father's hometown in Vermont after decades of living and working and bringing up their family in Munich. For her parents' generation, Munich would always be the city of Hitler, and a reminder of all those relatives put to death by the Nazi extermination agenda. Her grandmother had been a hidden child in Holland who had met and fallen in love with another hidden child, both originally from Munich. Astrid's mother had been born in Holland, but at a certain point, her grandparents had returned to live and work in Munich. Astrid could never figure that one out. But she had spent a great deal of time in Holland during holidays, visiting the families of the Christian people who had saved her grandparents. She loved all those 'cousins' who still lived and worked on their great-grandparents' dairy farms.

"I just want you to know, Asti," Emma began, "that with your parents down the hall, we will not be making love tonight. We are just too noisy."

Astrid laughed, came over to her beloved, and embraced her. They kissed.

"Okay, stop now, Asti. Don't get me excited. Your father is not a fan of mine, and although your sister and her husband and three kids make up for us not having children, I don't want to remind him that our lovemaking goes nowhere, produces nothing."

"You really think that my father doesn't love you?"

"He doesn't even like me. He doesn't approve of me. I'm too much of an intellectual for him."

"But he loves my mother, and she is an intellectual, who also taught in a university—German literature, in fact. You couldn't get more intellectual than that. My mother loves you, though. Of that, I am sure."

"It's true. She accepts me as another daughter. But your father..."

"I'm an intellectual, too, Em."

They got into bed, turned out the lights, and continued talking. "But you practice your profession, and he loves the fact that you help people. He's proud of you. I stopped practicing. I write books and I teach."

"He may just be a little intimidated by you. Many people are. They see you as the 'expert', which I have to say is true."

"But he shouldn't be. He's an intelligent, successful man who I am sure uses his head to design all those beautiful buildings he has given the rest of us to contemplate and live and work in."

"Oh, Em." Astrid moved closer and started kissing Emma's face and eyes and mouth.

Emma gently pushed her away. "Stop, Asti. I only have so much willpower. Your parents are driving to Holland tomorrow. You can do whatever you have in mind tomorrow."

"But I want to make love to you now. Just keep your mouth shut and try not to scream."

Chapter Seventeen

<u>In Toronto</u>
<u>Birgitte and Richard</u>

Francesca and her old friend Simon were in the kitchen preparing the lunch. Birgitte and Richard, Simon's husband, were talking in the living room, because neither of them ever set foot in the kitchen of their respective homes. Richard was not looking happy and Birgitte knew why. He was feeling insecure about Simon. Francesca and Birgitte had come to Toronto, Francesca to play Simon's piano concerto—first with the student orchestra of the University of Toronto and then with the Toronto Symphony Orchestra—and she, Birgitte, to conduct it. She had only been supposed to conduct the student orchestra, but when the conductor of the TSO had come to the university to hear the concerto for the first time, he immediately begged Birgitte to conduct the concerto with his orchestra as well. She understood its jazziness way better than he had, and he could tell that she was a great conductor in her own right, even though she was the first violinist of the Munich Symphony Orchestra. Birgitte had been delighted to accept. She hadn't really wanted anyone else to interfere with the way that she and Francesca conceived of the music. It had been, for her anyway, a great experience. It had been exhausting for Francesca—and not because of the music—but because of Simon. Francesca was in the kitchen letting Simon know that he had behaved inappropriately with her.

"She's really letting him have it, isn't she, Birgitte? Does she yell at you like that?"

"What? Never. Never. Francesca doesn't fight. We never fight."

"You never fight? Simon and I fight all the time." Richard looked ready to talk about it.

"Okay, Richard, what is wrong? Tell me. I live thousands of kilometres away from here and no one is ever going to find out about the precariousness of your marriage, no one at least who is in your vicinity."

"You can tell that we are on rocky ground, can't you?" *Well, that and the fact that Simon had declared to Francesca the other day that he had always loved her and still does, despite his eight-year marriage to you. What a dishonest thing to do! Marry a man when he knew that he loved someone else!*

"Birgitte, did Francesca and Simon ever sleep together when they were students here in the music department of the university?"

"What? Richard, you wouldn't ask that question if you knew Francesca in any way. Did Simon tell you that Francesca had a boyfriend, Colin, when she studied here?"

Richard nodded. "She had been with him since the age of sixteen, I believe."

"Francesca would never have cheated on Colin. It's not in her. She did eventually leave Colin, despite the fact that her parents believed they would get married. She didn't love him, but that doesn't mean she could ever have conceived of sleeping with another person. Not Francesca."

"I'm sorry for insulting her or you. It's just that I know that Simon is bisexual, and I am not! And—and Simon is *my* husband." Richard looked as if he were about to cry.

Birgitte took a deep breath. "Look, Richard, there is something you have to know about Francesca. What she is yelling at him about is something very specific."

"Oh? And what is that?"

"Francesca does not like to be touched in an indiscriminate way, not out of affection or anything else, especially in public. You must not touch her, her arm, her shoulder, her elbow, and God forbid you should put your arms around her, even if she played your concerto brilliantly."

"But she did play it brilliantly. *I* wanted to put my arms around her. I was ready to run from my seat in the brass section and hug her, too. You can't blame Simon for coming on stage afterwards. You were the one who called to him to take a bow."

"But Francesca does not like to be touched. Did you notice that even I, her lover, did not hug her, despite the fact that conductors often do those things?"

"You didn't even hold her hand up there."

"Exactly. Simon came between us and held our hands and then we took a bow together. But he touches her all the time. He puts his hand on her back and leaves it there! You can't imagine how hard that is for her. He touches her face. He sometimes touches her hair."

"Stop! Stop! I hate it when he does that. Oh, God, Birgitte, what if he actually loves her?"

Birgitte felt such compassion for this man. *Richard, you are in deep trouble.*

"He's never written me a trumpet concerto, or a sonata. He's even written her those little pieces which she sometimes plays as encores at her performances."

Birgitte nodded her head. *And she plays those brilliantly, too, I might add.* "Richard, I think that a marital counselor may be in order here. You shouldn't be fighting all the time anyway, despite your insecurity over Francesca. And don't worry. She's *my* lover and would never do anything...She doesn't love him like that. Today she might not love him at all. That would be my guess."

Chapter Eighteen

<u>Francesca in the Office VIII</u>

When she opened her office door and saw Francesca in the waiting room, Astrid realized that she had missed her. *She only left for a week! She didn't come to two whole sessions, and you missed her!? What is wrong with you? Em says that it is the way I am, and she wouldn't have me any other way. Can I at least smile at her, Em?* They both smiled at each other. Francesca looked a little pale. Thankfully she hadn't gone that far and Birgitte had been with her. *Well, let's find out what happened between her and her old friend Simon, the composer. I am sure she played the concerto admirably and her favourite conductor was at the helm. She was not so sure about Simon. He had written the concerto specifically for her. Is that usual or unusual? Did it mean anything?*

Francesca sat down in front of her and opened her mouth to speak, but nothing came out. Astrid waited.

"Who marries someone when they are in love with someone else, Dr. Paul?"

I was right. "Maybe because he knew he couldn't have you?"

"How...how did you know I was talking about Simon?"

"Well...uh..."

"Because you are just so smart and perceptive, not to mention a psychoanalyst."

"Good answer. Has Simon ever written music for any other specific person?"

"No. Only for me. And right now, he is in the middle of a violin sonata that he is writing for me and Birgitte. He's trying to get to my heart through my—"

"—Wife. Strange."

"Dr. Paul, I'm not trying to avoid a difficult conversation, but I want to say something completely unrelated. May I?"

"Of course. Go right ahead."

"I love it when you call Birgitte my wife. I can't tell you how it makes me feel. But you, of course, are going to want me to tell you how it makes me feel."

Astrid laughed. "How does it make you feel?"

"It makes me feel totally accepted by you. It's the most wonderful feeling."

"Others do not call Birgitte your wife?"

"Well, we never tell anyone about that little private ceremony we had in that bedroom in Florence. It was just her and me and these two ebony rings that I had bought. I asked her if she'd be my wife. It startled her, but she said yes. I put the ring on her finger, and then I gave her the other one and she asked me the same thing, and I said yes. It was kind of romantic."

"And since you don't wear them on the finger of Apollo but on the finger of Saturn—"

"—Well, they were too big."

"Am I supposed to believe that?" Francesca looked a little stunned. *Tell me the truth now, Francesca.*

"Okay, okay, I bought them too big; I wanted them to fit the middle finger because I didn't want anyone to know about us...yet."

"You never say that you are married, then, even to your friends?"

"It's possible that Birgitte has told Magda—you know, the cellist who now lives with Bradley. I don't know. Magda knows a lot about a lot of things. I tell Jordan stuff when we speak to each other. I am fine with Magda being Birgitte's good friend. When Ghita came back here after being in Montreal for that year, she told Magda how unhappy she was about leaving me. She really needed Magda. But Magda has never breathed a word of our situation to anyone."

"People don't know you live together and how you live together?"

"Well, some do now. I have to feel really sure about them."

"Okay, who knows?"

"Besides my mother and Stefano and Birgitte's parents? Well, Bradley and Magda, who are getting married. And you have to know that when Bradley lusted after me for a while at the beginning, he never touched me. The violinist, Linda, who sits beside Birgitte in the orchestra and replaces her when she conducts; and her husband, Konrad. There are two men who sit behind them, Philippe, from Marseilles, and Ugo, who is from Arezzo. They're a married couple and are not bisexual, and although Ugo and I love to talk with each other about all kinds of things in Italian, he never touches me. Neither does Philippe. Of course, it is possible that Birgitte has told them about me, that I don't like to be touched. She is very protective of me. Anyway, these are the people that Ghita and I consider our good friends. We spend time together."

"Are we going to talk about touching today, Francesca?"

Francesca took a sudden audible inhale. *I shouldn't be shocking you, Francesca, but it is what we have to talk about today, not about how much you love it when I call Birgitte your wife. Although it pleases me that I can give you that little bit of acknowledgement and acceptance. I am glad you told me. I should say that.*

"Francesca, it really pleases me to know that I can give you that little bit of acknowledgement and acceptance. Thank you for telling me."

"But we have to talk about touching, don't we?"

"We do. Did Simon touch you—"

"—So much, it was painful. You know, he even hugged me onstage when the audience was applauding. He was so pleased with himself. But it didn't give him the right to hug me."

"It does happen."

"Well, if it keeps happening to me, I might just have to stop performing."

"Well, we wouldn't want that. So we had better talk about it in more detail. What happened?"

"I'm not going to cry. Why should I cry? I yelled at him, you know?"

"You did?"

"On the day we left Toronto. My mother and Stefano drove us back to Montreal and we stayed there for a night and left from Montreal. But we, Ghita and I, were invited to Simon's and Richard's house for lunch first. I slept for twelve hours straight after that last concert."

"That often happens to you."

"But this time, I was so upset, that...that...We got back to the hotel, and I told Ghita that I wanted to take a bath, with her in it. And we did. She practically had to carry me to bed. Dr. Paul, I couldn't even make love to her. That never happens, no matter how tired I am. It wasn't just the tiredness. After the concert, Simon told me that he always loved me and still did. I was furious with him. Ghita and I went back to the hotel almost immediately after the concert, and I told her what he said. She had to wake me up the next day so we could go to Simon's house for lunch. When we got there, I went into the kitchen, where Simon was preparing the food, and the words just flowed out of me. Ghita told me that she and Richard heard me yelling and they talked about their pitiful marriage. She advised him to go into marital counselling, but he told her that Simon had refused."

"What did you say to Simon?"

"That there was no way that we could ever be a couple. That he had to stop touching me as if he owned me. That's what it feels like, Dr. Paul, when men touch me. They feel entitled or something. Like they own me. I belong to them." Francesca began to cry. "I don't belong to them. When I was a kid, my father did own me. Or at least I thought he did. And then one day, one night, he came to my room, and Colin was lying naked beside me. And I felt as if I had broken the leash. My father was shocked. And the next day I threatened him with telling my mother." Francesca was almost panting.

My poor, poor Francesca, I can't hold you now. But know that I feel as if I am holding you. All I can do is hand you a stupid box of tissues. You're right, Em, this is a terrible job for me. But I will never give it up.

"Take deep breaths, Francesca. I am here. Your father and Simon are on the other side of the Atlantic."

Francesca nodded. She didn't speak for quite a long while. "It feels as if I never want to talk again about anything. And I feel like I am crazy. This touching thing is so—"

"—So fundamental to who you are, Francesca? Of course it is."

"Will it continue to plague me forever?"

"I'm not that smart or perceptive, even though I am a psychoanalyst."

"But it could, couldn't it?"

"'Forever' is not a word I will ever use, since, in fact, I am a psychoanalyst and always have hope. And today, I am truly hopeful for you."

"Really? Why?"

"Remember when you said to me that you enfold yourself into this room and surrender yourself to me?"

"Yes."

"That's why."

Chapter Nineteen

<u>Francesca and Cora II</u>

Francesca's office door was wide open. She was sitting at her desk writing at her computer. She was writing about a painting that had been intriguing her for years. She had had so many thoughts about this painting, *Portrait of the Dwarf Nano Morgante* by Bronzino in the Pitti Palace, and she finally had decided that it was time to put pen to paper and reveal them. She thought that she might show it to Professor Green when she finished it. It seemed as if she would finish it fairly soon, because she just couldn't stop writing. She had done so much research on it when living in Italy and since all her notes were sitting there in her computer, she couldn't understand why she had never done it before—perhaps because it was such a famous masterpiece, and part of that polemic initiated by Vasari about the comparison between sculpture and painting, and she had never felt worthy. She stopped writing for a moment and realized that it was like her attitude to Chopin. She was afraid to play Chopin. How could she ever play him when Martha Argerich, the greatest pianist, was out there playing Chopin better than anyone ever could? Birgitte was urging her to play a Chopin concerto, with her as conductor with the Munich Orchestra, because Goldschmidt was intent on getting her to conduct more. Francesca believed that he was thinking of retiring, and he wanted to hand the baton over to someone he really trusted. But Birgitte was his first violinist. Could she give up that position to be a conductor? She conducted the student orchestra at the conservatory and taught violin there, not to mention starting the orchestra in their private high school in Montreal where she had taught history. She had conducted her in the Rachmaninov second concerto with the Munich Philharmonic, and Simon's concerto in Toronto. But she was now beginning to be a soloist as well. She, Magda, and Birgitte had formed the Munich Trio and had been playing at Bach Festivals and then had made that recording for Deutsche Grammophon. Why couldn't Birgitte have two professions: be the first female conductor of a great orchestra and have a career as a violinist? Last year Birgitte had played the Tchaikovsky violin concerto under Goldschmidt. He had twisted her arm to play the concerto, and it had been magnificent. After all, she herself did two things. Why couldn't Birgitte? She would have to discuss this with Birgitte. They hadn't really talked about it because Goldschmidt had never actually said he wanted to retire. But he was at least seventy-five, and it was bound to happen sooner or later.

The question remained whether she could attempt Chopin. She played Chopin when she was alone in the house, his pieces for solo piano. She was working on his third piano sonata at the moment. Birgitte had told her that at the concert given by the teachers at the Conservatory this year, she had told the director of the school that they would be playing again. The year before they had played the Franck sonata, and a critic had been in the audience. He had written a glowing review. He had said that she and Birgitte were so in sync with each other it was like hearing one instrument. He had also written that review when she had played Brahms, saying that it had been the most sensuous performance he had ever heard. That was because she was concentrating so hard on trying to hear Birgitte's violin. They had practiced it at home together for hours. It had been like making love to Birgitte. It was Birgitte's debut as first violin. The critic had also written that he expected that the Munich patrons were going to fall in love with their new Danish concertmaster. The article was called "Who is Francesca Oliver?" She wasn't supposed to play the concerto. The soloist who planned to play it first said she couldn't come to the rehearsal, and Birgitte suggested to the conductor that she, Francesca, could rehearse with them. She had, and then the soloist had cancelled the concert as well. So, she had been asked to be the soloist. And that was basically how her career had started.

Francesca looked up suddenly. Cora had just entered her office. She had been so engrossed in her thoughts that she hadn't noticed her student until she had tapped her knuckles on her desk.

"Sorry, Cora, I was thinking very hard about something and didn't realize you were standing there."

"I guess that's why you do great things, write books about art and play music." Francesca gave her an inquiring look. *What the hell did she mean?*

"Your powers of concentration. I have this feeling that you never waste a minute."

"I can waste time just as much as the next person."

"But you do so much. How often do you play the piano?"

"What? I...I...I play the piano every single day for hours. You have to understand. It's a question of need. I can't live without playing the piano."

"That's what I mean. And you teach us. And you write. You're writing something now, aren't you?"

Francesca nodded. "And you know what? If I manage to publish this article, I am going to play a Chopin piano concerto with the orchestra. You have no idea how terrifying that is for me."

"Why?"

"Because...never mind. I said it and so I will do it."

"You know what Melanie says about you?"

"What?"

"She says she wants to be you."

"No. No. That can't be. No one wants to be me."

"What do you mean? All your students admire you. You are phenomenal. I've heard you play the piano. Remember that concert at the Conservatory? You played a sonata by Cesar Franck with that willowy blonde Scandinavian violinist. She was a Botticelli-like Venus." *Birgitte, a Botticelli-like Venus?*

"Really? You think Birgitte looks like a Botticelli Venus? She certainly does not have hair that goes below her waist. Her hair just reaches her shoulders."

"I only said that to show off how much I learned from you in art history class. Anyway, I had never heard such beautiful music in my whole life."

"I think Franck should get the credit for that."

"But you made his music come alive."

"If you want to hear us again, you can come next month."

"I'd love to. I'd love to hear you play with the orchestra, too."

"I'll let you know if and when it happens."

"Uh...Francesca, can I sit down and talk to you?"

"Of course. Will it require that I shut the door?"

"Yeah, I think so."

Francesca stood up and went to close her door. She then rolled her chair closer to the one that Cora would be sitting in. She smiled at Cora.

"So, is it good news or bad news?"

"It's great news!"

"I'm so happy for you. Are you going to tell me about it or is it too private?"

"No, I want to tell you. I desperately want to tell you."

"Go ahead."

"You were right about everything."

"You mean about telling the truth?"

"Yeah, about telling the truth."

"And are you going to continue seeing her naked body?"

"Stop! It's not funny. You have no idea how scared I was. The thought of giving up that pleasure was terrifying."

"Okay. Okay. I'm going to stop talking altogether. You have my undivided attention."

"So, that night I was in our room, in bed reading, and Melanie came in almost in tears. She slammed the door shut and declared that Jeremy was an asshole, and she broke up with him. And I asked her why she was crying, since that was a good thing, because I had known all along that he wasn't any good. She proceeded to tell me that all he really wanted to do was go to bed with her and she had never felt like it. She told me that they actually had never had sex. I was surprised. I could not have imagined Jeremy waiting around for a girl to surrender to him. So, when she told him that she didn't want to see him anymore, he got really angry—as if she had deprived him of something he deserved. She was even afraid of him. Fortunately, his roommate came in at that moment and asked if he should leave, and she said no, that she was going to do the leaving. Not bad, huh? Then she proceeded to get undressed. I couldn't stop staring. I was so afraid that it might be the last time I would ever be able to have that privilege. Of course, after she put on her pyjamas, she got into bed with me. Francesca, I thought I might cry. I didn't want to ever say goodbye to her. You understand?"

"Of course I understand."

"Then she went on to say that she had never much enjoyed sex with men. Her previous boyfriends—there had been two—didn't seem to know what to do to make her come. Then she started to cry because she thought that something was wrong with her, because she only had orgasms alone."

"Are you sure that it is alright for Melanie that you tell me such intimate things about her?"

"I am sure it is."

Why was it so easy for this woman to talk about sex when she had so much trouble talking to Dr. Paul?

"She also said that the male anatomy was not so attractive to her, and that also scared her. And then she said the most startling thing. She said that sometimes she wished I were a man, because she knew she could love me."

"How did you take that?"

"I just turned to her and asked her why I couldn't just love her like a woman."

"Good for you."

"She looked at me in shock and then she asked if I wanted to kiss her. And we kissed for a long time. I restrained myself, if you must know. She said no one had ever kissed her like that before. And that was my moment. I told her that no one had ever loved her like I did. And that's all I'm going to tell you, because the rest is just between me and Melanie. But it felt so good, Francesca. I felt like I had been walking in a desert for three and half years and finally I was given water to drink."

"And is she as happy as you are?"

"Well, she's finally had an orgasm; several, actually."

"And she took to loving you quite naturally, then?"

"Well, I don't know how her parents are going to feel. But we are living in Munich, and they are living...I have no idea exactly where. She can't bring me home to meet them, but I'm not sure I want to. It will have to be a secret from them. It won't be that easy for her. But she says she loves me more than she loves the idea of pleasing her parents. And we owe it all to you. I told her that I talked to you about my problems beforehand, and that you had advised me to tell the truth. I think she wants to come here and thank you herself."

"She can come and see me anytime. And so can you. I am really happy for the both of you."

Cora was beaming. It felt good. Francesca suddenly had the feeling that she would like to make Dr. Paul feel good, but she wondered if that would ever be possible. She had such a long way to go. Well, at least she had started the journey.

Chapter Twenty

<u>Francesca in the Office IX</u>
"I have had the experience of making a student—no, two students—very happy. I am going to be a thesis advisor for one of them, although she is in the history department and not the art history department, but I was approved."

"I'm not surprised."

"Well, a few days ago, she told me that she was in love with her roommate, a girl, and had been for three and half years—she was miserable. I told her to tell the truth, because she couldn't feel any worse. Well, she did, and it all worked out. I had no idea it would work out, but in the end, I did a good thing, and it felt really good." Francesca stopped talking for a moment and took a deep breath. "She spoke so easily to me about sex. It was incredible. I will never be able to do that with you."

"Francesca, it doesn't matter how it exits from you. It just matters that you tell me eventually."

Francesca looked at Astrid in a rather guilty fashion. *Okay, what's coming now? Please don't feel guilty about something you have yet to tell me.*

"There's something I didn't tell you about Toronto."

"Oh?" Francesca looked fearful. *How can she be afraid of me? I guess because she never loved a parental figure before. Is she afraid she will lose me? If she only knew how hard I fight to keep her.*

"Please, please don't be angry with me."

"Francesca, I won't be angry with you. I promise."

"How can you say that? You have no idea what I'm about to tell you. It's important."

I shouldn't have said 'I promise'. I feel as if I could never be angry at her. There I go again—feelings. They are going to be my undoing."

"Francesca, remember when you said quite a while ago that it was so hard to tell me everything? It was when you said you concentrated on one thing in a session and something else never came up."

"I remember. I remember. We don't have to go into detail."

Astrid smiled. "It's true. We don't have to rehash it. Well, I accepted that—"

"—Excuse?"

"It was the truth. Not an excuse. It takes a while to trust another person so much that you are willing to tell the most hurtful things of your past."

"But I shouldn't be afraid anymore of you, that you will hurt me. You have never hurt me."

"I once asked you if it was important to you that you liked my appearance, and I think—no, I know—you took it as a reprimand for being superficial."

"I was afraid of what your reaction might be. I am still afraid sometimes. But I shouldn't be. It's not right."

"How is that? The emotion of fear is very genuine. There is no right or wrong."

"But it's not right. It's not fair to you, to the kind of person you are. I should know by now that you accept me."

"I do accept you, but I probably should not have said that I promise I won't be angry. It sounded too easy. It was making light of your genuine emotion of fear. I won't do that again. I understand your reaction. Thank you for pointing that out to me."

Astrid paused here. *Now let's get down to it.* "So, what did you leave out?"

"I saw someone in Toronto."

Colin? I was hoping you would.

"You're smiling. You know who it is. How do you know everything before I say it? Who are you?"

Astrid lifted her hands in the air and smiled some more. "I'm afraid I can't tell you that."

"You are a magician."

"Was it a good reunion?"

"Well, he came backstage after the performance with the Toronto Symphony. He came with his wife. Birgitte and I were in the room for the soloists, and an employee of the theatre knocked on the door and asked if I wanted to see this couple. I opened the door wider and there he was. I said Colin's name out loud, so the employee knew that I was familiar with these people and left. I was a little tongue-tied. I have to say I was just getting over the feel of Simon's body wrapped around mine. Birgitte was with me, trying to make it all better with Francesca, the child."

"Can I ask you a question?"

"Yes."

"Did Colin come towards you and hug you or kiss you?"

"Well, his wife was there, so no. She looked a little scared—you know, intimidated. Why would that be?"

"You are a *very* accomplished young woman, Francesca."

"Oh."

Astrid waited.

"I wouldn't have been uncomfortable with any type of physical contact with Colin. I had known him as a kid. We were intimate for years. His body is so familiar. And yes, I always had orgasms with him, in case you are wondering. And he loved me, legitimately. He wasn't married to someone else like Simon. And he helped me. I owe him a lot. But I am glad he was there with his wife, because after Simon's harassment of me, I was feeling fragile. They were holding hands. I liked them. They have two kids, and they are both elementary school teachers. All Colin ever wanted was to teach little kids. I was happy for him. And I know I hurt him by so abruptly going off to Siena to continue my studies. He had said he would go with me. Remarkable, eh?"

"He loved you."

"And I spent years lying to him about my feelings. I needed him and used him. And I started with Massimiliano almost as soon as I got to Siena. I never wanted to be without a man, just in case my father showed up. I was a horrible person in those years."

"Massimiliano?"

"He was my boyfriend in Siena. He was studying psychology. He wanted to be a therapist—God help his patients. He wasn't exactly stupid, but, well...he was certainly lacking in brain power."

"And you were with him anyway?"

"I had no expectations whenever I was in a relationship with a man. I just had to have one for protection. I think that at that point I was more afraid of my father beating me than fuck...Sorry, but I can't think of another word for it in relation to my father."

"I am not offended. Use whatever word you please...So, after you were sixteen and had started up with Colin, and you had already threatened him with exposure, he was still beating you?"

Francesca looked down, away from Astrid.

"Say it, Francesca. It's one little word."

"Yes." She started to cry.

I am so sorry, Francesca. What a monster.

"Please don't ask me why he was always angry with me. I wasn't giving him what he wanted. I wasn't playing in competitions. I wasn't making a name for myself. But I was practicing piano all the time. And then in Siena I was performing all the time, with chamber groups, as a soloist, and with the student orchestra. I was learning so much music. I don't know how I kept it all in my head."

"And when you switched departments?"

"Well, I continued to perform with the other students. I couldn't leave them high and dry without a pianist. And my father continued to pay my piano teacher for lessons. But one day, Luigi, the most respected and sought-after teacher at the Accademia Chigiana, told me he couldn't teach me anymore. I was afraid that it meant that my father had stopped paying him, but really, my mother would never have allowed that. And she didn't tell him for a long time that I was officially studying art history at the

University of Siena. But she would never have let him stop paying for my education. Never. She would have left him. But she didn't leave him until so much later. I never understood her. At any rate, had they split up then, my mother would have continued to support me. She had, after all, always supported her parents, when she was a nurse in Northern Quebec and later in Montreal. That's why she couldn't continue her studies and become a doctor. Long story."

"I hope you will tell me that one, too."

"But not today, although I know I have to, because it involves my grandfather." Francesca paused. "When I came back to Montreal, and started my PhD program...I know, I know, why the hell would I come back to Montreal, when I could have gone back to Toronto? I came back because of the piano, *the* piano, that beautiful Yamaha grand that my parents had bought me. I wanted to play *my* piano. Of course, now I play a Steinway grand in our house. It is such a great piano. Birgitte had bought it from a friend of hers who was moving away from Munich. Little did she know...Anyway, I was able to teach at McGill. I taught art history survey courses as a teaching assistant, and I could get my own apartment. And my mother bought me an upright piano so I could continue to play, but every now and then, I came home during the day to play my piano. And then I got that job at the high school and met Birgitte."

"Why did this Luigi stop teaching you?"

"He said that I was a better, more accomplished pianist than he was. That I had my own voice and didn't need him telling me what to do."

"Was that true?"

Francesca shrugged her shoulders. "Maybe?" There was silence for quite a while.

"Do you want me to go back to talking about Colin, Dr. Paul?"

"I understand Colin and your need for a boyfriend much better now."

"You mean because I finally told you that my father continued beating me. Again, I'm sorry that I left that out. I kind of think that you always know everything anyway."

"It doesn't matter what I know or think I know. It matters that you say it."

"Of course, Dr. Paul. Please—"

"—Don't be angry? Is that what you were going to say?

But Francesca couldn't say anything else because she was crying.

Oh, Em. What am I going to do? This woman is breaking my heart. I need you to save me from wanting to be her mother.

Chapter Twenty-One

<u>Astrid and Marisa</u>

After her last patient of the day, Astrid smiled at Marisa and shut her door. She climbed onto her couch and called Emma.

"Bad day, my love?"

But Astrid was already crying.

"Oh, my poor Asti. Can you talk?"

"Maybe not. I sometimes think you gave up your practice because I talk so much about mine. It would be like having two practices for you. I shouldn't be talking about any of this with you. Even though I am not your student, you are still my expert."

"Just tell me, Asti. If it's wrong, it's wrong. I am your wife. And I am here to make you feel better. I think we can live with the guilt. I hope we can live with the guilt... even if you should not be telling me the stories you heard today in your office. Did you see Francesca today?"

Astrid was still crying. "There are so many horrid people in this world. Why did her father marry and have children if he was only going to hurt his beautiful child? Why? Why, Em?"

"Asti, I'm home already. My book's been edited. It's out of my hands. I'm free to take care of you. Please come home. You can be my child for the rest of the day."

"Okay. See you soon."

Astrid got off the couch, went into her bathroom, and washed her face. *Oh, what the hell. So Marisa will see that I've been crying. It won't be the first time.*

She picked up her briefcase and put on her coat, took her keys, and opened the door to her exceptional receptionist.

Marisa looked up. "Sometimes I don't know how you do it. It was a trying day, wasn't it? I can see that—"

"—That I've been crying?"

Marisa just nodded. The phone rang and Astrid walked up to the desk and waited.

"Yes, she's here, Randall. I'll put you on."

Astrid took the receiver. "Yes, Randall. What can I do for you?" Astrid tried to sound cheerful but surely was failing.

"Can you forgive me? I behaved so horribly last time. I said such terrible things. I'm sorry. I take everything bad in my life out on you and then I tell you I hate you and never want to see you ever again. But I do want to see you. My wife says she won't live with me unless I continue to see you."

"Do *you* want to see me, or does your wife want you to see me?"

"*I* do. I really do. Can I come at my usual time on Thursday?"

"I'll check with Marisa." Marisa put him on hold.

"Am I still free on Thursday at four?"

"No, you have to see Randall," Marisa laughed.

"You mean you didn't cancel him when he walked out of here in a huff? I told you to."

"But I didn't, because I knew he was going to beg you to see him again."

"Really? Oh, Marisa, you are truly amazing. Pass me through to him again."

"I can see you then. Bye for now, Randall."

"Bye, and thank you. My wife just said to tell you she thanks you, too."

"Marisa, you are so wonderful. I don't tell you that enough. I couldn't handle this office without you. You speak English really well, and more than half my patients are English-speaking. You handle all the financial side of things. I never think about those things."

"Well, my husband is your accountant, and he has taught me exactly how he wants things done."

"You are totally discreet and guard my private life from...from...everyone. And most of all, you handle me and my emotions."

"You can be as emotional as you like Dr. Paul."

"Astrid, Marisa. You've been working here for fifteen years. I want you to call me Astrid."

"And I've been working here that long because you are so great to work for. And you are the best analyst in the business. I didn't cancel Randall because no one leaves you unless their analysis is well and truly over. Maybe not all analysts cry over their patients, but you do, because you feel so much. That's what makes you so great. The patients know how much you care. One thing, though. I once talked with Francesca about your running."

"You did?"

"How could I not? It was apparent that you had been running."

"And in the hallway, I did mention to her that I had been running a little slowly."

"Did you know that she ran the marathon last month?"

"No, I didn't. Did she finish?"

"Did she finish? She was the first woman after all the elite runners. She did say that she liked running but could live without marathons."

"That's interesting."

"Everything is interesting to you. She has an amazing body, that Francesca. So athletic. So strong. You, too. You are also athletic and strong-looking."

"Well, thank you. I wish I felt strong right about now."

"Tomorrow is another day, and maybe your patients will make you feel happier. Or maybe your wife will. Your patients will continue to get better because you are treating them. That's my opinion, anyway."

"Oh, Marisa, it was good to talk to you. Do you want to be my analyst?"

"No, you have one at home. I'm just here to cheer you on."

Chapter Twenty-Two

<u>Francesca in the Office X</u>

"I was a mess last time. I hate it when I have to tell you I left something out. I feel like a bad little girl. I was often the bad little girl with my father."

Oh, I hadn't thought of that. "So, when you were a bad little girl, and he hit you, was there something sexual about it?"

"Always."

"I see." Astrid was nodding.

"You are figuring something out, aren't you?"

"I am always figuring something out."

"Are you thinking about the pleasure/pain thing we've talked about?"

"Would you like to talk about that?"

Francesca sighed. "It's early on in the session to be talking about sex, don't you think? But okay. Here goes. When I first came to Munich, Birgitte had to use a lot of love toys with me. She had to penetrate me with a fake penis. She had to hit me. This is so embarrassing, I'm going to cry."

"But she stopped?"

"Pretty much. She doesn't fuck me from behind in the shower anymore, because she thinks of it as punishment. But sometimes, rarely, I ask to sit on that love toy, and she will let me because it isn't punishment. But now, I prefer to 'make love' and not fuck. Penetration with her fingers is special. I hardly ever ask to be penetrated with that plastic penis. I can't remember the last time she used it. Months. You're still thinking."

"Do you both consider it as progress that you do not ask for the love toy anymore?"

"Yes, definitely. It used to make me cry. I've stopped crying. I am with Birgitte now and my father isn't in the room with us anymore. Do *you* think that it is progress?"

"Yes, as long as you don't crave it and feel some resentment towards your wife for depriving you of a specific pleasure."

"I don't crave it. I am really really happy with our lovemaking now. My father is long gone. And that part of my body, about which we have talked already, is waking up, and I can feel a kind of bliss when she touches me there."

"And it was only after that incident with Simon that you couldn't make love?"

"I had to experience oblivion. I had to stop being conscious. I slept and slept."

"And the next day you were back to normal?"

"Well, the next night we slept in my mother's apartment, and it's small. Birgitte held me to keep me feeling whole, and I didn't initiate anything sexual. But as soon as we got back home, we didn't even make it up the stairs to the bedroom."

"So, you went two days without sex. Is that a long time for you?"

"Usually, we make love every day—making up for lost time—during the week when we are home from work, before dinner. Then we play music for several hours after dinner, and often we end up making love after making music. Dr. Paul, can we stop now—I mean, talking about sex? I feel as if I want to crawl under your desk and hide from your thinking mind. I am ready to talk about anything else, even really difficult things."

"Is there a really difficult thing that you have in mind now?"

"Unfortunately, yes. And I am so scared."

"Does it involve me?"

"Yes."

"Do you think you can talk about it?"

"It involves asking you something, like asking something from you."

"Like asking a favour?"

"Like a really big one that psychoanalysts would ordinarily not do."

What can that be? I have no idea.

"And how would you feel if I denied you?"

"It would be...it would be...I think I'd want to give up. I'd want to crawl into some hole and never come out. I need you to do this for me."

"It sounds like it. You're just going to have to tell me, Francesca."

"I know. And there's no way I can get around it. I need you there."

"You want me to be somewhere."

"Yes."

"Okay, start talking."

"Okay. Well, there is something I am afraid of. I am afraid of playing Chopin. I practice Chopin alone in the house, but I never play Chopin in public. Have you heard of Martha Argerich?"

"Of course. The world's greatest pianist."

"Well, she sort of owns Chopin, doesn't she?"

"You could say that."

"That's why I can't play Chopin in public."

"I have no doubt you can play Chopin. You are a virtuoso, Francesca. You will play him your way, and it will be beautiful."

"You think so?"

"I do. So, ask me."

"Well, Birgitte and I are supposed to play Chopin's first piano concerto with the orchestra here. She will be the conductor."

"You know that when you do play that concerto, I will be there."

"I know. This is different. This is asking you a real favour."

"Okay. Just ask me, Francesca."

"Well, Birgitte knows how scared I am. I have been suggesting umpteen other concertos. But the other day, when I was in my office writing an article about a famous painting by Bronzino, the painting of the dwarf Nano Morgante, I realized that I was writing almost automatically, because it is something I have been thinking about for years. But I have been scared to write about something so famous. Who the hell am I to have ideas about this painting? I am not worthy. It is the same way I feel about Chopin."

"I see."

"Well, a student came into my office, and I said to her that if I succeeded in publishing the article, I would play the Chopin concerto. Well, I have succeeded. I even translated the article into Italian, and it is going to be published in an art magazine in Italy."

"So now you have to play the Chopin concerto?"

"Yes."

"Are you practicing it?"

"Yes, but I am also practicing his third piano sonata, and Birgitte thinks that I should play the sonata at the concert that the Conservatory hosts every year for its teachers. Last year, although I am not a teacher, I played the Cesar Franck sonata with Birgitte, and it kind of started my music career here, because the conductor was there, and he told Birgitte to audition for first chair because the person in the first chair was retiring. And a critic was there, and he gave an unbelievable review of our performance and said that we should record it. This year with Magda we will probably be playing Mendelssohn's first trio. But Birgitte has asked the director to let me play the Chopin sonata even if I do not teach there. She said that I help her students because I accompany them on the piano when they come for a lesson to the house, and besides, I could be a guest because I have a certain...because I am no longer an unknown. The director has told me that all I have to do is teach one student. I will never teach piano, but Birgitte is right. If I want to play the concerto it is necessary for me to overcome this challenge first."

"Will the director say yes?"

"She can't say no to Birgitte. She can't lose Birgitte. She may be the chief of administration, but Birgitte is the heart and soul of the place. So I think it is going to happen in two weeks."

"And where do I come in?"

"You know how I say that playing the piano is another way of talking. And it makes me happy that you hear me expressing myself in this other language. If I said to you that I would be talking to you specifically the whole time, would you come and hear me play the sonata? I don't think I can play Chopin without you there holding my hand...metaphorically speaking. I really need you there, and now I am going to cry. I am sorry I am so dependent on you. I wish I didn't have to ask you this. Any other analyst would say no."

"Birgitte will be there, her parents, your mother, and Stefano, I presume?"

"Without Birgitte I couldn't even get on the stage. But without you, I think I would faint from fear. I have performed a great deal, especially in Siena, without any problem."

"But Chopin is different. You don't feel worthy."

Francesca was crying. *What would Em say? She would make conditions.*

"When in the evening would you be playing the sonata?"

Francesca lifted her head. She looked devastated. She had made a big admission, an admission of fear, of need, of unworthiness. And she had made a big ask.

"Towards the end. Either the trio would be the last thing, or my sonata. You would have to sit through the other teachers."

Astrid nodded. "Okay, here are my conditions. You will not speak to me. You will not acknowledge me in any way. I will listen and I will leave. Will you be able to see me there?"

"It is not a big hall. I will find you."

"And if you don't?"

"I will know anyway that you are there because you will tell me you are coming. I will bring you two tickets the next time I have a session."

"There is another condition. You will ask me nothing about it the next time you see me in here. You can talk about your feelings after, during, before the concert, but you will ask me nothing of what I thought. I may choose to speak about it, but it must come from me."

"I am used to you not saying a thing about a concert of mine. I am just always glad that you are there. I just need your presence because I will be terrified. I will need to feel..."

My arms around you. What am I doing, Em? Is this wrong? It does not feel wrong. It feels necessary.

"...That you are listening to me the way that you listen to me in here."

Chapter Twenty-Three

<u>Francesca in the Office XI</u>

After handing the tickets to Dr. Paul, Francesca, looking very humble, sat down and took an audible breath.

"Do I have to repeat the conditions, Francesca?" *Thank you, Em for letting me do this, and for accepting the conditions I imposed. I am sad that you will not come, but I may be able to convince you yet. Maybe you do not have to sit with me. Maybe you can sit anywhere you like. You can even talk to her afterwards. After all, you have met her. Am I jealous? I am definitely not well.*

Francesca shook her head. "I got the message, loud and clear."

"Are there assigned seats?"

"No, you can sit anywhere you like. But I will search the auditorium from the wings and try to find you." Then Francesca started crying.

"Is the practicing, the rehearsing, not going well?"

"I will be fine in the Mendelssohn. And I have Birgitte talking to me all the time about the Chopin. She is not shy to point things out, pick up her violin, and make a suggestion about how to play certain passages. It's funny, most people consider that the pianist is always the coach, but not in my case. Perhaps I stopped having a teacher too soon. I was twenty-two, I think, when Luigi spurned me. That's ten years ago. And I believe him now. He wasn't helping me much at a certain point. I remember him looking awestruck sometimes. He told me that he had never had a student like me before. I guess I should have gotten a new teacher. Maybe I should have gone to Julliard. My father wanted me to. But I wanted to live in Italy. I wanted to *be* Italian all the time, not just with my grandparents. And in terms of a music school, the Chigiana was fantastic. I lived music day and night. I got to become a musician. However, at Julliard, I could have met Birgitte and Magda. We sometimes talk about that. Who knows what would have happened? I might even have married Colin, just to be safe, however."

Astrid remained silent. *She is going somewhere. Just have to let her go there.*

"You know, sometimes, even when I was in elementary school, my mother let me go and spend, like, an entire week with my grandparents. I loved it. We spoke Italian all the time. And my grandmother corrected me and taught me the language. She did not speak a dialect. She was born in the southernmost part of Tuscany. My great-grandparents worked on a farm, and when land was being offered cheap in Quebec, they decided to leave Fascist Italy. They hated Mussolini when everyone else was in raptures over him...My *nonni* would get up in the morning and get on the bus and metro with me. They then walked the few blocks to school with me. And when I finished school, they would be there, and we would do the whole journey back to their house in the Plateau. Do you know that area of Montreal, too?"

Astrid nodded. *I am not interrupting her now.*

"Then my grandfather and I, if he wasn't feeling too bad—sometimes he didn't get out of bed, but eventually, it being the nineties, his psychiatrist found a good medication for him—would go shopping for food, and when we got home, the three of us would start preparing the meal together. We had so much fun. That's why I'm fine cooking and being in a kitchen. I like to be alone in the kitchen, though. Birgitte leaves me be, and I remember all those wonderful times with my grandparents. Sometimes I phone them when I'm in the kitchen. I love to hear their voices. At a certain point, my grandmother would say: '*Vai, Francesca. Vai a suonare il pianoforte, amore.* Go, Francesca. Go play the piano, my love.' My parents made sure they had a small apartment-sized piano for me to play. And I played for them. All the time I was with them, I didn't have to worry about my father. I could be free. Can you understand how important that was for me?"

"Francesca, are you really asking me that question? I do understand."

"Yes, you understand everything, even my need for you, my gargantuan need for you." The tears were falling. But she was able to talk.

Tell me about your grandfather, Francesca. Tell me about his depression. Why is he so important to you?

Francesca took a deep breath. Astrid waited. "When I was with them, I didn't feel like a crazy person. I felt more normal. There was nothing normal about my parents, not even my mother, who was a superwoman. You know why I have a European passport, why I am an Italian citizen, and I have been since the age of three, I think? My mother saved the life of the Consul General of Italy. He had been rushed in an ambulance to the hospital, where she worked, and my mother was the first person to see him. She examined him, diagnosed the problem immediately, called the surgeon, and told him to prep for a certain surgery. She scrubbed in, too, mind you. The medical staff completely trusted her, because she had seen who knows what up there in the North when working with Indigenous people in the hinterland. She had had so much experience at such a young age. When it was all over, and the patient was going to be fine, he begged her to tell him what he might do for her. And she asked him to make me and her Italian citizens. She hadn't been born in Italy, although both her parents were, so it would have been a little complicated. But in Italy, if you know someone, then anything is possible. I remember when I started teaching at the university here, and the person in Human Resources asked me for my documents, thinking that I would be giving her a Canadian passport, which I have, and telling me we would be going through some complicated procedures, and my paycheck would be somewhat delayed, I told her there would be no delay and handed her my European passport. She was so relieved. 'Oh, you are Italian! How wonderful!' So, my superwoman mother had saved the day as

usual, but it was better for me to be away from her than with her."
Now Francesca stopped her long monologue. She looked up at her therapist and waited for some sign from Astrid.

What does she want? What am I supposed to give her now?

"Francesca, I want to hear this whole story. Really, I do. Just tell me everything."

"Okay. I was just wondering if there was something in particular that you wanted."

"No, Francesca, I only want what you want to give me. Nothing more. And nothing less." Astrid began to laugh quietly. Francesca smiled at her.

"My grandfather is kind of a hero. He fought with the *partigiani* at the tender age of sixteen, at the age when I was just beginning my relationship with Colin—how trivial in comparison. You know who the *partigiani* were, Dr. Paul?"

For answer, Dr. Paul began to sing quietly, "*Bella ciao, bella ciao, bella ciao ciao ciao.*"

"Oh, God, Dr. Paul, I love you. I am so lucky to know you. I don't deserve you."

If you knew all my failings as an analyst, you wouldn't be so thrilled about me knowing who the partigiani *were in the Second World War in Italy. If I didn't have Em, I might not be able to help you. Besides which, I am Jewish. We tend to know these things.*

"He did all kinds of covert things to halt the Nazis. Sometimes he told me of his experiences before getting captured."

"But he was captured."

"Yes, he was, and fortunately for him, the Nazi soldiers never asked him to drop his pants."

There was a short intake of breath from Astrid. *Oh no. What is coming next? Am I going to cry in here, too?*

"Yeah, you got it. They would have killed him on the spot. Instead, they threw him into some kind of makeshift jail and tortured him—for weeks and weeks. They starved him. They put electrodes on his body, but as it happened, not on his genitals. But he didn't squeal on anyone."

Astrid's face was in her hands, and she was doing her best not to cry.

"Are you okay, Dr. Paul? I guess my story is pretty gruesome, but I can stop."

Astrid lifted her head. She was thinking of all those relatives of hers who had remained in Munich while her own grandmother and grandfather had been sent to Holland. They were all sent to their deaths. But Francesca's grandfather had survived.

"I am glad your grandfather survived."

"Well, it was in 1944, towards the end of the war in Italy. The Allies were pushing up the peninsula. And the Nazis were forced to leave. Fortunately, the Canadians happened to look in that underground storage facility where the *partigiani* were being kept, and they were able to liberate my grandfather. Otherwise, he would have starved to death. He was pretty much a bruised skeleton when they found him."

Oh, God, I am crying. She pulled a tissue from the box. "I'm sorry, Francesca, for my inability to control myself. Just go on."

"This is really getting to you. It gets to me, too, all the time. The thing is...The thing is...The horrible thing about me is..."

"There is nothing horrible about you."

"Okay, well...The sick thing about me is that...is that...my grandfather is the only man I have ever known whom I love. There is not another male on the planet whom I love. Not Colin, not Simon...not anyone. How sick is that? Is it possible that I am only capable of loving men who have suffered so much in their lives?"

"Okay, Francesca, I am now going to say something that I, as an analyst, should not be saying."

"I love when you say things you shouldn't. I live for those moments."

"I think you love your grandfather simply because he is lovable. Now I'm going to shut up."

Francesca was nodding her head. "He is lovable. I would have loved to stay with my *nonni* forever and ever and never have to go home. But how come I'm afraid that all men will hurt me like my father, instead of trusting that some men can be like my *nonno*?"

"Think about it, Francesca. Why don't you lay down on my couch?"

"I told you already."

"But I'm a woman."

"You mean I don't trust anyone, no matter the gender—well, not right away. I trust you and Birgitte."

"And that's a very good thing."

"So, it's all about my father *and* my mother. And they are way more important than my *nonni.*"

"Is 'important' the right word? You went to live in Italy because of your *nonni.* They are very important."

"I also went to get away from my parents and from Colin, whom I was hurting, but not loving. I wanted to be in that special place, like their home in Montreal. Maybe I just go around thinking that something is deeply wrong with me. Why did my father do those things to me? Why did my mother not see me? Why, Dr. Paul? Why? What's wrong with me?"

Astrid looked at the tear-stained face of her patient and remained silent. She just waited. A little bit of silence was a good thing at this moment. Let the room empty of all the sadness and tears, for she had shed some, too. Francesca placed her elbows on her thighs and dropped her head into her hands. *Just know that I am here, Francesca. I am here for you.*

Finally, Francesca raised her head. "I know what you are doing. You are waiting for me to answer my own question. For me to say that there is nothing wrong with me, that something was missing in my parents, something fundamental that made it impossible for them to be parents and take care of me the way they were supposed to. I can say that, but I can't feel it. I feel that something is wrong with me. The other day my student told me that the girl she loves said that she wanted to be me. And I immediately responded that that was impossible, because nobody would want to be me. Because that's the way I feel. I feel damaged, too. My parents damaged me. Didn't they?"

Astrid just nodded. She could not deny the truth. They had hurt this beautiful, sensitive creature, and now it was her turn to clean up their mess. *I hope I can do this. I want to do this.* What could she say to Francesca now? Francesca was waiting for her to say something. *Let's get her to talk about something a little easier.*

"Francesca, I think this is something we are going to keep returning to over time. It will take time to solve. And I want to solve it."

"Are you going to reveal something about your life now? Like you did the last time by telling me that you'd spent time in Canada."

Astrid smiled. "No, I was thinking more about your grandfather, about this man, this rather unhappy man that you love. It is so important that you love him. It says so much about you. It is such a beautiful, positive thing. Tell me about his depression. Was he able to function, go to work, and support his family?"

"No. My mother and her younger brothers, once they were teenagers, had to work after school to support the family. And my *nonna* could only work when he was feeling well enough to take care of his three children, when they were little, if she was out of the house. It was a terrible situation. I think the government helped somewhat. My mother should have gone to medical school, but just getting her nursing degree was a hardship on the family. So, when she became a nurse, she went into the wilderness knowing that she would not have to spend much money. They got housing and food. She flew all over the place, into the most remote places in Quebec to see her patients. And she sent home all or almost all the money she earned. A heroine, like my *nonno.*"

Was that sarcastic? I can't tell.

"Do you think she ever resents her parents for her childhood and adolescence?"

"I really don't. My mother is revered by everyone, besides her parents. She is so competent. She runs that emergency ward. The patients love her. The doctors more than respect her. She is Nurse Oliver. My grandparents changed their name from Olivieri to Oliver, thinking that anglicizing their name would be a wise course. Why would anglicizing your name in Quebec of all places be the smart thing to do? I tell my mother all the time we should change our name back to Olivieri."

"So, you do not use your father's name."

"Of course not. When I moved to Toronto at age eighteen, I officially removed Hunter as my last name. No way was I going to keep that name. I remember going with Colin and his father—his family lived in Ottawa—to officially change my name. You needed a witness, and Colin's father worked for the government. He knew exactly what to do. Colin kept saying I was angry with my father, because that's what I told him. And his own father kept saying that maybe next month I wouldn't be so angry with him. But we got it done."

"Did you tell your father?"

"I didn't speak to my father. I never spoke to my father if I could help it. I don't know what my mother said to him. I didn't care. I was an Oliver. I loved my grandparents, my Italian heritage. My father's parents lived in Calgary. We hardly ever visited them, and they hardly ever came to Montreal. My mother never changed her name. She was Nurse Oliver, but mostly Véronique or Véro, as the French call her. Her name is Veronica. But my mother works in a big French hospital. In her profession she is *Québécoise.*"

"I see. Tell me about your grandfather's depression."

"I have to say, Dr. Paul, that it scared me. I believed he was suicidal. Primo Levi committed suicide after experiencing the concentration camp."

"You believe Primo Levi committed suicide."

"I do. I really do. Because I was witness to my grandfather's depression. I believe in the logic of it."

"Okay, I accept that."

"But then, finally, the psychiatrist tried a medication that seems to work. He is much better. Maybe Primo Levi could also have been helped. I don't know. What he experienced was perhaps much worse, and it did go on for much longer. Have you read his books?"

"A few, but not in Italian, of course. Ironically, I read them in German translation. I should probably have read them in English."

"Your English is completely unaccented. Birgitte's English is pretty perfect, having studied in New York, but you know she isn't anglophone, whereas you sound American."

"My father is American. His last name is Paul. We spoke mostly English at home."

"So, you never changed your name, either. My mother is Nurse Oliver, and you are Dr. Paul. Got it." Francesca smiled. "I like that. And I like that it didn't pain you to tell me. I don't want you to suffer so that I won't."

That is such a sweet thing to say. It's the nicest thing that anyone has said to me all day. My last patient just told me he hates me. But he didn't walk out of the office. He stayed and finished his session, at least.

Chapter Twenty-Four

<u>Astrid and Emma</u>

"Professor Green?"

"Yes, Caroline."

"There is a Professor Francesca Oliver on the line from Art History. She wishes to speak with you."

"Okay, put her through."

"Francesca, what a nice surprise."

"How are you, Professor Green?"

"I am very well. Even better to hear your voice."

"Really? This time you remember me?"

Emma laughed. "And how are you?"

"Well, besides being terrified about a recital I have to play on Thursday night, I am feeling okay."

"Do performances scare you?"

"This one does. Anyway, I am calling you because an article I have written is going to be published soon. It's about Bronzino. And since I can print the final PDF version, I was thinking of bringing it over to you—I can leave it with your secretary—so you could read it, if you want to. I don't have to teach until two o'clock, so I can walk over now."

"I would love to read it. And you can tell the secretary—no, I'll tell the secretary that I want to see you. You can step into my office for a bit, can't you?"

"Of course."

******

Astrid unlocked the door of her apartment and saw Em sitting and reading something on the couch in their living room. Emma didn't even say hello. She seemed completely absorbed in her reading. Astrid unbuttoned her coat and hung it up. She left her briefcase near the entrance. She removed her shoes and walked silently over to Emma.

"What's going on, Em?"

Emma looked up. "I didn't even hear you. Just let me finish this last paragraph." Astrid sat down beside her. Finally, Emma let out a long exhale. "Wow!"

"What have you been reading?"

Emma put the printed pages down on the coffee table. Astrid picked them up. "Francesca's article on Bronzino, that artist you love. How did you get ahold of it?"

"She brought it over to my office."

"Really?"

"You're jealous, aren't you? You want her all to yourself."

"Stop it, Em. Life is difficult enough. I think I am becoming less and less able to do my job. It wears me down. Francesca told me today...Oh, never mind. I can't talk about it yet. Em, I actually cried in the office."

"Oh my God, Asti. You *have* to tell me."

"You can't be angry at me. You would have cried, too."

"Really? Me?"

"Yes. She was talking about her depressed grandfather. And now we know why. He was a *partigiano* at age sixteen. He's a hero in her eyes. He was eventually caught, tortured, and imprisoned by the Nazis for weeks on end until Canadian soldiers liberated him. He wasn't killed instantly because, as she said, 'They didn't make him drop his pants.'"

"Oh, Asti."

"I couldn't keep it together. My eyes teared and I wiped the tears away, but she saw."

"What did she say?"

"She just said that it always got to her, too. Kind of as if she expected me to react like that. I couldn't help thinking of all those people in my mother's family that were exterminated."

"Did you know she was Jewish?"

"Well, now I know that her grandfather was. She didn't tell me about her grandmother. But it was a surprise. And I learned that Oliver is her mother's name. She got rid of her father's name at age eighteen."

"Good for her."

"Is it a good article?"

"A good article? Are you kidding? It is a phenomenal article. And I am going to let you read it, although you can't tell her how you got it. I know she's an art historian, but she writes like a psychologist. She has that kind of analytical mind. And it's not boring. It's exciting to read. She knows so much about so many things, Asti."

"Are you going to come to the concert? Sorry to change the subject. It's funny. She needs *me* there. And I need *you* there. You won't have to sit with me or even come home with me. I will run out immediately after she plays, but I think you should talk to her afterwards. Please come. I won't sit beside some handsome guy and flirt with him. I will do what she asked and focus on that. Please come."

"Okay. Okay. I am really intrigued by this young woman. And you think her grandfather's depression is totally linked to his war experiences?"

"She thinks that he was suicidal until he got the right medication. She mentioned Primo Levi."

"Really. It's hard to know if the war was what caused her grandfather's depression, though."

"I'm not going to discuss it with her. I'm going to let her think what she wants. Besides, I can't let what happened to me today happen again."

"Yeah, but your crying was totally natural. Talking about Nazis and Jews and torture can do that. She doesn't think any less of you. In fact, I would bet she thinks more of you now."

"You believe that?"

"Yeah, I really do. I made dinner. Do you want to eat now?"

"Can we go to the bedroom for a minute? I'd just like you to hold me in your arms. I'm feeling kind of...I don't know...delicate, maybe."

"Oh Asti, I love when you ask me to hold you in my arms. You should ask me more often."

They got up and walked towards the bedroom. "And you have to read that article. Tonight. You understand?"

"I got the message. Looking forward to it."

In the bedroom, as soon as Emma took Astrid in her arms, Astrid began to cry. Emma held her as tightly as she could. "It's okay. I'm here. I love you now and forever."

"What's wrong with me lately, Em? I'm so emotional lately. I seem to want to cry all the time. And two patients recently have told me that they hate me. Why do they hate me?"

"Because stuff comes out of them when they are with you that they would rather stay buried. They don't really mean it. They are only expressing their pain."

"I guess so. But it's causing me pain, that's for sure."

"Asti, I love the person you are. I love the woman you are. I love the therapist you are. I know it's hard for you to be like this. But this is how you help your patients, by being porous. This is your way. And if you weren't like this, you wouldn't be helping them. The question is: Is it too much of a sacrifice?"

"No, Em. I have to do this job. I have to. As long as you love me now and forever."

"Then there is no problem. You've got me."

As she held Astrid in her arms, Emma knew there was something she had to tell her, her wife of twenty years, whom she had never told. "Asti, there is something I have to tell you, something I never told you, something I felt on the day we met."

Astrid broke away from Emma immediately. She sat up and crossed her legs in front of her. "How could that be? That was twenty years ago. How could you not have told me?"

"Asti, I was so in love with you. I didn't want you to think I was petty or anything. I didn't want you to know something about me that could have jeopardized our possible relationship. And then I thought that it didn't matter anymore. I forgot about it."

"Until today."

"Until you started talking about your patient's Italian-Jewish grandfather."

"Oh, Em, I guess you're not perfect after all."

"Shush. Don't be mean, you who are never mean. It was stupid."

"Tell me, Em. I need to know."

Emma sat up and faced her beloved, crossed her legs, too, and let their knees touch. "It's only about love, about me loving you."

"Just tell me. I'll be the judge of that."

"On that first day we met in Dr. Lang's seminar, and we were supposed to tell each other—all eight of us—about how we had gotten to this juncture in our lives, as soon as you opened your mouth, I fell in love with you. You were the most beautiful creature in the universe. I couldn't take my eyes, or ears, off you. I had come all the way from Baltimore to study in England at the famed Tavistock Institute. I was so excited about everything I was going to learn, and the only thing I wanted at that moment was to kiss you."

"And you did, about an hour later. You move fast, Em." Astrid smiled and touched her partner's knee. She moved her hand up and down Emma's thigh. "You overwhelmed me."

"You responded, though. You kissed me back."

"I was sex-starved at that point. I had broken up with my girlfriend from Victoria a year before."

"Okay, you keep telling yourself and me that. I felt all of you in that kiss, all of your longings, your emotions..."

"I wanted that kiss. I really wanted it. I couldn't believe it was coming from the most accomplished and sexy creature in the room. I was surprised at my own reaction to your kiss. It felt like I was 'swooning'. A maiden out of the nineteenth century! That's how I felt. Life would never be the same again. That's the effect you and the suddenness of that kiss had on me."

"Happy to make you swoon. But when we were talking and walking after that class—where were we going?—towards some more secluded spot, I presume, you said something that blew me away. It was the way you said it—your assuredness. It was...it was...if you were swooning, I was smitten."

They both laughed. Then Astrid held her arms out and leaned forward. As they embraced each other, their torsos fell towards the bed, and they ended up in a lying position. They kissed for a long time.

"Are you avoiding telling me, Em?"

"Yeah."

"Just say it, then. Then we can get back to the loving part and I can take your clothes off. I need to..."

"I know what you need to do..."

"So, talk, Em."

"Well, remember when you started telling me the story of your hidden grandparents, and your mother being Dutch, and meeting your father in Munich, where she went to study German literature and he to practice architecture in Europe after getting his degree, etcetera, etcetera?"

"Yes, I remember."

"Well after you told me that your father wasn't Jewish, and you were brought up without any religion—and neither was I for that matter, but both my parents are Jewish—I was wondering how you felt about your heritage."

"And you asked me, 'But are you Jewish?'"

"And you said, 'Of course, I'm Jewish', quite forcefully."

"So?"

"Well, it got me. I thought...I thought...I just said to myself, 'I love this woman.'"

"And that's petty?"

"Well, yeah. And it wasn't long before I just leaned into you. We were sitting outside somewhere, and people were walking by in front of us. And...and I kissed you without thinking. I didn't even think that I was blowing my chance with you by being so precipitous. I had no idea whatsoever if you were interested in women. I just did it."

"You caught me off-guard for sure. You almost frightened me. I moved away from you," said Astrid.

"You looked into my eyes for a very long time and then you came forward towards me until our lips met."

"And I kissed you back," said Astrid.

"It was marvellous. It was the best first kiss in history."

"And you were afraid to tell me that, I don't know, that I impressed you, for once, with my forthrightness? Was it the only time I ever impressed you?"

"Oh, Asti, you always impress me. You do what I had always dreamed of doing but can't. I can't be hour after hour in a room with a suffering soul drawing compassion from me. I admire you from the bottom of my heart. All I can do is write about it."

"And teach it and listen to others struggling to do this job."

"Yeah, well, I can do that, tell others how to do their job."

"You tell me, too. And I need you to."

"No, Asti, I just support you in what you do. I just tell you I love you."

Chapter Twenty-Five

<u>Professor Green (Emma) and Francesca</u>

After the Mendelssohn, which had gone really well, although she hated all the applause afterwards, Francesca was standing and waiting for the director to introduce her. Birgitte came up to her and touched her on the arm, something she normally would not do in public. She whispered to her: "Play it for *her,* Ollie. Put all your love into the piece for your spiritual mother." She just nodded. Then she walked onto the stage and took a slight bow. She didn't look for Dr. Paul, although she had noticed her before the concert had started. There was no way she would make eye contact. She had been expressly told not to.

She sat down at the piano. There was silence now. She looked at her hands on her lap and she thought these words: "*This is for you, Dr. Paul. There are only three people in this room: me, Birgitte, and you; but this is all for you.*" And she played as she had never played before.

When it was over, she was startled. The applause was thunderous. She had forgotten about all those other people. She continued to look down at her hands. Finally, she stood up and bowed. As she walked off the stage, she could see Dr. Paul in the aisle heading for the door. "*I did it, Dr. Paul. I am so glad you were here. I just talked to you. That's all.*" Then Birgitte, in tears, was pushing her out onto the stage. She felt as if she were in a dream. She walked out again. Everyone was on their feet. *Why?* She thought. She bowed and smiled. And then she walked towards Birgitte, who had taught her this piece, who had encouraged her over and over to play it. She looked at her and wanted to embrace her, this woman whom she loved more than anything in this world, more than Chopin. They just smiled at each other, and Francesca thought, *I love you.* Birgitte nodded and put her hand on her heart. The applause continued for a while and Magda asked her if she wanted to go out again, and she shook her head.

"You know you are going to have to mingle a bit," said Birgitte. If you don't, the Director will have my head."

"Okay."

The other teachers were coming around to her and congratulating her. She did her best to converse with them, to tell them that they had all played wonderfully, although she hadn't actually listened. Until she had to play the Mendelssohn trio with Birgitte and Magda, she had stayed alone in the little room off the stage with the door closed. She had needed to be alone. Now she would go out into the big room off the auditorium, where there would be a sort of party for the teachers, and talk to Birgitte's parents and her mother and Stefano. Cora and Melanie had come, too, and of course, Bradley. She took a deep breath and walked between Magda and Birgitte towards what, the slaughter? Had she played well? She only knew that she had been in a kind of trance, and then it was over. The first person to come over was the Director.

"I am so glad Birgitte twisted my arm. You were positively magnificent. And now I must tell a lot of parents that you refuse to teach here. You are certain about that?"

"I am, and thank you for letting me play."

"No, thank you for letting me listen."

And now her mother was hugging her, and then Stefano, too, hugged her, and Ghita's parents. Ghita went off with her mother and father. She heard them speaking Danish. How she loved that language. It had so much meaning for her. Thankfully, the hugging was now over. It hadn't been that bad. Cora and Melanie were delightful, as usual. She spoke to several others whom she didn't know. They were all enthusiastic about her.

Her mother and Stefano were exhausted, and Ghita's father didn't love driving at night. They were all going off to the country house in the woods where Ghita's parents lived. It was amazing what good friends these two couples had become. It was hard to believe. She and Birgitte would drive up there on Saturday and spend the weekend.

And suddenly, Professor Green was standing before her.

"What are *you* doing here?" she asked.

"What do you mean? I came to hear you. My favourite art historian giving a concert—I wasn't about to miss it!"

Francesca smiled. All of a sudden, she was happy, happy to be standing in front of this wonderful person, whom she hardly knew.

"I've heard you play before, you know...with the orchestra."

"Really? You never told me."

"Well, we just had so much to say about Bronzino." Francesca laughed.

"You know, before this concert I thought I would never laugh again. Thank you for being here and for making me laugh, Professor Green."

"My name is Emma, and you are to call me Emma from now on. And take it from me, you should play Chopin morning, noon, and night. Your performance was unbelievable. I know the piece and have never heard it played like that. You put your own stamp on it."

"Really? I actually didn't hear it while I was playing. It was like I was in a trance."

"And what were you doing in this trance?"

"Do you really want to know?"

"I really want to know."

"I was talking to someone."

"I understand."

"You do?"

"I do. You told me how nervous you were and that usually you aren't nervous about performing. Was it a way to make you able to perform?"

"I don't know for sure. I didn't have a choice. I felt compelled to have this one-way conversation."

"Do you remember what you were saying?"

"I was saying the notes of the piece. I was saying what I had to say in the language of Chopin."

Emma sighed. "You love this person, don't you?"

Francesca nodded.

"That's wonderful, Francesca. That's really wonderful. And that's why it was so beautiful. And we all loved you back."

"Really? Was it a good performance?"

"You idiot, Francesca. It was off-the-charts good, and so was your essay on Bronzino. I loved it. How do you do it, have two professions?"

"I don't know. I just have to play the piano and think about art. I don't have a choice. The piano has saved my life, for one thing, and...and—"

"—You love artists that make you feel."

"You are such a wonderful person. You know how to make others feel happy."

"No one has ever said that to me before."

"I can't believe that. The person you're married to has never said that? Well, anyway, you have just made me feel happy."

Chapter Twenty-Six

<u>Francesca in the Office XII</u>

Francesca came into the office with her head lowered. She looked scared, embarrassed, ashamed. She sat down and looked at her clenched hands on her lap.

"Thank you for coming. I couldn't have played Chopin without you."

"Do you want to talk about it?"

"If I start at the beginning, you will hear something that maybe you don't want to hear."

"Say it anyway."

Francesca looked up. *I mean it. Just say everything.*

"Well after playing Mendelssohn..."

God, that was beautiful.

"Birgitte came up to me and whispered something."

"Tell me."

"She said: 'Play it for *her*, Ollie. Put all your love into the piece for...for...'" Francesca closed her eyes. "I don't know if I can say it."

"I know you can. I will not be angry. But I won't say 'I promise'. Although I do."

Francesca smiled. She said: 'Put all your love into the piece for your spiritual mother.'"

I was not expecting that. But I'm not surprised.

"When you sat down you stayed motionless for a long time looking at your hands...."

"I was talking to you. I was telling you that it was all for you, that there were only three people in the room, but it was all for you."

Am I going to be able to keep it together today?

"Like a gift?"

"Maybe. Yes. Like a gift. The gift of words, except they weren't words. They were Chopin's musical notes. But I was telling you something. And I didn't realize what I was doing. I just played and you were there, like you are here. And then it was over. I had said it all. And the noise afterwards startled me because I had forgotten where I was."

I have to say this, even if Em might not like it. I have to be honest. I have to be who I am. "Francesca, thank you. Thank you for such a wonderful gift. I will never forget it. You spoke to me. I heard you." *Please don't cry. If you cry, you will make me cry.*

Francesca had been looking down, but now she raised her head. *You didn't expect that, did you, that you had communicated with me? Well, you did. And I have to say it.*

"Yes, you communicated with me. Is that so hard to believe? You communicate here. You communicate through music. I listen. I will always listen."

"And you knew it was all for you?"

"No, but I knew you were saying something to me in particular. I knew that. And I was listening for your voice as hard as I could."

Francesca leaned back in the chair and looked up. She stayed like that for a while with her head resting on the back of the chair. *Silence is okay, too. It is also a form of communication.*

"It was a big ask, wasn't it?"

"Yes, it was."

"Other psychoanalysts would not have complied."

"I don't care what other psychoanalysts would have done. You are stuck with me. I'm the one you have."

"I don't want anyone else."

"Good."

"I have such a long way to go. But I, at least, have started this journey."

"Yes, you have."

Chapter Twenty-Seven

<u>Astrid and Emma after the Concert</u>

"Asti, you don't have to put on any pyjamas. I would be taking them off, anyway."

Astrid smiled and got into bed beside her naked partner. "Are you glad you came?"

"Oh, Asti, she was mesmerizing tonight. I mean, she always plays beautifully, but tonight she transported me. She told me she was in this trance talking to someone. She didn't tell me it was you, but I knew it. And at a certain point, I said to her that she loved this person, and she said yes. I didn't ask her. I told her because I knew."

"It's going to make me cry."

"So what? If I had a patient who wanted to play Chopin for me personally, I would cry, too."

"I have these patients who hate me, but I have this one patient who—"

"—Asti, I told you. They don't hate you. If anything, they also love you. And you are helping them."

"I should listen if a patient says she loves me, but not listen when they say they hate me."

"Exactly. Come on, Asti. You know deep inside of you that they don't."

"Okay." Astrid sighed. "She did play so beautifully, didn't she? I loved listening to her, and I can't tell her how great she is."

"But I can, and I did. She told me that I was a wonderful person who knew how to make people feel happy."

"Really?"

"And when I said that no one had ever said that to me before, she was a little startled, and then said: 'The person to whom you are married has never said that?'"

"She thinks you are married to a man, I bet."

"Probably, but you told me that she liked it that you didn't change your name. I'm afraid that is what she thinks about you, too."

"Do you think she noticed that we have the same wedding ring? She's kind of observant, as you know, and that essay on Bronzino was amazing. She really sees."

"And hears."

"Em, when I think of her parents and what they did to her, I feel as if—"

"—You want to kill them?"

"Well, her mother does care for people, her father especially; I mean, Francesca's grandfather."

"Just not her daughter. Or not enough to pay attention to what was going on around her."

"I guess some people should not have children."

"But you are not so forgiving of me and my fear of having children."

"Oh, Em, I have forgiven you. I could not bear to think that I would have made you unhappy."

"So, in true Astrid fashion, my happiness is more important than yours?"

"Don't say that. Please don't say that. Don't ever say that."

"But I think it's true. You always put me before you. Don't you see that?"

"I just love you the only way I know how." Astrid moved closer to Emma and put her head on Emma's chest. "Hold me."

Emma put her arms around her partner. "You know why we never fight, Asti?"

"Why?"

"Because you are impossible to fight with."

"What do you mean?"

"Who could fight with you? You always say the right thing." Emma stroked her lover's back and thought about the next thing she wanted to say to Astrid. "Asti, I've been having thoughts about this triangle here."

"Are you worried Francesca might want to have more of a relationship with you?"

"No, I'm more worried about what it would do to you and your relationship with her. The situation is very delicate. And there is the question of dishonesty."

"Are you telling me that I have to give her up?"

"No, I'm not saying that."

"What are you saying?"

"I'm saying that maybe we have to be honest with her."

Astrid sat up abruptly. "You mean I have to tell her that I have been in love with this amazing woman for twenty years, and guess what, you think she is wonderful. Really?"

"It's something I have been considering."

"And then I will have to tell her that I always ask for your advice, and therefore you know just about everything about her."

"I'm not saying it will be easy, but I'm beginning to think that dishonesty is not the best policy."

Chapter Twenty-Eight

<u>Francesca in the Office XIII</u>

"I talked to my *nonno* yesterday."

"And how are they doing, your grandparents? Do they still live independently, or in some kind of facility?"

"Well, they're not young, but they love their home. They do the Italian thing. They have *badanti,* caregivers. Two of them. Each of them spends half the week with my grandparents, and sleeps there, so they are never alone. My *nonno* is well into his nineties. My mother and her brothers, my uncles, take care of everything, pay for everything. My father gave my mother a lot of money during the divorce, not to mention our house, which she sold. A lot of money, so she can do this, but I think she would like to stop working now and live with Stefano. She doesn't work full-time anymore because she comes to Europe to see me and Stefano. She's ready. She's worked so much in her life. Stefano would retire, too. They just want to enjoy each other now."

"But your grandparents are keeping her in Montreal."

"Yeah."

"So, how is your 'lovable' *nonno*?"

Francesca smiled. "Still lovable. We talked yesterday because I was in the kitchen cooking and I had a desperate need to speak to them—*be* Italian, you know...Dr. Paul?"

"Yes."

"Something strange happened last Sunday, and I am not sure what to do."

"Okay, tell me."

'You're going to think that this is stupid, but I think Birgitte was hurt."

"Your feelings or your wife's are never stupid, Francesca."

Francesca sighed. She nodded. "I know. Well, we were all at Linda and Konrad's place with Magda and Bradley, and Philippe and Ugo."

"And he doesn't touch you."

"No, he doesn't touch me. He talks to me about wanting to go back to Italy. Neither of them really likes Germany, but they play in a great orchestra, and how are they going to find two positions in a great orchestra in Italy? Also, they want a child, and it's so complicated for men, much more complicated than it is for women."

"Are we going to have that conversation one day, too, Francesca?"

"Oh, yeah, maybe even today. But first I have to tell you that when Birgitte and I were leaving, Linda told us that her five-year-old daughter thought that Ugo and I were married. After all, we speak the same language."

"Was your wife disturbed about that?"

"Well, she tried not to show it. But she didn't talk much in the car. And when we got home, it took a great deal of work to get her to open up. Not to mention the fact that I was worried she'd never make love to me ever again. But I managed, finally, to seduce her."

All of a sudden, the intercom went off in the office.

An emergency, thought Astrid.

"If it's an emergency..."

"Yes, Francesca. Marisa would not interrupt for any other reason." Astrid stood up and picked up her office phone. "What is it, Marisa?" Silence. "Okay, tell her a few seconds. I can call back later."

Astrid was glad her mother had phoned. Her father had been in a car accident, but her mother was now telling her that everything was fine. No major injuries. She breathed a sigh of relief as she put down the receiver. She sat down in front of Francesca and smiled. "All's well. Let's talk about Ugo and babies."

"Dr. Paul?"

"Yes?"

"That wasn't German you were speaking."

"No, it was Dutch. My mother is Dutch."

"You are amazing."

"Really? And what about you? How many languages do you speak?"

"Well, four now. My German is getting pretty good. And that book on your desk by Jenny Erpenbeck?"

"Yes?"

"I've read it."

"In German?"

"Yes."

"Shall we get back to Ugo and babies?"

"I hope your husband loves it when you speak Dutch to him, as much as I love it when Birgitte speaks to me in Danish."

"Francesca! You... I..." Astrid couldn't get the words out. Was she angry or scared? *I'm scared. I'm really scared. Am I going to have to have that conversation now, here, today? Am I ready for this? What am I going to do?* "Francesca, hang on a moment." Astrid rushed out of the office and shut the door. Marisa looked up in surprise, not expecting to see Astrid. Astrid was trying to breathe normally. She walked over to Marisa's desk, bent forward, and placed her hands on the desk.

"Is everything alright?"

"Not really. I have to think. I have to think about what I am going to do next."

"Can I help?"

"No, not really. I have to make a big decision. I just didn't expect it to happen today."

"Shall I call your wife?"

"Not necessary. I know exactly what she wants me to do."

Astrid pushed herself up and away from the support of the desk. She headed for her office, opened the door, and sat down in front of her patient.

Francesca looked stricken. "I'm sorry for what I said, Dr. Paul. Please, please don't throw me out. Please don't send me away. I don't think I can manage my life without you. I'm still a child." And then she was crying.

You don't know how much I'd like to be crying, too.

"Why did you have to leave the room, Dr. Paul? What did I do?"

"I had to think. I had to work something out."

"But you always do that, and you do it in front of me. And then I want to crawl under your desk and cry like a child."

"Is that what you want to do now?"

"Yes."

"Is that what you did after your father hit you?"

"Yes."

"I'm not going to hit you, Francesca, ever. Should I say that again?"

Francesca nodded.

"I'm never going to hit you. And, Francesca, when you were begging me not to throw you out, what were you also saying, but not saying?"

Francesca lifted her face from her hands. She took a tissue from the proffered box.

"I...I...don't know. I was saying...I promise to be good. I will never be bad again. Please don't reject me. If I'm good, would you be my—"

"—Be your what?"

"Do I have to say it?"

"I think you do."

"My mother." Then she was sobbing. She was completely bent over.

"Do you want to crawl under the desk?"

Francesca nodded.

"Well, you can't, because we have to have a very adult conversation now."

Francesca lifted her head up. "Are you going to send me away?"

"No. You will go away from here only when *you* wish to go away from here, although after what I tell you, you may just want to go away."

"Never!" She was adamant. The tears were gone.

"Okay, here goes." Astrid took a deep breath. "I do not have a husband."

"But you wear a wedding ring."

"I'm married."

"Oh. You mean...? You mean...?"

Astrid was nodding.

"And you had to go out of the room to think about *that*?"

"Francesca, none of my patients know anything about my personal life. It is not important to the work we do here. In fact, whether I studied here or in Canada, that my mother is Dutch and my father American, or that I am married to a woman, has absolutely no significance whatsoever. Am I right?"

Francesca nodded. "I just hope you love her as much as I love Birgitte, and she loves you as much as Birgitte loves me."

"Francesca, that was the nicest thing anyone has said to me all week." Astrid smiled.

"I just hope you are happy, because I—or we, who sit in this room—certainly do not make you happy. You have a debilitating job, holding the hands of so many damaged people."

You are going to make me cry, and the important part is coming next. I need all my strength for it.

"The reason why I left the room to think is because I have a very difficult thing to say to you now. You are always honest with me, right?"

"Except when I leave things out. But I eventually tell you. I almost lied to you about my wedding ring. But then I didn't. Dr. Paul, I always always believe you. I can't imagine you being dishonest with me."

"But I have left something out. For any other patient, it would have no significance. But for you, it does. It's not about me being married to a woman; it is about who—"

"—That woman is."

"Francesca, you really have a very unique brain."

"You're married to Emma Green, aren't you? You wear the same unusual wedding ring."

"Yes, Francesca, I am." Astrid put her hand on her heart. "So, this is your decision. If you are in any way uncomfortable with that fact, and you want to leave analysis with me, I can suggest someone else."

"Are you crazy!? You have done so much for me already, not to mention the fact that I respect you more than any other person I know, even more than your wife, who is so-o-o impressive."

Astrid smiled. *Don't leave me, Francesca. I want so much to work with you. I want so much to clean up your parents' mess. And Em will help us. She'll make sure I don't screw up.*

Then it was Francesca's turn to smile. "Dr. Paul, you have made me so happy."

"Because I'm married to a woman?"

"No, of course not. Because you're married to *that* woman, that brilliant, wonderful woman. Not that you're not brilliant and wonderful, too."

Chapter Twenty-Nine

<u>Astrid and Emma</u>

After Francesca had left, Astrid did not move for several minutes, but she knew that she had to speak to Marisa. She finally opened her door and entered Marisa's sanctuary. She walked over to her desk.

"Everything seems to have worked out okay after all. I never lost confidence in you, although you looked pretty scared."

"Marisa, thank you so much."

"For what? I didn't do anything."

"For just being here. You have no idea how grounded it makes me feel to know that you are out here. I needed to see you before I went back into my room. I needed to talk through my dilemma out loud. I couldn't do much if this room were empty of you. Please don't ever leave me to find another job."

"I love you too much to ever leave you."

"And now I have to go back there and lay on my couch and talk—"

"—To *your* analyst." Marisa smiled.

As Astrid walked back towards her couch, she turned around and said, "Marisa?" Marisa lifted her head. "I hope you know that I love you, too."

* * * * * *

Astrid was on the couch. She picked up her phone and called Emma.

"Hello, my love. Are you laying on the couch? You really don't have to. You can lay on our living room couch or on the bed, because I'm home, and I'm ready for you. More than ready. I can't wait to—"

"—Em, I did it."

"Did what?"

"That thing I've been so scared to do."

"No!"

"Yes."

"How did that happen? And how did it work out?"

"It had to happen."

"Oh, by the way, your mother called me to tell me that all is well. You must be so relieved."

"In fact, that is how it all started."

"Really? Tell me. You're sure you don't want to come home? I'll hold you in my arms. I'll kiss every part of your magnificent body."

"I'm exhausted, Em. It took so much out of me. In fact, at one point before I did it, I had to leave the room and be taken care of by Marisa."

"That hard, huh?"

"But I was still her psychoanalyst. I dealt with all kinds of other Francesca things."

"Good. And it all turned out okay?"

"Maybe because of you. She said in the end that I had made her happy. And I asked if it was because I'm married to a woman, and she said, no, not at all, but because I was married to *that* woman, that brilliant, wonderful woman. You were right. We had to do this. She's much too interested in you."

"It pays to be honest, sometimes. What would Melanie Klein say, do you think?"

"She would say that I should stop being a psychoanalyst."

"Did you ask her if she wanted to change analysts?"

"I did."

"What did she say?"

"Her exact words were: 'Are you crazy?'"

"Listen, Asti. You have to come home right now. Get off the couch. I don't want to be your analyst! I want to be your lover!"

Chapter Thirty

<u>Birgitte and Francesca</u>

"Philippe and Ugo want a baby, Ghita. I don't think they can afford to go to the U.S. and buy one from some private adoption agency."

"What about a surrogate mother?"

"I suppose that's a possibility."

The two of them had just finished practicing the first movement of the Chopin piano concerto, with Birgitte playing the music of the first violinist, and other instruments when possible. They had discussed each and every bar of music. Francesca felt tired. She had been correcting student terms papers and final exams, too. She was starting to enter the final grades into the computer. This year the students going to Florence would not be taking a course. They would just have the opportunity to see everything they had studied together with Francesca. Bradley, therefore, would not be coming. Anyway, he and Magda were fixing up the house they had bought two blocks away from their place. Philippe and Ugo were talking about finally buying a house, too. But Ugo definitely didn't want to live in Germany forever.

"I really feel for them," said Francesca.

"But not for us."

"It's different for us. *You* will be carrying the baby."

"But we won't know anything about the sperm donor."

"In Canada they are all medical students who have already had a child."

"That's not very much information."

"I guess not. What if we had a baby with them? I mean, if the sperm donor would be Philippe, for instance. We would know much more."

"And share a son or daughter who would have four parents? Really? Do you think it could work? The child would be musical, for sure. I never thought of that."

"The sharing might be complicated. How would it play out after the baby was born? The baby would have to be mostly with us, since you would be nursing him or her."

"There are always those pumps. Or we could all live in a bigger place."

"I only want to live with you. I can't even imagine living with anyone else."

"It would only have to be for as long as I was nursing. After that, they could live on their own and have the baby, let's say, every two weeks."

"I don't think I could handle them being around while you were nursing."

"They're gay, Ollie."

"Yeah, Simon was supposed to be gay, too."

Birgitte put her violin back in its case and came over to Francesca on the bench. "Move over. Let me put my arms around you." She did just that. "Stop thinking about him, my love."

"He was such a good friend, Ghita. I don't really want to know him anymore."

"Richard wrote to me today."

"He did? You didn't tell me."

"It just happened today. I'm telling you now. Do you want to read the letter? We can go upstairs, and I can show it to you on my laptop. You look exhausted. And I don't want to go to sleep without loving you a little bit." Birgitte kissed her on her cheeks, on her eyes, and then on her mouth. "Come, let's go to bed."

Francesca followed her up the stairs. In the bedroom, she turned to Birgitte and said, "I can't get over it so easily, Ghita. I feel sad all the time."

"Well, maybe you shouldn't read Richard's letter. There is so much sadness in it. He feels so betrayed. Simon does not want to go into marital counseling. And Richard is not fond of his therapist. I wrote to him and told him he deserved a therapist he could love. I think he should try a woman."

"And leave Simon. Simon married him all the while knowing he loved me. Who does that?"

Birgitte shrugged. "Someone who knows he can't have you. When I knew I loved you and came back to Munich, I thought I would die because I really believed I couldn't have you. My therapist and Magda suggested attempting a relationship with another woman."

"What did you do?"

"I went to this lesbian bar and let a nice woman pick me up."

"Really? Did you sleep with her?"

"She tried to get me to sleep with her. After one kiss, I told her I was in love with someone else. I couldn't do it. I only wanted you."

"Yeah, but Simon could do it. And he's ruined a good man's life."

"Richard's life is not over. He'll meet someone else. And then I met Gunther, and I stayed with him all the while knowing I would only ever be able to love you. I needed someone around sometimes."

"Could you have married him? Could you have told him you loved him?"

"Of course not. And you were with Peter."

"I was afraid to face the truth."

"We really owe Jordan a debt of gratitude."

"Ghita, every night before I fall asleep, I thank her. Every morning when I wake up, I thank her. Just to feel you beside me in bed is thrilling. Just to know that you are there." Francesca began undressing and then sat on the bed. "You know what, Ghita? I don't think I will be able to tolerate people handling you when you're pregnant, touching your belly...It's going to be so hard for me."

"Well, at least when Ugo or Philippe will touch my belly, they won't be interested in what's above it or below it."

Francesca dropped her head in her hands. "Stop! Oh, God, no. I can't even handle the image of them doing that. We can't do this thing, Ghita. We can never suggest this possibility to them. It would kill me."

"Well, then, we won't do it. What if my parents want to touch me? Would that be alright?"

Francesca nodded but still looked unhappy.

"And your mother? And Magda?"

"Okay. Okay. I get it. I will just have to steel myself, prepare myself for the worst. How do you live with me? I can't share you."

"Well, as you know, I'm not so great at sharing you, either."

"It will be nice to have you in Florence with me this year, although I am not so sure about you coming along with my students. My mother was different. I don't want my students to even think about who you may be to me."

"I am capable of wandering around by myself. And when you're free, we will have Stefano's apartment all to ourselves, because he and your mother will be wandering around the rest of Italy."

"Ghita, do you think I should go and visit Luigi in Siena before or after the ten days with my students in Florence? If I go before, we can go to Montreal earlier. I *have* to see my grandparents. Especially my *nonno.* He's ninety-five, and when Italy voted in a Fascist prime minister, it nearly killed him."

"You love the man, don't you?" Birgitte sat down beside her partner. She kissed her on her shoulder and then down her arm.

"The only man I could ever love."

"Don't ever love another woman."

"There is only you."

Chapter Thirty-One

<u>Astrid and Emma</u>

Emma unlocked the door to the apartment. She knew Astrid had gotten home before her. She wasn't in the living room. She wasn't in the kitchen. She wasn't in the study. So she went into the bedroom. Astrid was standing and staring out the window. Emma came behind her and wrapped her arms around her. Astrid leaned her head back.

"Em, I need to talk about something. I have a dilemma."

"Okay. Does it have anything to do with the fact that I know so much about your patient? Has she asked you yet?"

"No. She hasn't asked. I think she trusts us. I think she idealizes you a bit, as well."

"Really? I think I idealize her a bit, too."

"Remember we talked about wanting to kill her parents, or at least her father?"

"Should we hire a hitman?"

Astrid turned around and the two women embraced. "I need to talk to Emma Green, the expert."

"Asti, I don't know how to kill."

"I'm serious, Em."

"Okay, do you want to lie on the bed, or do you want to sit with me on the couch?"

"Let's lie on the bed."

"Should we take our clothes off?"

"Em, be serious. We can take them off later. First, we have to discuss a technical, philosophical matter."

Emma went over to the bed and propped up the pillows against the headrest. The two lovers lay down on their backs, with their heads resting on the pillows.

"This is about the fact that Francesca used to crawl under a table or a desk and cry after her father hit her—and did who knows what else. She still wants to do that. Do you know when I had to rush out of my room to think about whether to tell her the truth or not, I actually left her alone for all of two minutes, not more. When I came back in, she was a mess. I had really caused her grief. She thought I was going to kick her out. Basically, she pleaded with me not to reject her. I won't go into details. She was crying, and I was on the verge of tears myself, and terrified over what I had to do next. The horrible thing was she really wanted to crawl under the desk. This is not the first time she has mentioned that. I had to tell her—twice—that I wasn't going to hit her."

"Oh, Asti, the poor child."

"Yes, this incredibly sophisticated, brilliant, talented, accomplished, beautiful woman becomes a child in a moment when she senses that there is a threat from a parental figure. And believe me, I am a parental figure for her, except for the fact that she loves me."

"And you love *her*, or at least you always show her how much you care."

"Em, I know that this is going to happen again and again. There are two things that she is afraid to talk about, although she does: sex and me. It is in those moments when she complies and actually talks about these two subjects that she feels, at a certain point, the need to get away from me, from my 'thinking mind', as she calls it."

"And you want to know whether you should let her become a child, curl up into a ball, and hide under your desk."

"I said that I couldn't let her last time because we had to have a very adult conversation, the one about you. She grew up instantly. She listened and used her adult mental faculties extremely well. But I don't know about the future...She can't crawl into the shower anymore and curl up under the water, because Birgitte won't let her feel contaminated or dirty because of what her father did to her...I feel like I am in a fog, and I need clarity. I feel as if I don't know what is going on. I feel as if I can't see. I can't make any more mistakes with her. I can't lose my way. But, in fact, I am totally lost. And don't say 'Play it by ear'. I want to know if it is a mistake to give in to her need to relive those dreadful feelings and become a child. I knew what to do when she felt she had to take a shower after that awful conversation with the man I'd like to kill. I knew that I did not want her to feel that she was dirty or contaminated anymore. I just knew that I had to end that, and she got the message. And I was right. But this is different."

"Why is it different?"

"Because she is *not* dirty, but she *is* hurt, and I can't put my arms around her when she is experiencing the fear of a little girl being abused by her father. And her wife is incredibly understanding and exceptional as a partner to this traumatized woman, and they are doing so well now. They have overcome so many big obstacles."

"But?"

"This is not her wife's job. This is *my* job. Her wife is definitely keeping up her end of the bargain. I can't tell you how marvellous she is, but she truly is. But this wanting to revert to childhood is *my* problem, and I have to solve it."

"First of all, being in a fog is not a negative thing."

"It isn't?"

"Real therapy can get done even if you are in a fog. And you are doing real therapy with her, despite the fact that you want to be her mother."

"I hold myself in check, Em. I mean, I went to her Chopin concert because I knew it was the right thing to do. I let her express her love for me. It's a positive emotion, and you're right, I love her, too. But I am ever so conscious all the time that I am with her that I have to be her therapist. She knows I am not conventional, and we laugh about it. I believe I am capable of doing real therapy with her, but not when the atmosphere around us is viscous and soupy. Because I can't see the forest for the trees. Please be my expert, Em."

"I can't be your expert, Asti."

"Why not?"

"Because you are a full-fledged phenomenon. The therapy world is full of people like Massimiliano who need my expertise so that they won't destroy their patients. You are a breed unto yourself. I, for one, could not allow a thirty-two-year-old woman to crawl under my desk and become a child of twelve again. But you can, and something good could come of it. Because you're you. You're unconventional in your thinking. Ninety-nine percent of therapists wouldn't even contemplate allowing their patients to do that. But you are the exceptional one percent with the brains and the compassion to do it. Didn't she say to you that all other psychoanalysts wouldn't have come to her concert? And you said you didn't care what other psychoanalysts would do. Well, this is the same thing. You do what you feel in the moment could work, because you, and only you, could make it work. Asti, I believe in you so much. The only thing that disturbs me is that sometimes you walk around in too much pain. But at least then I can hold you and let you cry in my arms. Can I hold you now?"

"Yes, Em, please hold me. You can even take off my clothes."

Chapter Thirty-Two

<u>Francesca in the Office XIV</u>
There had been silence in the office for more than five minutes. Astrid was beginning to worry. *Here goes.*
"Since you found out who my wife is, has it become harder to talk to me?"
Francesca lifted her head and looked inquisitively at her therapist. "No, I don't think so. Once I had the feeling that I was talking to both of you, but the answer to that question is no."
Astrid breathed a sigh of relief.
"It's just that…You know we live in a society where everybody says that we *have to* forgive if we want to feel whole again. Well, I can't. Or not yet. I can't forgive my father, and maybe not even my mother, although that remains to be seen. I guess it worries me."
"So, you have bought into that notion?"
"Well, I can't be Jesus Christ, if that's what you are asking. But I do want to feel whole again." She paused here and then asked, "Are you worried that I'm worried that you ask your wife for her advice about your patients? When I play music with Birgitte I ask her advice all the time. I suppose if your wife were an expert in electrical engineering, I might be worried."
"Once I found out about your relationship with her, there is no way that she would ever give me advice about you. Do you understand that? There are things we can do and things we can't do. And anyway, I am not one of her students."
"But you are her wife, and some things come naturally. Anyway, I understand, and I have complete faith in you."
I don't know if I deserve that.
"Dr. Paul, is it essential that I forgive my father? I really can't stop hating him."
Neither can I.
"That's a very big question."

"I know. Sometimes there are whole days when I don't even think of him anymore. Because of Birgitte, because of the way she loves me."

"What I hope for is that there will be many many days in a row when you don't think of him."

"But that has nothing to do with forgiveness."

"No, it doesn't."

"So, you don't feel I need to be all forgiving and warm about him?"

"No."

"Is this one of those moments when you defy your training and say things you are not supposed to say?"

"I guess it is."

"I love you for that." Francesca looked down at the floor. When she lifted her head, she looked unhappy and not very loving at all. "Will it always hurt, like a stabbing pain in my chest? When I was little, really little, but after he had started up with me already, I used to feel a real physical pain in my heart at night in my bed. It was the strangest thing, and it worried me. I used to think that it would kill me, that I would die from that pain."

Oh, Francesca. This is one of those days when I will have to go home to Em and beg her to hold me.

"Tell me more."

Francesca sighed. "What if I can't?"

"Francesca, I've told you before, I accept who you are today, and if you can't tell me, it's alright. You'll tell me another time."

"But I need to please you."

"No, you don't. I will never retaliate. You know that what we do here is good for you, and that is all I care about."

"But why do I always feel so bad?"

"Always?"

"There is a corner of me, even in my happiest moments, when I am playing music with Birgitte or making love to her, that hangs on to that memory of me as a child enslaved to my father, and I can't get rid of it. It is like a very hard stone, like the stone that the ancient Egyptians used to carve their gods, to give the idea of absolute permanence. It won't dissolve no matter how much...no matter how much..."

"No matter how much...?"

"No matter how much you...you...no matter how kind and thoughtful and caring you are with me. You give me so much and...and...do I ever move forward? I seem to feel stuck in that moment in time after he used me or fucked me or hit me."

"Tell me how it felt."

"I felt depleted. I felt deflated. I was just skin with nothing inside me. I love the feel of people's skin. I remember that I loved Peter's skin. But mostly I love Ghita's skin. I love touching it with my fingertips. You know how cellists completely embrace their instrument with their bodies. And Ghita cradles her violin almost as if it were her baby. What is so special about her music is the quality of her tone. There's something uncanny about it. And wind players, my God, they make music with their breath. It's extraordinary. But you can't talk about the tone of my piano. It is what it is scientifically. I can't embrace or cradle it or blow into it. But each pianist touches the keys differently. I know that."

"So, it's all about touch."

"Yes. And I touch the keys in my own way, and I think it makes a difference. For example, Martha Argerich does something with her hand that is unique. It's like she rolls it over so that there is a different intensity at each moment. I love that. I don't do that. I can't. But I must do something else, something that makes my touch my own."

Astrid was nodding. "Okay, I understand."

"And I think it's because of the way I feel about skin, since I felt that that was all that was left of me after my father did what he did. And when he hurt me, when he hit me—and he hit me harder and harder as I grew older—I really felt my skin. And that's how I knew that I was still alive." Francesca was almost panting now. Her breathing was no longer natural.

"Francesca, take slower breaths. You can do it. Please try."

"I don't know if I can." She was sobbing.

"What if you lay down?"

"You mean on your goddam couch?"

"Yes, would it relax you?"

She shook her head adamantly.

"Okay, what about the floor? You have to slow your breathing down. I don't care where you do it. Anywhere you want. The carpet is very clean. Please, Francesca. Could you do it for me? I know it's a very big favour, but I'm worried."

As soon as she said that, said that it would be for her, Francesca got up from her chair and rolled it away. She bent down and got under the desk, curled up in the fetal position, and continued to cry. She faced out towards the room. *I may not be allowed to touch her, but I can be at her level.* Astrid got up from her chair and rolled it away, too. She sat down on the floor, crossed her legs, and faced her patient. *What the hell am I doing? I'm making her slow down her breathing. I would so like to touch her, like a mother, but I can't.*

"Slow your breathing down. Breathe more deeply if it is possible. I'm here, Francesca. I won't let anyone hurt you. Just listen to my voice. You were so brave today, telling me how you felt as a child. And I understand so much more now. And I see you playing the piano in my mind. I am watching you as you touch the keys in your own special way. That's better now. You are breathing more normally. You can cry as much as you like. Your sobs are like words. You are talking to me. You are communicating with me as you always do. You are enfolding yourself into this room and letting it envelop you. It is cradling you. It will never hurt you." Her words were having the desired effect. Francesca knew she was there sitting on the floor in front of her. Eventually she opened her eyes. She haltingly extended the fingers of her right hand until they touched Astrid's knee. It was barely a touch. Her knee, of course, was covered, and there was no skin, but Astrid knew what she meant. She smiled at Francesca, the little girl. *Now get up and become a woman again. I know you can do it.* Her patient began to move. Astrid picked herself up and returned to her chair. Francesca followed suit and sat down to face her.

"What just happened to me, Dr. Paul?"

"You became a little girl again, and that is fine. I accept all of you."

"I heard every word you said to me. I will never forget what you just did. Who are you? How do you know exactly what I need and when I need it?"

Astrid smiled. "And let's not forget where." Francesca almost laughed.

Chapter Thirty-Three

<u>Astrid and Marisa</u>

The day was over, and Marisa was still at her desk figuring out something to do with numbers. Astrid took one of the chairs in the waiting room and placed it beside Marisa's desk. She sat down.

"This is unusual Dr. Paul, I mean Astrid. I'm calling you Astrid now, right?"

"Right."

"So, what's up?"

"A few nights ago, Em and I had some friends over for dinner. And Mark, one of them, asked me what my hourly rate was. Emma just started to laugh. Nobody really understood, but I did. And then she explained to them that I had no idea what I charged. And it's the truth. I just explained that I did my thing, and you did yours."

"Okay. Do you want me to tell you what it is now?"

"No, I just wanted to say that it was really embarrassing."

"I'm so sorry."

"I know you take care of everything in this studio. You pay the rent here. You pay all the bills. I never go into the bank. You can sign cheques, too. I know you are exceptional at your work. And I know that you take care of me as well. In fact, at the end of the month, money goes into my bank account, and your husband, who is the accountant and our—mine and Em's—financial advisor and broker, does whatever he does, so that in around twenty years when we retire, we can live a comfortable life."

"Yes, that's all true."

"At tax time, you and Guido come over to the house, Emma makes a delicious meal, and afterwards I sign some papers. He tells me that I will be getting a raise, you will be getting a raise—cost of living. Then he and Emma go into the office to talk investments etc., and they leave you and me to—"

"—Have some girl talk."

"And I love those moments. I love talking with you about your kids, about our lives, about our feelings. I really love it. But I have come to the realization that the three of you, in some way, infantilize me."

"Astrid, don't say that! Not to me, anyway. I'm the one who sees you when you walk in here in the morning, especially after your run, looking bright and beautiful. I'm the one who sees you at the end of the day, when you look as if you are carrying all the sorrow of the universe on your shoulders. I'm the one who sees that you have been crying. I am not ever going to let you worry about anything financial. I don't want you to ever be burdened with the trivia of this office. There is a line of demarcation between what goes on behind your door over there and what goes on in here. This part is my domain. You have enough troubles. And I *want* to take care of you."

"Oh, God, Marisa, you are so good to me. And obviously this is the way I want it to be, otherwise it wouldn't be this way. So I have to ask you a question. Please be honest. And if the answer is 'no', then I will do whatever it takes to right the wrong."

"Okay, ask me. And I'm sorry if I sounded angry. I'm not angry. I'm just convinced that this way is the right way for us."

"Yes, it is the right way for us. My question is...my question is: Do I pay you enough?"

Marisa started to laugh. Astrid looked confused. Astrid was sitting forward with her hands on the desk. Finally, Marisa put her hand on Astrid's and said, "Astrid, you are adorable."

"What? I'm forty-seven years old. I haven't been adorable in ages."

"Trust me, Astrid, you're adorable. And yes, you pay me a great salary. You know Caroline?"

"Emma's secretary Caroline?"

"Yes."

"*You* know Caroline?"

"Astrid, it has been years that we have been communicating with each other. You say to me, 'Can you call my wife?' and I call Caroline. Emma says to Caroline, 'Can you call my wife?'"

"I see."

"Over the years we have become great friends. In fact, Guido and I, and Caroline and Leonard, go out together very often."

"Really?"

"Really. Well, the university does not pay her anywhere near as much as you pay me."

"But just because the university exploits her doesn't mean I pay you enough. Does she take care of Em the way you take care of me?"

Marisa laughed some more. "All good secretaries are therapists in their own way."

"But surely, Em doesn't need a therapist the way I do."

"Astrid, you are a very very special woman—sensitive, kind, and what's the word your wife always uses?"

"Porous."

"Yes, porous. You make me feel for you. I feel as if I always want to give you a hug. And I love that about you, that you care so much. I wouldn't work for anyone else. But you know how your wife does not suffer fools."

"Yes."

"Well, who do you think she talks to about all the idiots in her department, and in the university administration?"

"Caroline. And me."

"I'm sure she does. But Caroline has to cheer her up, too."

"Is Caroline happy working for Em?"

"Of course she is. She also wouldn't work for anyone else. And Emma is usually right about the assholes she works with. You know what happened at the meeting of the tenure committee two days ago?"

"No."

"Some idiot asked Francesca how many concerts she would be giving in the next academic year. As if the quality of her teaching would be different."

"What did Francesca say?"

"She shrugged her shoulders and said nothing."

"Did they give her tenure?"

"Of course. Emma would not have had it any other way. And she really let that stupid administrator have it."

"I had no idea...I had no idea about any of this—I mean, of the relationship my wife has with Caroline."

"So, yes, the university should pay her more. But my salary—"

"—Is commensurate with the quality of work you provide me? Is it really?"

"Yes. And my husband would not have it any other way."

"Good. And when you stay late?"

"You pay me overtime."

"Good. Does Caroline get overtime?"

"No, but Emma gives her a cash bonus at Christmas, one that she pays herself."

"I love my wife. Could I pay you a cash bonus, too? I never thought of it. How much does she give her?"

"Two thousand Euros."

"Okay, I'll do the same."

"I just told you that you are way more generous than the university."

"I don't believe you."

Marisa started to laugh, and Astrid joined in.

Chapter Thirty-Four

<u>Francesca in the Office XV</u>

"I am going to Italy in two weeks for two weeks. First, I am going to Siena to see my teacher, Luigi, for a few days and then I am going to spend ten days with my students in Florence and in other parts of Tuscany. The university is arranging it."

"Is Birgitte going with you?"

"Yes, but I haven't decided if she will meet my students. I am still uncomfortable with students knowing anything about my private life. But I did do something very much unlike me a few days ago. You might even be proud of me, but I'm not sure."

"Okay, tell me."

"Well, after our rehearsal with the orchestra for the Chopin piano concerto and the symphony that Birgitte is also conducting with the orchestra, Goldschmidt wanted to see us both in his office. We sat in the two chairs in front of his desk. They are not far apart. Basically, he wanted to tell Birgitte that she would be conducting more often next year; she could choose the repertoire, and if she wished for me to play the piano with the orchestra, she had his blessing. He told her she would still retain her job as first violinist, but that there would come a time when she would probably be a soloist and a conductor rather than a member of an orchestra. He was going to have her be the soloist in the Mendelssohn violin concerto next year. So it was kind of momentous news. And then he looked as if he was contemplating saying something else. He started talking about our performance of the Franck sonata last year at the Conservatory. He said he couldn't get over how together we were, how well we communicated. He agreed with the critic that it sounded like we were playing one instrument. He said, 'How do you do it? I know you are great friends, roommates in fact, but the way you two play music together is uncanny.'"

"Oh, my God, Francesca, you did it!"

"I did. I took Birgitte's hand in mine—she nearly fell out of her chair—and said we were way more than roommates. I mean he isn't exactly of a generation that accepts these kinds of things readily, but I wanted to be honest."

Em, can you believe it? Our honesty with her bred more honesty.

"How did he take it?"

"Well, he was stunned at first. And then he said, 'It wasn't obvious at all.' He added that Philippe and Ugo are so obvious. And then he said he was happy for us. He said he loved us like daughters. But he wasn't going to say more just in case he said something politically incorrect. 'You should know that my wife is a New York Jewish feminist, and she would have my head if I made some kind of remark that could be construed as disparaging towards women.'"

Astrid laughed.

"And you know what? The time is coming soon when we will have to be more open."

"Are we going to have that talk about babies now?"

"Birgitte really wants to have a baby."

"And how do you feel about it? Will you ever want to have a baby?"

"Birgitte is definitely going first. She had a great childhood and wonderful parents..." Francesca hesitated. "I did not."

Astrid kept still. *Let her talk.*

"You know my mother never told me that she loved me when I was growing up. She would say, 'I love the way you play that Bach sonata.' And it wasn't her way of saying she loved me. Not even my *nonni* declared that they loved me, although they showed it. It was never said. I have only ever said 'I love you' to two people, Birgitte and you, and I was already almost thirty. I never thought about my grandparents in that way. Now I know I love them, because I have felt love with Birgitte and you, but when I was a child, I just wanted to live with them and get out of my house..."

Francesca stopped her monologue and took a deep breath. "I think I want to say something now, but I am not sure why. It concerns Birgitte and something she said to me. Maybe if I told you, we could try to figure it out together."

"Of course. Tell me whatever you want, and we can try to understand your feelings about it."

"Okay. After I played the Brahms second piano concerto with the orchestra here and Birgitte played first violin for the first time, when we were going home, she asked me to drive the car. I didn't drive much initially because I didn't know the city. She was very quiet for a while, and then in tears, she began to talk. It was quite an admission...confession, I'm not sure what to call it. She started talking about the fact that she had sometimes been worried that she never loved anyone, I mean in a romantic sense. She said to herself that she was afraid to feel vulnerable. And then she told herself that it didn't matter, because what she loved most in the world was music and playing music. She didn't need to love a man. She was fine the way she was. And then she met me. And then I came to Munich. And we said we loved each other. But, in the back of her head, there was something else that she wasn't saying, not to me, not to herself. But after we played the concerto, the thought leaped to the front of her head. And then she started to really cry. At the apex of her profession, at the time, being first chair of a great orchestra, she had the thought that she loved *me* more than music, more than playing music. She said it was frightening to be so vulnerable. I knew that feeling, because I had said I loved her on the phone from Montreal, that I loved her heart, body, and soul." Francesca stopped. "Why am I telling you this?"

Astrid did not speak. She waited.

"We are going to do that again. You are going to make me answer my own question. Well, first I have to say that at this stage I no longer feel vulnerable when I tell Ghita how much I love her. I just tell her because I want her to know. She deserves to know. I am a difficult person with my history, and she wants me anyway. So, I tell her...Okay, I'm just going to say something else to give you more background. At a certain point Ghita stopped going to her therapist. After this revelation she went back. Then she stopped for a while again. But when we were in the middle of that pleasure/pain thing, and she was scared of herself—scared of hurting me, scared of the fact that she really wanted to be a tiger in the bedroom, that she enjoyed it—she went back, to kind of get confirmation that it was alright to be like that and make love to me like that."

Astrid was nodding. *More is coming. Now she is going to talk about me and what happened in here last week.*

"I don't want to cry now, Dr. Paul. I want to stop crying in here. I thought that maybe since I did what I did in here last week, I might always be an adult from now on. But that's an illusion."

"Francesca, I will never reject the child in you. I will never reject you when you wish to cry. We have to do this, because you have to vomit out all that toxicity. Every bit of it. And I don't care where you are in this room when that is happening. I don't care where I am, either."

"But how can I become a mother, if I'm still a child?"

"And you think that all mothers, all good mothers, are always mature and self-contained and never cry like a child? Come on. You, with that incredibly unique brain of yours, know better."

Francesca nodded. "But having had a mother who didn't love me...No wonder I want you to be my mother." And she started crying.

Astrid waited. And then she thought better of her silence. "Francesca, I want you to talk now. We have come this far today, but I know that you know you want to and must go further. I am listening. I am not going to send you away. I am never going to hit you. What are you afraid to talk about?"

"What happened last week..." She took a deep breath. "I know that you are saying all these beautiful things to me because you are beautiful. But I don't feel I deserve you. I told you. I feel bad. And you are good. How can we be in the same room together? If I vomit that toxicity, I will contaminate you."

"Okay, Francesca, let's go back. Tell me about what happened in the room here last week that is making you feel so vulnerable to me."

"I touched you."

"Why did you touch me?"

"Because I couldn't talk yet. My voice couldn't work."

"Can you say the words now that your voice can work?"

Francesca shook her head.

"Is it something you've never said to me before?"

"No. You know I've said it to you before, but I've never touched you. I said it to you when I played the piano for you."

"When you touched the keys in your own special way."

Francesca nodded.

"But touching is more intimate than saying it," commented Astrid.

Francesca nodded.

"Dr. Paul, you know I love you. I've said it over and over. But I worry that touching you was too much—yes, too intimate. But you have to believe me when I say that I was not asking anything of you in that moment. I was only thanking you for what you had already given before I even asked. And I didn't have the voice to tell you that I love you and I cherish you. But you always know what I mean no matter what I do and I'm afraid that...I'm afraid that...it was too much and that you will reject me."

Oddly enough, she wasn't crying when she said all these things, all these amazing things. *Too bad I can't tell you that I love you, too, and that gesture of yours meant so much to me, and Em is always worried that I want to be your mother. Can I tell her that her gesture was meaningful to me?*

"There's something else that I was telling you."

"Yes?" *What could it be?*

"I may not be very articulate. But I'll try to say it."

"Please try."

"I don't want you to be angry with me."

"Have I ever been angry with you?"

"No, but I once scared you and you had to go out and talk to Marisa."

"True. Is this going to scare me?"

"I don't think so. I just have to be able to say it."

"Okay, try."

"I wonder if you think I love you because of what you do for me, because of how good you are to me. I know very little about you except for a few extraneous facts, although the fact about Professor Green is a pretty big one. However, I never see you interact with other people, only with me. Except for Marisa, and I know she loves you and admires you so much, she'd lay down her life for you. And it is truly apparent that you love her."

No kidding. What a big brain you have, Francesca. You are unbelievable.

"Was it okay for me to say that, because what's coming next is even bigger. I haven't offended you?"

"It was okay. You haven't offended me. Talking about love never offends me."

"I was afraid of what could happen after I touched you. But I couldn't help myself. Then when I sat up and looked at your face, I felt calmer, reassured."

"You mean the expression on my face?"

"No, I mean your face. Usually when I am crying or afraid of how you will react to me, and especially if I think you might eject me from your office, I'm looking down. I should look at your face more often." Francesca stopped. She took several breaths.

My God, this is interesting.

"Go on. You are being extremely articulate."

"I haven't gotten to that part, that difficult part. You see, although I know next to nothing about you and your life and how you are with others, except for me and Marisa, I feel that...I feel that..."

Please continue. I really want to hear this.

"I feel that I love you because of who you are. Your face tells me who you are. I look at your face, not at the expression on your face. Am I making sense?"

"Perfect sense."

"I don't know you. But I feel that I know you. And I love you because you are that person. And...and...and...when I touched you, I think I wanted to tell you that. Even if I had a voice at that moment, I would have touched you anyway, because I thought I was telling you more—not just that I loved you, but that I loved you for who you are, not for what you do, and how you help me."

Em, you have to let me tell you about this and about what happened in here last week . You don't want me to talk about Francesca anymore, but this is important, and I won't be asking your advice because I've already done it. Please let me talk to you about this.

"You're not saying anything."

"That's because you have more to say."

"I do?"

"I think so."

"What about?"

"Just think. Go back to last week. What else happened here?"

"You told me to lie down so that I could relax and not have a full-blown panic attack. And you said to do it for you even if it was a big favour. And I did it for you."

"Did you want to do it?"

"Of course I did. I just wanted to lie under your desk and cry and feel my skin so that I would know that I wasn't going to die from my father's hands and his body and his...his..."

"Use whatever word you want."

"I can't. Can I say genitals?"

"I get the picture."

"So, I was reliving those moments from my childhood. And that was a good thing?"

"Good or bad is irrelevant. Do you think that it was necessary?"

"To stop having a panic attack?"

"No, in a more general sense, for your present and your future."

"Uh, maybe. Well, yes, I do."

"Why?"

"Because I didn't die. And I know that I won't ever die of his mistreatment, despite what he did to me. I'm going to live and I'm going to be me, sometimes like a child, sometimes like an adult and...and...you'll always be there for me. And so will Birgitte. And you won't judge me. You will let me be me, and I will always love you because you're lovable."

"There, now you've said it all."

Chapter Thirty-Five

Francesca in the Office XVI

"Dr. Paul?"

"Yes?"

"When I go to Italy, can I talk to you on Zoom like always? I mean, we will be in the same time zone."

"Yes, of course. Just take care of it with Marisa. And when you come back, I will be on holiday. Marisa will tell you when I'll be back. Alright?"

Francesca nodded. "After Italy, Birgitte and I will be going to Montreal for a while anyway. My mother has taken the plunge and is retiring. So is Stefano. Most of the time that we will be there, they will be hiking in New Zealand with Ghita's parents. But really, I am going to be with my grandparents. My grandfather, a few years back, had a heart attack on the very day that Italy voted in a Fascist prime minister. It nearly killed him."

"Oh, Francesca. How horrible. All those years of sacrifice. All those years fighting Fascism and the Nazis, and then...and then that woman gets elected. I am so sorry."

"My *nonni* have met Birgitte once before when we went to play Simon's concerto in Toronto. But I am not sure about meeting them again. Anyway, thank God she is Danish. And last time she brought her violin; we played some Bach for them, and then she got a call from her parents. She was speaking Danish, and my grandfather, you could tell, was really relieved."

"They don't know about you and Birgitte?"

"My mother has strictly forbidden it. My *nonno*'s health is too fragile. And she knows best under the circumstances."

Astrid nodded. "How about the fact that you live in the city of Hitler? How did he take that?"

"Well, I just explained to him that Munich is a city like any other in Europe, and as cities go, a pretty good one. And besides, he's proud of me. I teach in English at an American university. My students are for the most part American, and I speak English all day."

"Does he know you speak German now?"

"I haven't told him, but I have lived here for almost two and a half years. I'm sure he assumes—no, he knows I speak German."

"Right."

"In some ways, it's strange to be living here. I like Munich, and I love Birgitte. What happened here happened a long time ago. But not for my *nonno*. For him, it's like yesterday. But I think about it. I try to imagine Germany in the time of Hitler and Italy, as well, in the time of Mussolini. My great-grandparents, my *nonna*'s parents, left before the racial laws came into effect. Italian Fascism never really had that component of being based on the hatred of other people before Hitler came into power. In fact, the most important woman in Mussolini's life was Margherita Sarfatti."

"Who was she?"

"Well, she was a famous art critic. She published an art magazine, and if she said an artist was great, his fortune was made. She knew all the Futurists. Her husband was Mussolini's lawyer. He got into a lot of trouble when he was younger, and he needed a lawyer. Their love relationship was well-known."

"And she was Jewish."

"Yes, a Venetian Jew. And when he was forced to bring in the racial laws, Mussolini sent her and her children to Buenos Aires. She didn't come back to Italy for a long time."

"But he died with Clara Petacci."

"So? I don't know how important she was to him, but Mussolini was kind of a boor before he met Sarfatti, and she was an educated, sophisticated woman of intellect. She changed him, I believe. But then she wrote a book about him. She believed in what he was doing. How weird is that?" Francesca sighed. "Sometimes my grandfather wakes up in the middle of the night, crying '*I tedeschi! I tedeschi!* The Germans! The Germans!' Oh,

God! I'm not really thinking, am I? I'm not offending you, I hope. I mean you were born here. This is your home. I'm sorry, Dr. Paul. It's funny. I think of you as someone unassociated with any particular place. You're a woman of the world and you speak English like an American."

"You're not offending me. The word '*tedesco*' comes from Deutsch, does it not?"

"Yes, it does. And the Jews from Germany, Eastern Europe, and Russia were called the *Tudesco* Jews, or more commonly Ashkenazi Jews, to distinguish them from the Portuguese and Spanish Jews, some of whom then moved to Holland to be free, because of the Inquisition." Francesca stopped suddenly and looked up at her therapist. *Your incredible brain is spinning, isn't it?*

"So, Francesca, your grandmother is also Jewish?"

"Yes."

"And you and your mother identify as Jews?"

"Yes."

"Okay, Francesca, ask your question. It's bursting out of you. I've been asking you questions. You have the right to ask me."

"I'm afraid. Couldn't you just tell me?"

Would it be so terrible? But then I will have to go into the story of hidden Jews. Do I want to go there? What would Em do? But I got myself into this mess by asking her about her grandmother. It's my fault. I have to pay the price. Why can't I remain anonymous with this woman? Why do I always get into trouble with her?

"But if you ask, I won't feel so terrible about breaking the psychoanalytic oath. I won't say no to you." And then Astrid began to laugh. "What is wrong with me, Francesca? I think you're just smarter than I am."

Francesca was laughing, too. When they stopped, she finally asked her question. "Are you Jewish, Dr. Paul?"

"Yes, I am. But my family did not go to Holland during the Inquisition. My grandmother and grandfather were born here.

They were sent to Holland as hidden children during the Nazi regime. They grew up in separate Christian families, met in high school, and married. My mother was born there. And I'm not telling you anything else, because *all* of the psychoanalysts of old are going to fire me, not just Freud and Melanie Klein."

She and Francesca continued laughing for a while. *Em, I am about as unconventional as one can get, but my patient is laughing.*

Then Francesca got serious. "Dr. Paul?"

"Yes."

"There is another question I want to ask you."

"Then you have to know that I have the right to decline to answer. Is that alright?"

"Yes, it is. But I want to ask it anyway."

"Go ahead."

"You remember when you left the room to talk to Marisa, when I said what I said about speaking in Dutch?"

"Yes, I'll never forget."

"And I've said that I felt you were scared, and you admitted it."

"I did."

"I don't really understand why it scared you so much. Why were you scared?"

Astrid sighed. *Come on, Astrid. Give her an answer.*

"I was scared because once you knew the truth I had to ask you a very difficult question, difficult for me, too. I had to ask you whether you wanted to continue analysis with me."

"Did you doubt that I would wholeheartedly want to stay with you?"

"I'm not sure. But I knew that I didn't want you to leave. I knew that I wanted to continue to work with you. I knew that I wanted you to talk to *me* about your childhood, your father, your mother, your life."

"Because you wanted to help me?"

"Of course, because I wanted to help you."

"Because you knew you could help me."

"Yes, because I knew I could help you and I didn't want someone else to be the one listening to you."

"Because you are the best person for me."

"I can't really say that. There are a lot more conventional, strict analysts out there who know what they are doing, and I don't always know what I am doing. If you don't follow the rules, you can get lost in the fog. And then I have to feel my way through. I can't depend on my knowledge and my training. Was that a good enough answer? It was certainly the truth."

"You always tell the truth. And I love you for telling me the truth. And I would rather be here in your fog than in any other classical analyst's clarity. I love your fog. Dr. Paul, I will never leave you until the moment when I have spewed everything out. Until the moment we are both satisfied that all that toxicity is out of me."

Did I just do that, tell her how I work? Work with my feelings, with my gut, and not with my head. Oh, Em, what are you going to tell me? Please don't divorce me over this.

Chapter Thirty-Six

<u>Astrid and Marisa</u>

When Astrid exited her office, Marisa was also getting ready to leave. They looked at each other, and Marisa knew.

"What's wrong, Astrid? Can I be of help?"

Astrid sighed. She shook her head. "I don't know."

"Anyone tell you they hate you today?"

"No, my patients seemed quite happy with me today."

"Then what is it?"

"You want the truth?"

"Of course I want the truth."

"It's my wife. I'm afraid she may divorce me."

"Astrid, come sit over here near my desk." She pulled a chair closer to her desk and sat down in her own seat. Astrid sat down.

"You know that I am not a very orthodox therapist."

"I know that. It's what makes you so great."

"I told the truth today about the way I work."

"Did the patient mind?"

"Not at all. She said it suited her just fine."

"So it's your wife you're worried about."

"And I can't lie to her. I have to tell her exactly what I said. It felt right at the time to speak the truth, but then afterwards, I thought of what Em would say. And I feel sick about it. Lately she's been saying very positive things about me and about how she has faith in me. But I may have gone too far to the other side of orthodoxy. What is wrong with me, Marisa? Why am I like this?"

"You are like this because you are special. No one is like you. And your wife admires you. We all admire you because you are so authentic, real, and independent. I believe you know what you are doing. Stop doubting yourself. Go home and tell your wife that you told a patient the truth today and it all worked out. Tell her you're glad you told the truth. So what if another therapist would not have said those things? You are better than all of them put together."

The tears began to trickle down Astrid's face. She was nodding. "Okay, I'll do that. I shouldn't be afraid of Em. She is so loving and gentle with me. Just like you." Astrid smiled. "I don't deserve you, Marisa."

"Shut up. Let's lock up this office and go home."

Chapter Thirty-Seven

<u>Astrid and Emma</u>

"Asti, what's the matter? You don't look good. Are you getting sick?"

Astrid came into the living room where her wife was sitting and reading a book. She pulled off her shoes and dropped her briefcase next to the door. She practically ran over to Emma. "Hold me, Em. Just hold me."

"Of course. Come over here." Astrid knelt on the floor in front of Emma and dropped her head into her lap. She wrapped her arms around Emma's waist. "Just let me stay here for a while. I don't want to talk yet. I'm afraid."

"Of what?"

"Of you."

"Okay. We don't have to talk. But just know that it doesn't matter what you did today, or what you said today in your office. I will always love you." Emma stroked her lover's back. She bent over and kissed the top of her head.

Finally, Astrid pulled herself up and stared into the eyes of the most important person in her world. She turned around, sat, and leaned her back on Emma's knees. "I know you don't ever want to do this again, but I have to tell you what has been happening with Francesca last week and this week. I *have to*. And I will not be asking for your advice, because it already happened, and I am glad it did."

"You let her crawl under your desk."

"I didn't just let her. I practically begged her to go there."

"Okay, tell me, but I'd rather be facing you. Come into the bedroom and I'll hold you in my arms."

"Okay."

They went into the bedroom and lay down. Emma was on her back and held her arms out to Astrid, who lay her head on

Emma's chest. Emma wrapped her arms around her. So Astrid told the story of what had happened in her office the week before. When she got to the point where Francesca touched her, she sat up and showed Emma what happened. "It was like in slow-motion. She stretched her arm ever so slowly towards me and touched my knee like this." Astrid touched Emma on the knee with all her five fingertips.

"Oh, my, what a remarkable gesture of love! You did something truly amazing, Asti. You are a magician."

"It was kind of a transcendent moment. I have never felt anything like that in all my years practicing this profession. But I couldn't tell her. I couldn't tell her that I love her, too."

"Asti, she knows. She just knows."

"And today she told me something even more startling. She said she touched me to show me that she loved me for who I am, for the person I am, not for what I give her. Can you believe that?"

"I can, Asti. She does know you, because you let her see you."

"We had an unbelievable conversation today. Suffice it to say that we told each other that we were Jewish, and we laughed with each other. But then she got serious and asked me why she made me scared the other day. Why did I have to run away to talk to Marisa?" Astrid dropped down again and placed her head on Emma's chest. "Hold me, Emma, because now I'm afraid."

"Afraid that I'll stop loving you?"

"Afraid you might even divorce me."

"You're being ridiculous. Just tell me."

"Please put your arms around me."

"Okay. Okay."

"I told her the truth. I told her I was afraid she might not want me to continue seeing her. I told her I want to listen to her talk about her childhood, her mother, her father, her life. And basically, that I didn't want anyone else to be listening to her. But she understood that I want to help her, and I know that I can."

"Okay, I'm not divorcing you yet, my love."

"And then she said: 'It's because you're the best person for me.'"

"And you said you were."

"No, I did not. I said that sometimes I didn't know what I was doing. People who are classical analysts follow the rules and know what they are doing. People like me, who do not follow the rules, sometimes work in a fog and have to feel their way around. And she said she'd rather be in my fog than anywhere else, that she loved my fog. But basically, I was telling her I work with my feelings, with my gut, not with my head. I told her the truth about the way I work, and...and...and I'm afraid that you will think less of me because I admitted that without thinking. It was just me, Astrid, in a room with Francesca, and I wasn't being her therapist. I was just being me. But she needs Astrid, the therapist."

"No, she needs Astrid, the kind, generous, foolhardy, wise, daring woman she loves, and the woman who loves her back unstintingly. You are the right person for her because you could say all that to her, be honest with her. She doesn't want a law-abiding therapist who could not get down on the floor with her and talk to her in a voice filled with love and understanding. She wants you because you are you. How you could not know that I would love you for your magnanimity and compassion is astounding to me. Don't you know me, Asti? I'm your wife, for Christ's sake. I have lived with you for twenty years."

"You really mean that? You really mean I did the right thing?"

"You did the Astrid thing, which is the best thing, is always the best thing. Stop doubting yourself. Stop judging yourself!" Emma stopped talking and hugged Astrid to her. "I love you so much, Asti. I want you to love yourself."

"Oh, Em, it feels so good to be here in your arms. All the sadness of my office disappears when I lie in your arms. I couldn't do my job without you."

"I'm never leaving you, Asti. Don't worry. These arms belong to you and only you."

Chapter Thirty-Eight

<u>Astrid and Marisa</u>

Astrid walked into the waiting room after her run and gave Marisa a big smile.

"Someone isn't getting divorced!"

Astrid continued to smile, and then said, "I guess not."

"Astrid, you are so...I'm not saying it."

"Why not?"

"I don't think you like it."

"Just say it!"

"You are so adorable."

Astrid laughed. Just before she walked into her own room, she turned to Marisa and said, "No one knows that Francesca is a patient of mine, do they?"

"Of course not. Why would they? Not even Caroline knows. It's none of her business."

"But you told me that Caroline—"

"—Said some young art history professor was up for tenure."

"How did you know she was talking about my patient?"

"Astrid, Francesca is Italian. I'm Italian. We talk to each other in our language in the few minutes she has before you open that door. We talk about Italy, her job. She tells me what she is doing. I figured out that Caroline meant Francesca. I'm rather smart, you know."

"And I am stupid. You are such a marvel."

"Stop calling me that."

"Well, if you can call me adorable, I can say anything I like about you."

"I'd love to hear her play the piano with the orchestra tomorrow night. Guido never wants to go."

"I've forgotten to get a ticket for Em."

"You don't go with her?"

"No, I've been going with my sister for years and years. Check to see if there are any seats left. You can sit with Em."

Marisa sat down at the computer and checked. "There are two seats together in the parterre."

"Use my credit card. My treat. Now I must take a shower."

"Wow! Thank you, Astrid."

Chapter Thirty-Nine

<u>Francesca in the Office XVII</u>

"Marisa was rather enthusiastic about last night. I guess she liked my performance."

"Were you afraid she might hug you?"

"I like Marisa a lot."

"Francesca, were you afraid she might hug you?"

"Not really afraid. A little uncomfortable. But the phone rang, and then you opened your door."

"And how did *you* feel about your performance? Is Chopin still difficult for you emotionally? Were you nervous?"

"Well, when you play with an orchestra, you are very busy, busy listening to everyone else, busy watching the conductor, as well as touching the keys of the piano. You don't have much time to worry about stuff. Yeah, but I did worry before, although I practiced for hours and hours in the house alone and with Ghita, who is a marvellous coach. We worked everything out beforehand. She didn't want me to be nervous about anything."

"But were you?"

"You mean, did I feel unworthy? Yeah, I felt unworthy. Is that what you meant?"

"Well, you just answered a very important question...This is what I think. If we want to listen to music live, then we will be listening to all kinds of performers, and none of them has had the ear of Chopin himself. Don't you have just as much right to perform him, to interpret him, as any other musician?"

"I guess so. Okay, I want to be worthy of him, but I can't just expect that I will be. I have to work at it. I have to live his music all the time to understand it."

"Do you? I mean, live his music all the time?"

"Well, I think a lot about other things. I play other composers. But he's in my head a lot. I hear him. Can I ask you a question?"

"But remember I have the right to refuse to answer."

"I accept that condition...When it came to last night, I had Birgitte right there. I saw her all the time out of the corner of my eye. Everything she does makes sense to me. And she gives me confidence." Francesca sighed and hesitated momentarily. "I also knew you were there. And it was important. I feel you even though I can't see you. I know I sound crazy. How can I feel you, sense you in a huge concert hall? I concentrate...Birgitte knew to wait for me to give her a sign that I was ready. I only signalled my readiness to her when I felt your presence inside of me...I'm not making a great deal of sense, am I?"

"Are you trying to get me to tell you that I talk to you, too, when you perform, or just before you start performing?"

"No. That's not my question at all."

"Okay, ask this question."

"So far, I have only performed Chopin when you have been listening. It has meant so much to me that I can play for you, that I can express my feelings to you in this way, that I can touch the keys of the piano in a particular way, and you will understand what I am saying. I guess...I guess I need you to understand me. And I am happy when I am talking to you in that way, playing music...My mother loved the way I played the piano, still does, but I don't play for her. Ever. I never thought about expressing myself to her. She doesn't really know who I am...and I don't know if I really care.... I'm going round and round here and getting nowhere. I can't seem to articulate my thoughts today. If I had a piano in here, I'd sit down and play for you. But I have to talk. I have to say it. Let me think for a moment."

"Take as many moments as you wish. I also listen to you when you are silent."

"Really?"

"Really."

"And you watch my body."

"And I watch your body."

"You don't seem to be writing stuff about how I move my body as much these days."

"That's true. My memory is working well these days, very well."

"And there has been so much stuff going on between us lately in here."

"You could say that."

"I hope I don't make you too unhappy."

"Francesca, what do you mean?" *Why, oh, why does she feel this way? Em says she knows I love her. But does she?*

"I mean...I mean...I'm not sure what I mean. I guess I don't want the toxicity inside me that is coming out now to overwhelm you. I sometimes feel that I should let it out as slowly as possible so that it won't hurt you in any way. You don't want me to suffer. Why should I make you suffer?"

"Okay, let's be honest here. Sometimes you do make me very sad. I am human, and your father was vicious to say the least, and your mother totally absent. And you have talked to me in your special way, whether through words, body language, or tears, and I *have* understood. I hope to be able to always understand your many languages, including your musical one. But you also have to know that I want *all* of it, *all of it*, not just the pretty parts. I want the screwy, dirty parts, as you call them. I want them. So, despite your fear of contaminating this room, it is your job to give them to me, no matter how they come out, how fast or slow they come out, how inarticulate they come out. Understand?"

Francesca nodded.

"Say it."

"I understand. I will always tell you everything, even the screwy dirty parts. Because you want them."

"Am I making you unhappy now?" Astrid asked.

"No, I don't think so. And you're telling me I shouldn't think about making *you* unhappy. I should just concentrate on communicating."

"Right."

"This is not my question, but did you hear any of the screwy, dirty parts last night?"

Astrid began to laugh. "I wouldn't tell you if I did."

Francesca began to laugh, too.

"So, are you ever going to ask me this question?"

"I don't think you can really answer it."

"Well, I can try...if I want to, that is."

"Yeah, right, your condition."

Astrid and Francesca laughed some more.

"So, although we did not talk that much about this performance of mine before the concert, compared to the last time, I really, really thought about you when I was on that stage. It was Chopin, and I needed you inside of me. That's what I have been trying to tell you. The question I have been asking myself, and now will be asking you, is what does all that mean? What if I'm asked to play Chopin in Rome? Will I be able to?"

"If I'm not there."

"Even though I couldn't see you, I knew you were there and listening to me. If I'm in Rome, you won't be there. I want to play Chopin, and I want you to hear me. But I may not be able to have both those things. It's funny, Dr. Paul, I feel like crying now, but I'm not."

Astrid nodded. *I have also noticed that you're not crying. What does that mean?*

"So what you are saying is that it's physically impossible for me to be at all your future concerts. And you are not sure if you will be able to play a certain composer if I'm not there."

"I can chicken out. I can say I'll come to Rome, but I'll have to play Mozart."

"Is that what you want?"

"No, what I want is you." Francesca hung her head. *But she's not crying. Oh, Francesca, I know you want me. You're allowed to want me. Can I say that?*

"Dr. Paul? Did you notice something different last night?"

"Yes, I did. When you were taking a bow, you took your wife's hand. She looked surprised."

"I didn't tell her I was going to do that. I didn't know I was going to do that. But afterwards, when I realized how much of her went into that concert, I wanted to make her happy."

"And touch for you is a big deal."

"And she knows it more than anyone...except for you, of course."

"Francesca, I think you have something more you want to say to me now. Am I right?"

"I don't know. But you're usually right." Francesca took a deep breath. "Okay this whole discussion of you being there or not being there is symbolic, isn't it? It's like saying that you not being able to be at all my concerts is like you not being able to be my mother. I have a choice, though. I can choose not to play Chopin. But I don't have a choice about whether you can be my mother. I don't have that choice. I will never have that choice. And I have to live with it."

"I would like you to play Chopin, so I guess we have some work to do."

"Dr. Paul?"

"Yes."

"There's something else, isn't there? I didn't say the whole thing, did I?"

"Are you ready to say it? Because if you are not, I can wait."

"Well, I'm thinking it."

"Can you put all the words together for me?"

"It's the screwy, dirty part of me. Are *you* ready for it?"

"I told you I am. Go ahead."

"Not coming to all my concerts is also like one day never seeing you again. One day, you and I will stop seeing each other."

And I will miss you, Francesca. Very much.

"I guess part of me doesn't want that day to ever come. I think I'm going to cry now."

Chapter Forty

<u>Francesca and Birgitte</u>

"Ghita, I did something really crazy." The two women were sitting up in bed. It was morning, and they were talking about going out for a run. Birgitte was all for staying at home on this Saturday morning, and Francesca was all for running.

"What are you talking about?" Birgitte turned towards her lover and touched the top of her head, then began stroking her face.

"Um, well, I got a call from Benoit, our agent, in Paris. Apparently, the Director of the Conservatory called a friend of hers from Berlin. He works for the Berlin Philharmonic, and she told him to come hear us play the Chopin piano concerto, and he came."

"Really?"

"Benoit told me that he made an offer to have me play a Beethoven concerto in September—in fact, in the first concert of the season in Berlin."

"Oh my God, Ollie! That's fantastic! Do you not want to go?"

"Oh, I want to go, but...uh...I made a condition. I told him I want to knock the socks off those Berliners."

"What did you do, *meine Liebe*?"

"I told them that Berlin needed a female conductor to start their season off. I would come if you would be their guest conductor."

"You did what?! You made a condition with the Berlin Philharmonic? Are you crazy?"

"Ghita, the idea of the Berlin Philharmonic is also revolting to me."

"What? What are you talking about?"

"When I think of that orchestra, I think of all the Nazi soldiers in their uniforms filling up their auditorium and listening to hyped-up nationalistic German music." Francesca put her face in her hands. Then she sat up. "I told Benoit to be an agent, to be *your* agent. '*Mais, vous savez que Mademoiselle Thorssen est violiniste.*' I told him he was an idiot and that you had been the conductor of a great orchestra—maybe not as famous, but great nonetheless—when that scout had come to hear me play. And then he thought about it and said maybe that was a great idea. A female conductor! A first in the history books! So, he went off to pen a letter and be an original-thinking agent. Are you angry?"

"I think you're crazy." Birgitte turned away from Francesca and leaned back on the headboard. "But what if it happens? Maybe you're a genius. Which concerto would you want to play?"

"The second or the third. So far, I'm leaning towards the third, but Maria Joao Pires has that one sewn up for sure. How can I compete with such artistry? She's magnificent and I love her." Francesca sighed. "I met her once. She came to Siena. I guess Luigi had called her. She heard me play a Bach Partita. She told me she was impressed."

"Ollie, you keep having more and more stories to tell me from your short life, and I can't keep up."

"I want you so badly to conduct when I play."

"You're just so dependent on me." Birgitte started tickling her.

"I guess we're not running. Stop it!"

Chapter Forty-One

<u>Francesca in the Office XVIII</u>

"So, Birgitte and I are going to Berlin to play an all-Beethoven concert in September. I'll be playing Beethoven's third, and then she will conduct the fourth Symphony, at my request."

"What? How did you pull that off?"

"Yeah, I know. A female conductor. She's going to be famous. My agent called and I said yes to the concerto, only if..."

"Francesca, you amaze me. They could have said no."

"They could have. But history will be made. Hard to reject that."

Astrid smiled.

"And they are announcing it already. They want people to get psyched up," said Francesca.

"The auditorium will be overflowing."

"Yeah, to see the woman I love."

"And you, too."

"Not so much. I'm a nobody. I'm *not* Maria Joao Pires."

"Hm-m-m."

"What's that supposed to mean?"

"Well, are we going to have that conversation about feeling unworthy?"

"I don't really want to. But you're pretty influential *and* persuasive."

Astrid waited.

"I've been wondering..."

She's changing the subject.

"I've been wondering..." Francesca stopped and looked uncomfortable.

"I want it all."

"I know, all the dirty, screwy parts." Francesca sighed and lowered her head. It took her minutes before she raised it and looked at Astrid.

She has to see my face. Come on. What is my face telling you?

"I've been wondering if my father ever hit my mother. There, I said it." The head dropped down again.

I've been wondering, too. Come on, Francesca. Look at my face. You are not responsible for your mother. If he hit her, it's not your fault.

"What if, what if he did, and if I had told her about what he was doing to me, I could have saved her a lot of...a lot of...pain."

What am I going to say to her? Is she crying? I can't tell. Does she want to crawl under my desk?

"Do you believe that your mother's possible pain was your responsibility?"

Francesca lifted her tear-stained face. "I don't know. I just have all these 'what-ifs' in my head. But when I was a kid, I didn't think about stuff like that. I just thought of all the ways in which I could avoid him. Am I a terrible person? I mean, I was terrible to Colin. I used him."

"Francesca, let's talk about real stuff. Were your parents ever alone in the house without you?"

"Well, yes, when I went to my *nonni*. And at other times. My father did everything clandestinely. Just because I went to bed at midnight and my parents were already in bed together, it didn't mean that he wouldn't come to me at two in the morning. I was not safe during the hours of sleep. He would just wake me up. So he could have done things like hit her when I was asleep."

"Did you ever hear them argue?"

"Yeah, a little bit. I just played the piano more loudly."

"So you think he could have saved up his anger for later on in the night when you were out of the way?"

"My father is a sneaky person. Of course. He saved up anger, for sure."

"Do you think you could ask her now?"

"Well, then I would have to tell her that he beat *me*. I'm not up for that yet. Look how long it took me to tell *you*. And it's my job to tell you everything. I mean, that's why I'm here. Revealing stuff from the past to my mother...I kind of think that it's over. Or I'm wishing it's over. But maybe what you're saying is that it's not. Dr. Paul, you're scaring me. Do I have to?"

Oh, Francesca, I certainly don't want to scare you.

"Okay, Francesca, where do you stand? Are you more for the fact that he hit her or more for the fact that he didn't?"

Francesca wiped her face with a tissue. She thought, *Look at my face, Francesca. Is it saying that I accept you totally?*

Francesca squirmed in her chair. "I think he did."

"Why now, Francesca? Why are you thinking of this now?"

"I know I've told you that I didn't tell her to protect her. I felt that. It's the truth. But now, years later, I'm afraid that I didn't protect her at all. All that effort of keeping a secret for nothing. Also...also I see her with Stefano, and I wonder what my life could have been like if he had been my father. What kind of person would I be today? Certainly not this baby crying in your office, this baby who wants to crawl under your desk. How do you put up with me?"

"Are you still afraid that I might reject you?"

Francesca couldn't speak. The tears were coming fast and thick. She nodded her head.

What do I say to her?

"Francesca, look at my face. Come on. Do it. Please look at me."

"I can't. I'm afraid...I would like...I would like..."

"You have my blessing." Francesca stood up, moved her chair away, and lay down on the floor under the desk, facing towards the room. She curled up into a ball. She sobbed.

Astrid stood up and rolled her own chair away. She sat cross-legged in front of her patient. *Francesca, please don't be afraid of me. I won't reject you.*

"Francesca, you are not a terrible person. I am sorry that my words don't really stick, but I will say them again anyway. You are not a terrible person. You were never responsible for your mother's pain, and I will never reject the child in you. You did not have enough of a childhood. And if you need to be a child in my office...you can be a child in my office. I will always accept you. Unfortunately, Stefano wasn't your father. Unfortunately, you had the father you had. You may feel bad because of that father, but in this room, you are just Francesca, not the child abused by her father. You are so much more. And this room is a sanctuary. I would like for it to soothe you. Think of Birgitte wrapping her arms and legs around you, keeping you whole, keeping you from splintering and fragmenting. You will not shatter in here. This room is a sanctuary."

If you don't stop crying, I'm going to start crying. What am I not saying? Astrid, be smart. Figure it out.

"Your mother was going through a hard time. She married a horrible, vicious man. She was confused. So she hid away from everything by working. And she hurt you. She can't hurt you anymore. Neither can your father. You have a wonderful life here. You chose the right person for you. You were brave enough to declare your love for her. You are reaping the rewards. Nothing can hold you back. You are a phenomenal musician, a phenomenal art historian, and a phenomenal teacher, and most of all a phenomenal lover and wife to another phenomenal woman. Now take big breaths. Slow your breathing down."

Please stop crying. I have no words left. In the silence that ensued, Francesca began to breathe more deeply. Finally, she reached her arm out and touched Astrid's knee. This time, her fingertips stayed a little longer.

Chapter Forty-Two

<u>Francesca and Birgitte and Owen</u>

The concert in Berlin was over. Francesca had played two encores. After the symphony, Birgitte got a thunderous standing ovation. Birgitte had made history.

They were in the room for the soloists off the back of the stage. They were hugging each other. Their parents had not yet shown up to congratulate them. It was wonderful to be alone. And then there was a knock at the door. They both walked towards the door, and Francesca opened it. When she saw who it was, she took a big step backwards. Her face turned white and Birgitte was afraid she would fall. She held onto her wife to keep her steady.

And then in German, she asked Francesca who it was. But she already knew. The man just barged into the room, making the two women retreat. Finally, Francesca spoke.

"You can't be here, Dad. I don't want you here. Go away."

"What do you mean, you don't want me here? I'm your father. This is my place. You can't make me go away. The reason *you're* here is me. Without me there would be no concerts, no fame, no fortune. I am responsible for all this." He made a circular motion with his arm. "You can't stop me from being here. You owe me everything."

Francesca looked dumbfounded. She was silent.

Birgitte stepped up. "She owes you nothing. She got here because of her talent, hard work, and love of music. She is a great musician, and...and...you're not wanted here."

Francesca's father looked as if fire was going to burst out of his nostrils. "Who the fuck are you to tell me where I'm wanted or not?" He pushed her. "Get out of my way. I am talking to my daughter."

Francesca woke up and raised her voice. "I am *not* your daughter. I have not been your daughter for years. I hate you and I want you to leave."

"If you don't, I will call security," added Birgitte.

The father glared at the daughter, and suddenly lifted his arm to strike her across the face. But Francesca was too quick for him. She raised her arm, caught his on the wrist, and stopped it mid-flight before his hand was about to land on her cheek. Her father stood in shock. She was obviously stronger than him. He pulled his wrist away from her. He looked defeated and small and old and unhappy. The big man of her childhood was no longer there. He was shrunken and lost. He could not hurt her. He could not control her. He turned around, opened the door, and walked out. His ex-wife, Stefano, and Birgitte's parents appeared in the hallway.

"Owen, what are you doing here? You have no right to be here. Francesca has not invited you. Go!"

He kept going, his face a vision of failure and embarrassment.

Francesca's mother flew into the room to hug her daughter. "I'm so sorry, my love. I had no idea." She had tears in her eyes.

"It's alright, Mom. He didn't hurt me." She broke away from her mother. "Let's leave. Okay?"

"You were amazing, Ollie," Birgitte said to her partner. "He will never bother you again. You broke the bully's back." Birgitte explained to her parents in Danish that Francesca's father was *persona non grata* to both Francesca and her mother.

* * * * * * *

In the bedroom of the hotel, Francesca stopped being the amazing woman who had challenged her father to a duel and had won. She felt weak and sick.

"Okay, okay, my love, let's get you to the bathroom before you vomit on the floor." Birgitte took her wife by the arm and directed her to the toilet. Francesca got down on her knees and Birgitte pulled her hair back. She held her head with both hands.

"You were an Amazon in there. You reduced your father to ashes. He became a hollowed-out ruin. You crushed him. I am so proud of you."

When Francesca had nothing left to vomit, Birgitte started running a bath. Francesca brushed her teeth and took off her clothes.

"You're getting in with me, Ghita, aren't you?"

"Of course, *meine Liebe*. I just want to be with you." Birgitte undressed and followed her beloved into the bath. "Ollie, I think you really did it. He looked sick and demoralized. He didn't have the strength to...to...thrash you. I know you used to have boyfriends just in case he showed up. But he won't be showing up anymore."

"I'm sorry he pushed you, Ghita. I didn't move fast enough."

"Don't fret over that...You know what? Let's take a shower and let me wash you, all of you, and your hair, too. And then you can wash me, too. You always like that. I remember doing that when you first arrived from Montreal. I could not get over your body, how much I loved it and wanted to touch it. We hadn't made love yet, but we had kissed in the entrance to the house, and you said that no one had ever kissed you like that. You said that when a man kissed you it was like drowning inside his mouth. But my mouth was the perfect size."

Francesca smiled. "I love you, Birgitte."

"And I love you."

* * * * * * *

They were home. The parents had taken off to Birgitte's parents' place about sixty kilometres from the city. Francesca had managed to talk to everyone quite normally in the morning, and on the plane. She said goodbye to the four of them and seemed quite cheery, since the concert had been such a success. It was early afternoon on Friday.

As soon as they entered their house, Birgitte asked: "Do you want me to call Dr. Paul's receptionist? Maybe she can see you later today."

Francesca nodded. She knew that she had to work this out of her system, or she would be no good to anyone, not to Birgitte and not to her students on Monday morning. But she couldn't do the calling herself. It was as if she had lost her voice. She walked towards the stairs. She turned around to look at her wife. She held her arm out. Ghita took her hand and drew her into an embrace. They kissed.

"Go to the bedroom and lie down. I'll take care of this." Francesca climbed the stairs.

Birgitte took out her phone and called Marisa. She said it was an emergency.

"You mean the concert did not go well?"

"The concert was the greatest success of our lives, but what happened afterwards was disastrous to Francesca."

"As soon as Dr. Paul finishes with this patient and emerges from her room, I will tell her. Today she has a six o'clock appointment, but I am sure she will let Francesca come at seven. I will have to ask her. One of us will call you back."

Chapter Forty-Three

<u>Francesca in the Office XIX</u>

When Dr. Paul came out of her room, both Birgitte and Francesca were sitting in the waiting room. Dr. Paul motioned to Francesca to come inside. Francesca rose, walked over to Dr. Paul, and gave her a tiny smile.

I feel as if I want to hug her. I told her I wouldn't let her father ever hurt her again and I failed. I feel as if I lied to her. How can she ever forgive me? I will nurture her tonight. I will demand nothing of her. I will let her be. The room will hold her. And hopefully she will return to her wife as a whole person, a functioning adult. Good luck, Astrid.

They both took their seats. Astrid waited. Neither spoke for a long time.

"It was a great concert, Dr. Paul."

"I read the review. It was historical in every sense. I want to say I am happy for you, for the both of you, but I guess I can't."

Francesca took a deep breath. "Birgitte says that I was an Amazon with my father. I completely defeated him, and according to her, he will never show up again."

Astrid did not speak. It was not her place to speak. *Just tell me everything, Francesca. I am listening. I am here.*

"You're not talking."

"I'm here to listen."

"Do you know why I go to the gym and build my muscles and run, Dr. Paul?"

"Tell me."

"I have to be strong. I *have to* be strong. I don't have a choice. I can't depend on a boy or a man to take on my father if he ever shows up. I must do it myself. I must fight back. Do you understand?"

"Perfectly. But I did not know that. When you play the piano, you always wear something sleeveless, and I can see your muscles rippling." *And it is so beautiful. I love what you wear onstage. You look so compact, strong, and beautiful.*

"Most people do strength training because they want to look good; they want to be fit. I do it because I just might have to stave off my father. It is not unconscious motivation. I am very conscious. I have a purpose."

"And it paid off last night?"

"Yes. When you spoke to Birgitte, she didn't tell you exactly what happened?"

"No, she just told me that he showed up after the concert in the soloists' room."

"So, I have to tell you what happened?"

"You don't have to tell me anything. I make no demands. You can talk about anything or not talk."

"Yes, you listen to my silences. You are so special, Dr. Paul. I am so glad I know you and can be here with you in this room."

"But I made you a promise I couldn't keep."

"What promise?"

"I told you I wouldn't let your father hurt you."

"Dr. Paul, you always keep your promises. You said he couldn't hurt me in here, in your sanctuary. But the world out there is not a sanctuary."

How kind of you, Francesca. Where is all this wisdom coming from? When is the breakdown coming?

"I *am* strong, but I don't feel strong today. I used up all my strength last night. Did you know he pushed Birgitte out of the way because he had to get to me. He was such a bully. He was claiming that all I've ever accomplished is due to him. And when I told him I didn't want him, that I hated him, that I wasn't his daughter anymore, he lifted his arm to strike me."

"Oh, Francesca, I am so sorry."

"But I reacted fast. I lifted *my* arm, and I caught his wrist, and he couldn't do anything. He couldn't move it. I was stronger than him. He looked sick, unhealthy, defeated. He was no longer a big, strong man, able to punish his little girl. My mother says he has nothing now, except all his money. His girlfriend in Toronto left him. He is an empty shell."

Francesca suddenly stopped talking. She was thinking. "Dr. Paul?"

"Yes?"

"Have I wasted my life being afraid of such a broken man?" Her voice cracked as she ended her sentence. "He spent his life hurting me. He spent his life taking whatever he could from me. And I am sitting here feeling used, weak, and powerless. Am I the broken one? He's inside me, Dr. Paul. If he's empty it's because he emptied himself into me, night after night after night, before I even understood what he was doing to me." Francesca bent over and dropped her face into her hands. She was crying, whimpering, moaning, and ultimately weeping.

How did she go from Amazon to child in one second? That man has penetrated every corner of her being. She physically feels this man's power over her. How can we right this wrong, this injustice? The sobbing was getting more and more pronounced.

"Francesca, do you wish to climb inside yourself and roll yourself tightly into a ball?"

Francesca nodded, slipped out of her chair, and sank beneath Astrid's desk. She curled up. She was shaking.

Astrid pushed both chairs away, sat down on the floor, and crossed her legs. *I just may cry tonight. Em, help me keep it together. I don't know if I have the fortitude.*

Francesca seemed to be moving closer and closer to her. It was because she was trembling so much. Ultimately, her forehead just touched Astrid's knee, and she kept it there. *What am I going to do? Does she need my voice? It's her body that seems out of control. Oh, God, I think I am going to do something unthinkable.*

Astrid raised her hand and delicately with her fingertips touched Francesca's head. It was like an electrical current that ran from her into her patient. Francesca stopped moving uncontrollably. Astrid allowed her palm to rest on Francesca's head. She kept silent. She just sat there, unmoving, her hand only resting. She heard soft moaning come from her patient. The tears were still flowing but there was no more shuddering. They sat there for many minutes. But Astrid did not remove her hand. It was working. She had done something once unimaginable, but it was working. She didn't care how long she had to stay there. *Em, you can admonish me. You can fire me. You can try to make me give her up, but I am not moving. This is about Francesca's body being pulverized by her father year after year. The only way to heal her is through her body. I love and respect you, Em, more than anyone in the entire world. You can yell and scream at me all you want later, but I am doing this. This is what is called for in this moment. And I am obeying the call. How did I get here? All my years of study, and I am sitting on the floor beside a thirty-two-year-old woman who has accomplished so much in her life, and I have placed my hand on her head. Because I need to help her, and this is the only way.* She felt the tears flow down her face. She brushed them away with her free hand, very carefully, so as not to disturb her patient. And she waited for the child to become a woman again.

"Dr. Paul, I have to tell you something, but I don't want to get up yet."

"You don't have to move. I can stay here as long as you like."

"I feel as if I have regressed decades."

"That's okay. I accept all the different Francescas at all stages of her life."

"I must tell you what happened when we came home today, and we were waiting for you to be free to see me."

"Tell me."

"Birgitte and I took off our clothes and she held me skin-to-skin. She tried to make me whole after my father attacked me. I used to feel that he was splitting me, breaking my body when he penetrated me and pounded my insides out of me. It was a strange and painful sensation, but I always associated that feeling with sex, until I met Birgitte. But I told you before that in the beginning of our relationship I needed her to penetrate me and punish me by hitting me."

"How did she hit you?"

"She took a ping pong bat into the shower, because the skin hurts more when it's wet, and pounded me on my bum. I wanted her to hit me elsewhere too, but she couldn't and wouldn't. And then she would penetrate me from behind with the fake penis."

"Vaginally?"

"Yes. Never anally. My father never did."

"Did she really hurt you?"

"Yes. But it was so familiar." Francesca stopped and cried some more. Astrid just sat there with her hand on Francesca's head.

"This is a safe place, Francesca, and you can tell me anything. I will never judge you."

Francesca responded to her voice, and she seemed to stop crying. "Remember I told you that it had been months and months since she had to do that? I think it was almost a year before today. I asked her to...to...do it again today. I made my beautiful lover do something despicable because my father barged into my life yesterday."

"Did she?"

"Yes, she did, until she couldn't anymore. She just dropped the bat and sank to the floor. And I sank with her." Suddenly Francesca sat up, but she still cowered under the desk. There was no contact between them anymore. She pulled her knees up and wrapped her arms around her legs. She dropped her head down onto her knees. "How could she still love me? She says she does. I believe her. But I'm afraid that one day, she will just have enough of me."

"She's sitting out there in my waiting room worried sick about you. She loves you. Trust me, Francesca. And you give so much to her. I know you do."

"How do you know?"

"I have eyes and ears. I heard her on the phone today. I saw her in the waiting room."

"How do you know that I give to her?"

"I know because I know you. You have given yourself up to me in this room, and so I know you. Do you think that you know me?"

"Yes, I think that I know you."

"Well, the same goes for me. Because we meet in this room, and you share your story, and something incredible happens. We begin to know each other. And you haven't lost any ground. Just because you asked your loving wife to hit you today does not mean that everything you have accomplished here has disappeared. It hasn't. You have grown so much."

"Because of you. Today you made me feel something I have never felt before."

"Really?"

"You touched me. No one has ever touched me like that. No one has ever healed me like that. You are a healer. Okay, this will sound corny, but you touched my soul. And you healed me almost instantly. I don't care if I sound crazy. I believe it."

"Are you ready to be a grown-up now? Do you want to sit in a chair?"

"Who would have thought that sitting in a chair would represent being a grown-up?" responded Francesca, the grown-up.

Chapter Forty-Four

Francesca and Veronica

On the Saturday following the Berlin concert, Birgitte and Francesca drove up to Birgitte's parents' country home. It was beautiful there, and since Francesca had seen Dr. Paul the evening before, she was much more relaxed. At a certain point in the afternoon, Francesca's mother asked her if she'd like to take a walk with her along the trail in the woods. Francesca assented and the two of them went off together.

Francesca wondered what her mother wanted to talk about. Did she want to talk about her ex-husband? Did she want to talk about her daughter's feelings? It seemed not.

"Francesca, I don't know if you realize this, but your father...he...during our life together—"

"—Hit you?"

"So you do know."

"I had no idea then. I only just figured it out. The thing is, I'm in therapy now with an exceptional person, and...and...I'm getting pretty good at figuring things out."

Veronica sighed. "What an awful life I gave you. When you moved to Toronto, you used to keep asking me if I had left him yet."

"You didn't leave him until you were in your fifties."

"I know. I took a long time to learn what was best for me."

Francesca nodded.

"But, my dear, according to Birgitte, you were fierce with him. You stood up to him."

"And I stopped him from hitting me."

Veronica came to a standstill. "You mean he didn't just sexually abuse you? He hit you, too?"

"Yeah, Mom, he beat the crap out of me."

"Oh, no! Oh, my dear. I had no idea."

"You had no idea about anything. You lived in your own little world of the hospital, of *nonno* and *nonna,* and that was about it. You listened to me play the piano. I can't forget that."

"Francesca, do you hate me, too?"

"No, Mom, I don't hate you." *I can't find it in me to love you, though.*

"Stefano keeps telling me I should also go into therapy." The two women resumed walking. "His son, the psychiatrist, knows everyone in Florence. But I don't really live there yet, full-time."

"You have to spend time with *nonno* and *nonna.* I was happy seeing them this summer. *Nonno* is so frail now. But he is still *nonno.*"

"He didn't figure out about you and Birgitte, did he?"

"No. But *nonna* is younger and she lives in today's world. She knows what's going on. I could see her watching us. We were careful, but I think she knows."

"Yeah, there is something electric between the two of you. I am so happy for you. You found the right person."

"Birgitte wants to have a baby, Mom."

"I can't wait! And what about you?"

"Maybe. But she's going first."

"You could do the procedure in Montreal, and I could be there. I do know the best doctors. Hell, I could do the procedure myself."

"I know you could, but Birgitte will do it here. Munich is her home. And her parents live here."

"Yes, yes. That's how it should be. But I am available, if for any reason..."

They continued walking through the trees, and Francesca wondered why she could never be nice to her mother. After all, her mother had suffered, too. She just didn't understand her mother. Perhaps she never would. But at this moment in time, she thought that that was something she wanted to do. But it was just so hard for her to be with her. She felt as if she were being repulsed backwards, away from her mother all the time. Why did her mother give so much to other people? How—no, why—does such a giving person deny basic care to her daughter? And there was that question again. Was something wrong, intrinsically wrong with her, not with her mother, but with her?

Chapter Forty-Five

<u>Francesca in the Office XX</u>

"I'm not mean to my mother, but I don't treat her well. She asked me if I hated her, and I said I didn't hate her, which is true, but I almost feel repelled by her. I don't want to get anywhere close to her...She admitted to my father hitting her when I was a kid. I hadn't asked her. She just came out and said it, and I told her that I had just figured it out, with your help. Now she knows I'm in therapy."

"The conversation made you unhappy?"

"It made me realize I don't understand my mother. And I don't understand how such a giving person left me out in the cold. Is something wrong with me, Dr. Paul? Not with her, but with me? How could she have continued to stay with that man well into her fifties?"

"Okay, lots of questions. Which one should we deal with first?"

"Why did she stay with him?"

"Okay, let's start there. How would you characterize your mother's life in a few sentences?"

"She saves people. I only need one sentence. She saved her parents from destitution because my grandfather couldn't work. She gave up the dream of becoming a doctor for her parents. She saved the lives of so many people in the wilds of the North. She continued to save the lives of people in Montreal. She saved my student in Florence."

"And you mentioned that in the nineties, your grandfather had a psychiatrist who finally found a medication that seems to work. Did that psychiatrist appear out of nowhere?"

"Of course not. My mother knew him. Okay. So now she also saved my grandfather from debilitating depression."

"Do you think she also sees herself like that—as a saviour, I mean?"

"Good question. It's possible." *Think, Francesca. Use that amazing brain of yours.*

Neither Astrid nor Francesca spoke for a while. Francesca was deep in thought.

"Oh my God. You're saying that maybe my mother was trying to save my father. She stayed away from home because he was heavy with his hands, but she didn't leave him because she had hope that she could make him change. Really? But I am sure he hurt her, physically as well as mentally. Why would such a woman put up with that? She was suffering. If she was bruised, she knew how to cover things up, being super-nurse. But she couldn't cover it up from herself." Francesca continued to muddle over her own words. Astrid stayed silent. "You mean she liked suffering? Or maybe she was so used to it, she thought there was no other life for her. She always suffered. She always sacrificed. Staying with my father was the ultimate sacrifice."

"I've never met your mother."

"But *I* know her. *I* believe that this is possible."

"Francesca, the ultimate sacrifice was not staying with your father."

"It wasn't? Then what was?"

Astrid waited and waited.

"*I* was the ultimate sacrifice. She sacrificed me for him, for the possibility of healing him. But why?"

"Well, she didn't know about the abuse."

"But she left me totally alone, totally neglected. Why didn't she love me?"

"I don't think it was a lack of love. She saw you as herself, as someone who sacrifices for the greater good."

"You mean she didn't distinguish me from herself? She saw me as part of her."

"You did come out of her."

Astrid did not want to leave it there. She wanted to say more.

"But quite frankly, if any of this is true, it doesn't matter."

"It doesn't?"

"Well, does it change how you feel about your mother, now that you may 'understand' her better?"

Francesca shivered. "No, not significantly. Then why did we go through all this? You always have a reason." Again, Francesca was deep in thought. "It does change the situation somewhat. I see her as an ordinary suffering soul. She was a mother, my mother, and not a very good one. But she didn't neglect me because she saw me as defective. She couldn't help herself. She wasn't, or isn't, very introspective. She just lived out her life in her own flawed way. I don't like it that I was the one sacrificed. I can sort of feel sorry for her." Francesca sighed. "It's better to be someone like me who examines her life, isn't it?"

Astrid smiled. "Well, you do give me a reason to get up in the morning. People like your mother do not."

"Who are you, Dr. Paul?"

"I can't really answer that question, can I?"

"I know one thing."

"And what is that?"

"I know that I love you, but not to the detriment of my mother. My mother may not separate herself from me. But I feel very separate from my mother. I can never admire her, although everybody else does. I can't idealize her."

"And me?"

"Oh, now you are going to make me cry. Do we always have to end up there?"

"Where?"

"Where I tell you how I feel about you."

"You often tell me how you feel about me."

"It's one thing to say you love someone. It's another to say you idealize someone."

"Did I hurt you, Francesca?"

"No. You make me realize so many things. And I feel indebted to you. You have healed me. You have touched me. Okay. I can't answer that question. I don't know if I idealize you. I know I want you to be in my life." There was silence for many minutes. "I want you to say something, Dr. Paul."

"About how I can be in your life?"

"Maybe. I know you can't be my mother. I know that."

"What about how I am in your life, now?"

"I love the way you are in my life. I may feel miserable sometimes examining my life. But I do it with you. Being with you this way is my reward. For what, I don't know."

"What about for all the effort you put into this relationship?"

"Really? You mean for the 'surrendering myself to you' part?"

"What do you think?"

"I'm not that sure when I come here, I feel as if I am trying. I just am who I am with you. Isn't it you who does the trying? I mean, you let me be whoever I am at the moment. You let me be a baby. You let me show you my screwy, dirty parts. You came to hear me play Chopin when I was more scared than I had ever been in my whole life. *You* try. *You* give. Oh my God. Maybe I do idealize you. I don't want to cry now, Dr. Paul. I don't want to be a baby."

"Okay then, stay in your chair and try to be a grown-up. Can you do that?"

"I think so. But a part of me just wants to crawl into that space under your desk and have you..."

"What?"

"Heal me by touching me."

"But you're not doing that."

"I'm not."

"How are you not doing that?"

"By trying to be an adult."

"That's right. Francesca, you do try in here. You do make an effort. When I 'healed' you, as you say, you didn't have the strength at that moment to try. And you're right. I decided it was time to give you a rest from so much trying. What did you do in here today? You tried to figure your mother out, and in the end, you felt differently. You figured something out about yourself.

When you see your mother next time, do you think you will feel repelled by her?"

"No, probably not. I don't know if I can love her. I think I may one day be able to forgive her because she wasn't capable of being someone else, someone I wanted her to be. You know what?"

"What?"

"I don't want her to be anything anymore. I have to accept that this is the way she is.

"Francesca?"

"Yes?"

"You are one hell of a great 'tryer'."

Chapter Forty-Six

<u>Astrid and Emma</u>

Astrid could not wait to get into their apartment. As soon as she entered, she called to her wife, "Em. Em, where are you? I need you."

Emma came out of the kitchen to see Astrid putting down her briefcase and then stretching her arms towards her. "Is anything wrong?" asked Emma.

"Absolutely nothing. I just couldn't get this morning out of my mind, and I want a repeat experience."

"Asti, I am not lying on the kitchen table again. I just finished scrubbing it."

"But wasn't it exciting? I couldn't control myself."

"That's the story of your life, Asti."

"I guess that's true. Now kiss me."

They kissed. Astrid was already fondling her beloved.

"Okay, let's get to the bedroom before you pull me down to the floor. The table was hard enough."

"But you enjoyed it, didn't you? You certainly sounded like you did."

"I loved it, Asti. I love when you get uncontrollable. Now, can you hold on for another ten metres?"

Astrid took Emma's hand and pulled her towards the bedroom. They fell onto the bed.

****

When their activity was over, Astrid slipped away from Emma and sat on the farthest edge of the bed.

"Where are you going, my love?" asked Emma.

"I...I...have to tell you something. It's been sitting inside me for a few weeks, and it has to come out. I can't keep it from you any longer. You may divorce me."

Emma groaned. "And all this beautiful sweetness was just to butter me up?"

"No, Em, of course not. I would never do that. I just wanted you so badly, I couldn't help myself. That's just the way I am."

"I know, my love. But could you come back here? I don't just want to look at you from afar. I want to stroke you still. Please?"

Astrid shook her head. "I've got to get this out. It's killing me. It may kill you. I did something which many would say is unthinkable."

"But you don't think it is."

"I don't. I had to do it. It was the only way to reach her."

"Francesca?"

"Yeah." Astrid actually got up from the bed and started walking around.

"Well, Asti, at least I get to watch your naked body in action. You are beautiful to watch. Have I ever told you how much I love your—"

"—Shut up, Em. This is serious." Astrid stood at the foot of the bed and dropped her arms to her sides. "I know we aren't ever supposed to talk about her. I know that. But this is different. It's really about me."

"Okay, no more preamble. Just go."

"Well, after her concert with the Berlin Philharmonic, she and Birgitte were interrupted in the soloist's chamber by a knock at the door."

"Asti, could you please not talk as if you were writing a mystery story."

"Okay. Okay." She started walking again. She told the story of Francesca's fantastic performance at the back of the hall with her father. "The next day she called for...actually, it was Birgitte who called for an emergency appointment."

"I remember. You stayed really late that night. But you didn't tell me. You seemed very preoccupied, but I didn't want to push you. And you didn't make love to me that night."

"I'm sorry, Em. I'm so sorry. I was scared."

"I could tell. Why do I scare you? I'm never going to divorce you. I have accepted your style of therapy. I approve of it!"

"Well, maybe not this time."

"How has the therapy been going since then?"

"Very well, actually. In fact, I feel more and more in control of myself. Of course, you are always talking to me inside my head. And I do listen to you...sometimes."

Emma started to laugh. "God, I love you, Asti."

"Promise you'll love me after I tell you?"

"I promise. I promise!"

"I'm not sure I believe you."

"Asti, stop whining and get back to bed."

"I can't. I have to defend myself on my feet."

"Defend yourself from what? From me? You're not being reasonable. And stop crying."

Astrid continued her walk around the room, talking to the room, and not directly into Emma's eyes. "At a certain point, Francesca lost it. She went into a meltdown. She told me heartbreaking things about her and her father."

"She crawled under your desk."

"But this time it was different." Astrid stopped and stared directly into Emma's eyes. "She was shaking uncontrollably."

"Were you on the floor?"

"Of course I was on the floor. Her shaking caused her to move forward a little bit, until her forehead bumped into my knee."

"And you sweet-talked her in that Astrid voice that could melt an iceberg?"

"I didn't say a word out loud. I was talking to *you* in my head. I kept defending my actions to you in my head." Astrid came forward and kneeled onto the bed. "Em, her father had done revolting things to her, and it was her body that needed me, not her mind. Em, I placed first my fingertips on her head, and it was as if electricity passed between us. She stopped trembling. And then I laid my entire palm on her head and left it there I don't know for how long. Finally, she started speaking, but didn't move. And neither did I."

There were tears in Emma's eyes.

"She revealed so much in that moment. In the end, she moved away from me towards the back of the space under the desk. She brought her knees up, like this, and wrapped her arms around them. And then I asked her if she wanted to be a grown-up and sit in the chair. She made a sort of funny remark: 'Who knew that being a grown-up meant sitting in a chair?'"

"Astrid, you are a phenomenon."

"You always say that. But this time it was different. And you know it." Astrid rose again from the bed and moved backwards.

"Stop, Asti! Stop moving away from me!" Emma got up now and rushed over to her partner. She put her arms around her. "You have to stop thinking this way, that I will necessarily scold you for being way out there. I know you are way out there. I accept that this is the way you work. And probably, no one else could work like this. Don't you know how good you are at this way of working? Your patients grow up in your care. They regress and then they move forward. And what is this crap about electricity! Come on, Asti. What came through was love, plain and simple. That is what you give in your non-orthodox ways. It doesn't matter how you give it. That you give it is enough. No, it's more than enough. You give yourself. And I will never divorce you!"

Chapter Forty-Seven

<u>Francesca in the Office XXI</u>
When Astrid came out of the office in between sessions, Marisa informed her that she had given Francesca an emergency appointment with her at six.

"First I called your wife to see if you were free, and she said you were."

"Who called?"

"Actually, this time it was Francesca and not Birgitte."

"How did she sound?"

"It was hard to tell—maybe a little teary; she made it clear that she could wait until her regular appointment, but felt she had to work something out with you. Her exact words were: 'I don't know how I feel.' Did I do the right thing, Astrid?"

"Of course you did. I trust your intuition. Always have, always will." Astrid sighed and wondered what could have moved Francesca to request an emergency appointment. Then her next patient walked in the door.

* * * * * * *

When Astrid emerged from her office, Francesca was there with Birgitte. They both stood, and Birgitte hugged her wife. She guessed that Birgitte knew that Francesca needed it, and to hell with being discreet. Marisa said she would lock the outer door when she left.

Francesca barely looked at her, which was unusual. She always gave her a sign of some sort, even in her most difficult moments.

They sat. Francesca immediately bent over, placed her elbows on her thighs, and covered her face with her hands.

This is not good.

"Please, Francesca, tell me something. Give me a hint. I want so much to help you."

Her patient lifted her head and sat straight.

"Marisa told me that you don't know what you feel. I am sure you are feeling something. Just start talking and I'll try to zero in on your feelings."

"I'm feeling completely and totally dumbfounded. I never imagined this...Every time I have come here unexpectedly it has been about my father and how he has treated me."

"This is true. There was the recorded conversation and then there was Berlin. Has he done something worse?"

"You have no idea." Francesca looked devastated. "I don't understand, Dr. Paul. I don't understand. Or maybe I do. And this time I'm responsible."

"Are we speaking of an event?"

"Yes."

"Tell me. Stay as calm as possible and try to tell me."

Francesca opened her mouth to speak and couldn't.

"Okay. Let me ask you questions. Will that work?"

Francesca nodded.

"You said 'this time I'm responsible'. Can you explain that statement?"

"When we were in Berlin, when he came into that room, he was himself. He was a bully. He pushed Birgitte, a stranger, out of his way."

"Does he know about you and Birgitte?"

"I doubt it. How could he know? He calls my mother once in a while and shares some information with her. She was just the person who conducted the orchestra, as far as he was concerned."

"So it has nothing to do with your relationship?"

"For him, the only relationship is him and me. He wanted to hit me, and I wouldn't let him. That is what is important. I changed our relationship. He could no longer be the bully who took what he wanted."

"This is true. Did it make a difference to you afterwards?"

"Yes." Francesca nodded. "I think so. Dr. Paul, this is so confusing."

"Do you want to be a child? Shall we start on the floor?"

Francesca thought about it for a while. Then she shook her head.

"Then just tell me. Just say it. As quickly as possible. Alright?"

"Okay. My father was in his office on the fifteenth floor of this building in Toronto. It is not a very new building. You can open the windows..." Francesca was breathing shallowly and noisily. *Oh my God. He opened the window and jumped to his death. Should I ask her? I don't want to torture her. It is not that important that she says it. Someone has to say it.*

"He opened the window, climbed out, and fell—no, flew—to the pavement. My father is no longer with us...physically, anyway." Then she started crying. "This man made his exit with a flourish. He will continue to haunt me forever. I have hated him...and now I am crying. I don't know what to feel, Dr. Paul. Was it my fault? Does it matter? I didn't give him what he wanted once I grew up. When he owned me, he took what he wanted. But when I was old enough to have a choice, I rejected him. You know what? I don't believe he ever felt guilty for what he did. His responsibility towards me was getting me to this stage where I performed for the world. That's all. The rest of me never counted. But this last rejection was too much. Because it showed how little power he had over me. In the world, he has power. He owns stuff. He built this engineering firm and created things we use. Then he started buying real estate. Guess what? Irony of ironies. His lawyer, who knew that we were estranged, and was understanding because he made it clear that my father was a bully in everything, told me that this building he jumped from, this building...I can't believe it. It's too macabre. I own this building now. Can you believe that? I own the building from which he committed suicide. And who knows how many others? And apparently, he arranged everything before he died. The lawyer told me that his accountant said that my father was completely solvent, and everything is written according to who gets what. In other words, my mother and me. I don't want any of it. She can have it all. I just want my life back. I just want to understand what is going on. And...and...did I do this to him? Did I make his life so meaningless because he couldn't control me, couldn't punish me anymore, that he decided to fly out of a window?" She stopped her monologue. The tears were coming fast and furiously. "Who lives to be able to punish someone? If he could have punished me for the rest of his life, would he still be alive?"

"Francesca, listen to my voice. Just take deep breaths. We will answer all of your questions together. We will figure it out together. I will help you. You are not alone. We can do this. Is there anything you want now that I can give you? Do you want to crawl under my desk?"

"I think I'm going to be sick."

"Okay, come with me." They both stood up and Astrid opened the door to her private room. Inside there was another door. She opened it and Francesca ran for the toilet, got down on her knees, and started vomiting. Astrid knelt down beside her. She pulled her long hair away from her face and over her back. She held her head as Francesca heaved. "Francesca, you're safe here. We aren't going to let that man plague you forever. We will figure everything out. Get everything out now. Get all that sickness out of you." *I wish I could tell you that I will always care for you, that I can make it better, but I can't. I can only be your therapist. I'm so sorry.* "Are you finished? Yes? Okay. You wash up now. I will leave you alone and go back into the other room. Take as long as you need."

Astrid rose. She felt unglued. She felt depleted. And what had she done? Next to nothing. She had listened, but she hadn't solved anything. This woman wanted solutions. Could she, Astrid, find them? She went to her chair and sat down. She rolled it over to her desk, and put her elbows on her desk and her head in her hands. She wanted to cry. She wanted to hug the woman who would soon be emerging from her bathroom. *Why? Why can't I embrace her and show her I love her? Why?* As soon as she heard movement from the other room, she pushed her chair away from the desk. She knew that white face that was coming towards her. She had seen it before. And she loved it. She smiled at Francesca.

"Do you want to continue to sit with me, Francesca?"

Francesca nodded. "I need you now, Dr. Paul. I need you more than ever."

"Well, you have me. Without conditions." Her patient smiled. *At least we have that joke.*

"Dr. Paul?"

"Yes."

"Could you talk to me? I just want to hear your voice."

"Do you want to get down on the floor?"

"No, I think I have been down on the floor enough today. I'm sorry for what just happened. I know you think that it's like sweating and it's good for me."

"It *is* good for you, and you don't have to apologize. It's another way of talking, of opening yourself up to me. I want all of your father's secretions to go down the toilet where they belong. He was a very sick man. And some of his sickness you absorbed. But now you're getting rid of it, in so many ways. And there will never be new secretions for you to digest. Think of it that way. And none of it is your fault. He was sick way before you came along. And he hurt people all the time he was alive. So now, when we work through your relationship with your father, it will be finite, because there is nothing new to absorb. Now you only have to let the words come out of you. And I will be listening, as I always have. Because I want to know. I want to know everything. I want you to be free of him. You will be free of him. First you have to go to Toronto and get rid of all that real estate that you don't want. It can be done. Your mother and Stefano and Birgitte will help you.

I know you want your life back. Just make the life you want now. Don't think about all that money. Your mother will know how to use it for the good of others. You can even be a part of that if you want. And when you have children, they will need some of that money, I'm sure. And if they love music and art, you can bring that whole world to them. You can give them so much."
Francesca's eyes were closed. Astrid could tell that her words were relaxing her. Her patient was breathing normally. "Francesca?"
She opened her eyes.
"Yes?"
"Are you still thinking of having children?"
"Birgitte has an appointment next week for insemination. My mother offered to do the procedure herself in Montreal, but Birgitte wants to be where her parents live. She wants her own mother around."
"And when it's your turn?"
"I will go to Montreal and let my mother do it. She wants to. I suppose that is something I can give her."
"Good idea. I suppose she can't do it here."
"But the kid will be born here anyway. Or maybe in Italy. I'm not sure. But I want it to happen. And you're right. I have to use all that money for something."
"Did the lawyer give you any indication—"
"—About how much there was? He said I couldn't even imagine it. So I'm not trying."
Astrid smiled.
"My mother started this project in Montreal, a shelter for battered women near her old hospital, since she got so much money after the divorce. The place can now expand, and she can use the entire building, hire more social workers. It will make her happy. Me, too. It will be her way of getting out all of my father's secretions...Dr. Paul?"
"Yes?"

"You are so wonderful to me. I'm so glad I'm stuck with you. How do you always know what to do?"

"Francesca, I told you. Half the time I'm walking in a fog, but you lead me out of it. I just trust you. You know what to do."

"Really?"

"Yes, really. I am so glad I'm stuck with you, too."

Chapter Forty-Eight

<u>Six months later</u>
<u>Francesca in the Office XXII</u>
"Isn't it great to watch Birgitte conduct with her stomach out 'till here? A woman conductor and a pregnant one, no less."

"The audience just loves the way she always runs onto the stage and up the stairs of that small podium. They love her. Munich is so happy with their Danish conductor."

"I don't know how much longer they will let her conduct. They may be afraid that something could happen. There will be guest conductors for a while, I guess. And guess who's doing the vomiting lately?"

"Not you."

"No, not me."

She seems well-grounded today, but last time I felt something was brewing, as if she had forgotten to say something or had left something out. Come on, Francesca, give me those dirty, screwy parts.

"I've been thinking about..." She stopped. "Dr. Paul, I'm feeling guilty."

"Towards whom?"

"You."

"Did you not give me a dirty, screwy part of you last time?"

"Well, maybe partially. But I don't understand myself. I'm feeling as if I'm in a fog, and if I don't get this out, you'll never be happy with me."

"Francesca, the goal is not to make me happy."

"I'd like to make you happy. I don't want to feel stuck. But I am."

"Why do you feel you're stuck?"

"Because I can't say certain things to you."

"Well, you've only been really ambivalent about revealing things to do with sex and me. And yet, you do all the time. What do you mean by 'stuck'?"

"I mean I'm afraid of what I'll say to you. I'm afraid of your reaction."

"Which is it? Are you afraid of what you're feeling, or are you afraid of my reaction?"

"Both. But I'll never know how you're going to react if I don't say it...Remember when I told you about being with Birgitte in Montreal?"

"You've told me so many things. Remind me."

"It was when I was really scared of my feelings for her. I was scared but not really conscious of my fear. I was living like now in a fog. You know what that's like."

Astrid laughed. "I guess you could say I'm an expert."

"Well, I don't want to be here in this fog, and only you can lead me out, except I think...I think...it has to do with you. I'm not sure."

"Tell me about Birgitte in Montreal."

"Well, we used to go swimming together at a pool."

This she's never told me.

"Maybe I've never told you this. I always wore my bathing suit under my clothes, so I didn't have to change in the changing room."

"Because of what your father said to you?"

"I used to think that people would just know what he had done to me in the past. I mean, I had no marks on my body anymore from the beatings. I wasn't living at home. But I thought that the way he treated me...well, that my body wasn't mine. He controlled it whether he was there or not. I was almost thirty, Dr. Paul, and I didn't own my own body. Anyway, Birgitte did the same. She wore her bathing suit. It was just faster for her, I guess. We'd be in the pool faster. So we swam side by side. We did our lengths. I remember liking that, her beside me, but I didn't know why, or maybe I did…When we got out of the pool and went inside the changing room, I went straight to one of those small booths where you could lock yourself inside, get naked, and change into clothes. Ghita never did that. She just took off her bathing suit in the changing room, dried herself, and got dressed."

"You didn't want her to see your body, your body that wasn't yours, your body that had all those invisible scars?"

"I'd be lying if I said that was true."

What is she getting at? What is she trying to tell me?

Francesca looked very uncomfortable. She sighed. She moved about in her chair. She looked as if she might cry. "Okay, I'm going to tell you. It's a dirty, screwy part of me."

"I want it, Francesca. Tell me."

"I was really afraid of seeing Ghita's body."

Okay, now I get it. We are going to talk about sex today. And me?

"I mean, I wasn't saying that to myself. I was just sensing that I wouldn't be able to take my eyes off her, that I would be staring and staring. So I just hid from her body. I knew it had nothing to do with appreciation of her beauty. It had to do with a sexual feeling. And it scared me."

"Had you never felt that way about a woman before?"

"Maybe, but not like this. My feelings for Ghita, my emotions, were powerful. I don't think I ever felt like that with anyone else. We had just started to play music together and it was like heaven. I can't describe to you how close I felt to her. I had never felt like that with anyone before in my whole life—not even Jordan, who is also beautiful, but her body, her physical being, didn't move me like Ghita's did."

"Do you think that Birgitte felt that closeness when you played music together?"

"Now I know that she did, because she told me when I first arrived here from Montreal, on that first day we were together and were discovering each other's bodies. But I think I knew somehow that she felt it, too, in Montreal. We just understood each other in the music. We didn't say it to each other then. We didn't say anything. Ghita was more aware than I was, because when she came back here, she was terribly unhappy. She thought she would never be happy again."

"And she went into therapy."

"And she tried to be with another woman, but she couldn't. It took Jordan to wake me up, to tell me that I was emotionally gay. But I didn't really understand my body. I didn't really have a body until I met Birgitte. Colin was pleasant, but our relationship wasn't emotionally engaging. And Massimiliano, well, he was just one step higher than an idiot. I felt nothing for him."

"And Peter?"

"He came just after Birgitte. I guess I needed someone. He was okay. Sex was pleasant. I liked his skin...and his body. He was kind of pretty. He made me feel normal, or almost normal. I only broke off with him after I called Birgitte and told her how I felt."

"And Simon?"

"Simon was my gay friend. I knew he was sleeping with guys. Colin was never afraid of my relationship with Simon, although I would never have cheated on Colin with anyone. Colin was good. It was nice to be with a good man. My father was bad, and Colin was good, but then I had to go to Italy. I just had to."

"And what about your body when you were with Colin?"

"Well, I knew he was into my body, but I didn't really understand. Sex was a blur. Of course, it was different than with my father. I had orgasms. But I still felt as if my father, whom I hated, owned my body."

"Okay, Francesca, where are we going?"

"I don't know. I have no idea. I just have to tell you this. I have to talk about sex today."

"You said that it might involve me in some way. What does that mean?"

Francesca took a deep breath. "Can I talk about another incident? About something Ghita said?"

"Of course. We can work our way back to this."

"Remember the first time you met Ghita, here in the office?"

"Yes, the day of the recording, when you told your father he wasn't a regular father."

"This is embarrassing. And I am afraid you may be angry."

I won't be angry. But there's no point in saying that. Just talk, Francesca. You're doing so well. You're not crying, and neither am I.

"Well, when we left...You were amazing with me. You told me about Montreal and studying in Canada. I thought you were the most brilliant person in the world. We got in the car and the first thing Ghita said was that...was that...you were so attractive. And, to tell the truth, I wasn't shocked. Are you offended, Dr. Paul, because the next thing may be more offensive to you?"

"I'm not offended." *I'm fifteen years older than the both of you, so I am surprised.*

"You're sure?"

"Surprised but not offended."

"Okay. Then I asked her in a really normal way if she had undressed you, and she answered in a really normal way that she had."

My, my, she undressed me.

"Are you okay about that?"

"You really asked her that, and she really said that?"

"Yes. And she meant it. I sometimes undress people, too. Yesterday on the street, this young guy in tight black jeans was coming towards me. I didn't exactly undress him, but I enjoyed looking at him from the waist down."

"Is that the same as undressing someone?"

"Well, it's sexual. I had a sexual feeling, and Birgitte obviously did, too. But it seemed so normal to her. I think I was trying to be funny. But she took it seriously."

"Were you jealous in any way?"

"No. I understood her." And then there was silence.

Are you trying to say that you sometimes have a sexual feeling for me, too?

"Are you trying to tell me that just like with Birgitte at the swimming pool, you have had a sexual feeling for me, too?"

"I don't know," Francesca wailed. "When you have touched me or when I have touched you, I just felt understood. I felt healed. And after my father's suicide, you just took care of me. Ghita takes care of me, holds me so I won't break apart and shatter, lose my physical contour. But then, as you have pushed me to reveal to you, sex takes place after that. It happens. I become aroused by her body surrounding me." Francesca covered her face with her hands. "I don't understand. How could I want you to be my mother and at the same time have a sexual feeling for you?"

"Okay, Francesca, I am going to ask you a very difficult question now. Are you ready?"

"You're going to ask me if I have ever undressed you?"

There's that amazing brain of yours. "Yes."

"Do you remember a long time ago, I came once first thing in the morning, and you were coming in from a run. And then I told you that you looked beautiful?"

"I do remember that session. I believe I hurt your feelings."

"But I misinterpreted your question." Francesca took a deep breath. "Then. That was when I undressed you. When you were dressed in your running clothes."

She's not crying. She's not begging me not to throw her out of my office.

"Francesca, do you often have random, fleeting sexual feelings for someone you think is beautiful?"

"Not when I was younger. Not when I was hating sex with my father."

"Okay, afterwards, after you changed your name?"

"Maybe, but not often. More often, after I was with Birgitte, because sex became a beautiful, happy thing."

"Did you feel guilty if you undressed someone? Did you feel as if you had betrayed your lover?"

"Uh, no. I would tell her. We would joke about it. She would tell me, too."

"Like when you asked her if she had undressed me."

"Yes, like that."

"Francesca, do you ever feel that you might betray Birgitte in the future? Is it something you could possibly contemplate?"

"No, never. I will always love her."

"So, these random sexual feelings, like that one for the young man in the street, occur because you are human, and will always find some people attractive and some people not attractive?"

"Yes, I guess so. But you're you."

"And you find me attractive."

"Yes, I do. But I love you and I respect you and I trust you. Is that different?"

"Is it? Aren't you still human?"

She's thinking. She's getting the message. Should I say something?

"Dr. Paul?"

"What?"

"Do you think I could try to lay down on your couch now?"

"What? You want to do that?"

"Yeah, just to see what it's like."

"Really?"

"Well, my father is really dead, and I'm human. I'm a human woman. And so are you. A very attractive, beautiful, caring, gentle human woman, who will not hurt me. So, can I?"

"Go ahead."

Francesca climbed up on the couch. "It's not so bad. I'm not scared. You don't scare me anymore, Dr. Paul. Does that mean anything?"

Yes, it does. I think it means that you are ready to leave me. But am I ready?

* * * * * * *

"Professor Green?"

"Marisa, hello. What's up?"

"Uh, it's your wife."

"What's the matter?"

"She's in her room, probably lying on the couch, but not talking to you. Her last patient left maybe fifteen minutes ago. I think she is really upset. I knocked on the door and asked if she needed anything, and she said no. She wanted to be alone. I think she was crying. I think you should come and get her."

"Did she come in her car today?"

"Yes, because it's a running day and she had to bring her clothes."

"Okay, I won't take my own car. Stay until I come, if you can."

"I wouldn't leave her. Don't worry. Maybe I'll go and ask her again if she needs me. Maybe I could talk to her."

"You can tell her I'm coming. But thank you for taking care of her."

"Bye, Professor Green."

"Bye, Marisa. See you soon."

Chapter Forty-Nine

<u>Astrid and Emma</u>

Emma barged right into Astrid's office. Astrid turned to her.

"Em, what are you doing here?"

"Marisa called me. Come, I'm taking you home. Get off that couch."

"I'm okay. Really, I am. I just had to think, and sometimes I think best on my couch."

"I don't care. Get off that couch."

Astrid sighed deeply. "Okay, Em. You didn't have to come."

"Of course I had to come. You're unhappy and I'm your wife who loves you. Come, let me hug you."

Astrid let herself be embraced by Emma. She tried not to cry but was failing.

"Oh, Asti, sometimes this job is just too much for you."

"But you could call what happened today a great success for me."

"Tell me."

Astrid moved away from her lover's embrace. "I had the feeling, and I'm pretty good about these things, that Francesca is ready to leave me. I believe she is really ready."

"But you're not."

"Maybe not."

"But, Asti, it's amazing. She's a traumatized victim of horrific abuse, both sexual and physical, and you have helped her significantly. She's ready to take her first steps without you. This is the goal. You are a brilliant therapist. I admire you so much. Let's go home now so I can take care of you better."

Astrid just nodded and followed her wife out of her office. Marisa had left. Astrid locked the door, and they went down in the elevator to the garage. She handed Emma the keys and got into the passenger seat. Emma manoeuvred the car out of the garage and into the street.

"Asti, I hate this car. It's a piece of junk. You have to get rid of it. Immediately. We're going this weekend to look at new cars."

"We are?"

"Yes. I've had enough of it. I think it's dangerous."

"Okay. There's a Fiat that I really like."

"Asti, we live in the country that manufactures the best cars in the world, and you want a Fiat?"

"Yeah, I like it."

"Alright. Alright. I'll buy you a Fiat! As long as it's new!"

"You're going to buy me a car?"

"Yes, I am."

"I can buy my own car."

"But I don't trust you. You'll hesitate. As soon as you tell me you like driving it, I'm writing the cheque."

"Please stop treating me like a child, Em."

"Are you about to cry, my love?"

"I think so."

"Let me get you home as fast as possible. I want all those tears for me. I don't want to share them with the world. Are you going to tell me what happened in there with Francesca?"

"She lay on the couch."

"She did what?"

"She lay on the couch and declared that she was no longer scared of me."

"That's incredible!"

"I know. It was."

"But how did she get to that point?"

"I really shouldn't tell you now. After she abandons me, it will be better. We're not supposed to talk about her."

"Do you feel like she will be abandoning you?"

"Yes. That's exactly what it feels like. And it's going to happen soon. I can feel it. She will also be encouraged—and rightly so—by Birgitte to try to be a full-fledged adult."

"But she is. You just support her. You don't infantilize her."

"But I have touched her. And when she was vomiting in my bathroom after her father's suicide, I took care of her like a mother. I knelt down beside her body and held her head. I didn't question what I was doing for a second. I responded naturally to the situation the way I wanted to. Afterwards I wanted to hug her. I wanted to tell her that I loved her."

"Asti, you don't have to tell her that. She knows it. When you love someone, Asti, you show it. No one could miss it. Besides which, you are the most loving person I know. I am so lucky to have found you, to have you in my life. I couldn't imagine living without your love."

"I'm going to miss her, Em. I can't be in her life in any other way."

"Not for a while, since she may need you to be her therapist later on. And you must give her the opportunity to come back to you in a moment of crisis. Asti, how old is her grandfather?"

"Old. Very old and weak. I think he's ninety-six."

"You must remain her therapist, then, even if you don't see her. She is going to need you one day. And you will have to be there."

"I know. But you will get to see her anytime you want."

"This is true."

Chapter Fifty

<u>Five years later</u>
<u>Astrid and Birgitte</u>
Marisa and Astrid were preparing to leave the office for the night when the phone rang. Marisa answered.

"Birgitte, hello! Is everything alright?"

Oh dear, is Francesca in a meltdown?

Marisa handed the phone to Astrid and shook her head to show that nothing was wrong.

"Hi, Birgitte, what can I do for you?"

"Hi, Dr. Paul. I'm calling because I have to ask you something. I kind of have to ask for your advice. I want you to tell me what to do in a hypothetical situation."

"Is it really hypothetical or is it real?"

"It could be real. It could really happen. All of this was supposed to be a surprise for you. Emma, Marisa, and I had it all planned, and then I got scared about something, so it's not going to be a surprise. I'm sorry."

"This is intriguing."

"Well, you know how a few weeks ago Marisa told you that she needed a holiday, so you decided to close the office for two weeks starting Monday. And then Emma told you that she had planned a little vacation for the both of you but said it was a surprise, and she wasn't telling you where you were going."

"Yes, I remember all that. So all the secrecy had to do with you?"

"Very much so. I planned it all. I know that Emma said it was for your birthdays, because you hadn't really done anything special when you both turned fifty two years ago, and all that is true. But it is also a surprise for someone else."

"For Francesca."

"Yes, I want to give her the best surprise she could possibly have. I want to give her the greatest gift—you. She misses you terribly, although we are doing fine, and she is so happy being a mother. I guess you know that Roberta is four and Marcello is two and a half. Well, on Tuesday, we will be in Rome—now we are in Florence with the kids and Veronica and Stefano—and Francesca is going to be playing Chopin's second piano concerto, and I will be conducting, and...and...I know you've talked about this before with her, the possibility of playing Chopin without you in the audience. But you *will* be in the audience."

"Oh, Birgitte, I think I'm going to cry. I can't believe it. I'm going to Rome to hear her play Chopin. And she doesn't know."

"No, because I have been telling her that she has to learn to play Chopin when you're not there. She is really scared. But the rehearsal went great. She was on top of it. But as Tuesday gets closer and closer, she seems to be slipping. She's losing confidence. But I really believe I shouldn't tell her. This is something she must learn now, or she'll never play Chopin, and she should! She is magnificent, Dr. Paul."

"Okay, so what is the advice you want from me?"

"I was thinking that I won't tell her, but on the night of the concert, if I can't get her on the stage or she doesn't seem to be able to perform, then I will tell her that you're there at the last minute. What do you think? I want so much for her to play Chopin more and more, but this fear of being unworthy is so strong in her. I know if I tell her you're in the audience, she will be fine. She will play for you as she has done in the past, and she will be her brilliant self. Or I could tell her now and then we wouldn't be having this problem. I don't know what is more important."

"I think you do know what is more important. Be honest with me."

"You mean...you mean...for me, what is important is that she learns that she is definitely worthy and will be able to play Chopin just like she plays Bach." Astrid heard Birgitte sigh. "Okay, so I won't tell her. And if I see that she can't perform, I will tell her on the night of the concert."

"Yes."

"Dr. Paul, I know why she misses you. You are amazing. She loves you so much."

"And, Birgitte, if it happens that she is sitting at the piano and can't begin to play, you tell her that I'm in the audience, and you also tell her that I love her, that I told you to tell her that."

"Okay, I will. You've made me so happy. You have no idea. And we are spending time with the two of you in Florence as well, going to the museums together. Do you want to meet our children?"

"I would love to meet your children. And...and...Emma is okay with all this?"

"Yes. You should talk to her. She said that you and Francesca have to stop suffering so much."

"Well, how interesting."

"And on the night of the concert, when it is over, someone will come to your seats—he'll be standing in the aisle waiting for you—and he will take you backstage to see us. Okay?"

"That's great. This is all too much to absorb. And when we get off the phone, I'm going to kill Marisa."

"Bye, Dr. Paul. See you soon."

"Birgitte, my name is Astrid."

"Okay. Bye, Astrid."

"Bye, Birgitte."

****

"And, Marisa, you've known all along?"

"Yes. I mean, that's why I told you I needed a holiday at that specific time, so you guys could go to Rome and Florence at that specific time."

"And it's Emma Green-approved? Me meeting her family? Me having Francesca in my life, so to speak?"

"Yes, I think that's what your wife really wants. I mean, you kind of saved the woman, you did your job, you brought her back from the brink. And in the process, something happened to the both of you, something which rarely or never happens—or so far, I haven't seen it happen—you really began to care for her in a different way. Francesca wants you in her life, and I know that for a fact because we talk sometimes."

"So much secrecy, Marisa."

"I know. I'm sorry. Can you forgive me? I couldn't betray her. I couldn't tell you when she called."

"It's okay, Marisa. I understand. Don't feel bad...I think I have to sit down." Astrid took one of the chairs in the waiting room and brought it towards Marisa's desk. "You're right, though. Something developed between Francesca and me, something which is not supposed to happen."

"Who says it's not supposed to happen? You're human. And you helped her. That's what counts. I think you worked with her the only way possible and no one else could have done it, in my opinion."

"How come you know so much about her?"

"I told you. We talk. She told me things."

"Okay. Now I have to go home and talk to my wife."

"I'm sure she knows that you and Birgitte have talked tonight."

"Really?"

"I bet Birgitte is talking to her right now."

Chapter Fifty-One

<u>In Rome</u>
<u>Francesca and Birgitte</u>

"Come on, Ollie, we have to go out there now. Pull yourself together. Play it for her. Put all your love into it for your spiritual mother."

Francesca said okay and followed her out. The audience started their introductory clapping. When she got to the piano, she turned and smiled at the audience. Birgitte ran up the stairs of the podium, also turned to the audience, and slightly bowed. Then she fixed her eyes on Francesca, who was seated with her hands on her lap and head down. Birgitte waited for the nod.

But nothing happened. She waited some more and then turned and walked down the two stairs and went over to the piano. With her back to the audience, she whispered to her partner: "She's in the audience, Ollie. I arranged it. And she told me to tell you that she loves you. Now, are you going to play that goddam piano, or do I have to hit you over the head with my stick?" Francesca looked up and smiled. She nodded. Birgitte made her way back up the podium, faced the orchestra, looked at Francesca, and started to conduct.

Francesca blew the audience away. The applause was deafening. It was hard to believe. She had been so absorbed in her dialogue with the orchestra, with Birgitte, and with Dr. Paul, that she had forgotten where she was. She was glad it was over. But it had been exhilarating. She loved Chopin. She loved Birgitte. She loved her children. She loved Dr. Paul, who apparently also loved her.

Chapter Fifty-Two

<u>Astrid and Birgitte at the start of the concert</u>
"Why isn't she playing, Asti?"
"She doesn't know I'm here." *Please, Birgitte, tell her.*
Birgitte climbed down her podium and went over to Francesca. The audience began whispering.
"It's going to be okay, Em. Birgitte is telling her I'm here and that I love her."
"Oh, Asti, you are incorrigible."
"It will get her to play." Astrid was smiling. She knew that Francesca would be marvellous. And it made her happy that Francesca now knew how she felt.

Chapter Fifty-Three

<u>Astrid and Francesca after the concert</u>

Francesca was removing all the makeup from her face. She had already changed her clothes. Birgitte was nowhere to be seen. The symphony she had conducted had been brilliant. What was she doing? Why wasn't she back here? Francesca thought that it would be nice to see Dr. Paul now, but also knew that there was to be no contact, as stipulated years ago. And the question remained: Would she ever be able to play Chopin without her?

There was a knock at the door. Francesca froze for a moment, remembering a knock that had taken place years ago in Berlin. Now she was alone. But her father was also dead. She walked over to the door and opened it. Birgitte stuck her head in.

"I have a surprise for you, Ollie." She moved out of the way, and there was Dr. Paul. "Emma and I are going to stay out here. This is all for you."

Francesca stepped back into the room. Astrid walked in and shut the door. Francesca stared at the face that had healed her.

"Francesca, I know you don't like to be touched. But I haven't seen you since your grandfather died. I was wondering..."

But Francesca was already in her arms. They hugged each other like long-lost comrades. They both cried.

"Dr. Paul, I can't believe this."

Astrid moved back from their embrace. "You can't call me Dr. Paul anymore. I am no longer your therapist. You are no longer my patient. I am just Astrid now, and you are just Francesca, this incredible, brilliant pianist who plays Chopin because she is worthy."

"Pleased to meet you, Astrid." The two of them shook hands.

"Can I please, please hug you again, Astrid?"

Astrid put her arms around her. They cried some more.

"Shall we sit down, Francesca, and have a little talk?"

"But you're not my therapist anymore."

"That doesn't mean we can't talk to each other. What it really means, to me anyway, is that I can be freer."

"Meaning that I was always free?" The two women sat down.

"Were you? Perhaps freer than I was, because I was supposed to behave according to some code."

"But you never really did. Were you like that with all your patients?"

"Of course not. I think I am different with each of my patients. But you learned more about me than I guess I was comfortable with, certainly more than Emma was comfortable with."

"Oh...But you decided to tell me all those things."

"Yes, I did."

"Did you ever regret that you did?"

"Not for a second. I was just afraid that I would have to give you up. And that, I didn't want."

"How did you know that you wanted to work with me?"

"Francesca, I am a very emotional person. I just felt that I wanted to be in a room with you, having a relationship. And I cared about you. And I loved your brain, your extraordinary brain. Emma would always say that I just loved *you*. That was also true."

"Really? From the beginning?"

"From the moment you refused to lay down on my couch."

"That was literally at the beginning."

"There was just something so intriguing about you. But I knew that it was not good, and I wanted—no, I needed—to get to the bottom of it. And then, well, I used to tell myself that I wanted to clean up your parents' mess. I'm going to meet your mother, aren't I?"

"Well, according to Ghita, you guys are coming to lunch on Thursday, so yes, you will have to meet my mother. But she's okay now. She's in heroine mode. The women's shelter in Montreal is working out well. We're going to open another one in Ottawa, maybe in Quebec City."

Astrid nodded. *Be open-minded, Astrid.* "There is something I've always wanted to know, Francesca. Can I ask you perhaps a difficult question?"

"I promise I will answer truthfully. I don't know how to be any other way with you."

"When you use the word 'heroine' for your mother, is there something sarcastic in that designation? I mean you don't see her the way you saw your grandfather."

"No, not the way I saw my grandfather. I was always very sarcastic about my mother's heroic exploits when I lived with her. I was a teenager, and I often hated her—very often. But after, when I moved out and went to study in Toronto, I began to see her a little differently. I never saw my father. I never talked to him. But I always talked to her. She called me all the time. But my mother is good. She does good."

"She just never took care of you."

"Are you going to find it difficult to meet her?"

"Perhaps."

"But you're Astrid, the kind, the noble, the gentle, the compassionate. I think you will find it in you to feel compassion for her."

"Yes, I think that's possible." Astrid smiled and looked at the woman in front of her—the woman, sometimes the child, whom she knew so well.

"What does it mean that you can't be my therapist anymore?"

"Francesca, I just hugged you and cried with you."

"But what does it mean for us?"

"Francesca, do you want me to be in your life?"

"Of course I do. I would do anything to have you in my life."

"Okay, but you can't come to my office anymore and be my patient. When you stopped seeing me, I told you that if you were to have any sort of crisis you could always come back."

"And I came back for a while when my *nonno* Marcello died. There was lots of stuff I had to talk about."

"Look, Francesca, if you ever need me in the future, I will be there for you, as Astrid, not as Dr. Paul. It will be different, but I will never reject you. You can call me and talk to me, come to my house and talk to me—Astrid, the person, not Astrid, the psychologist."

"I don't care, I just want to be able to talk to you, see your face once in a while, feel your love."

Astrid smiled and reached up her hand to touch the face of this extraordinary woman. "Is it okay for me to touch you like that?"

"Astrid, besides my children, I love two people in this world, my wife and you. You can always touch me. Your touch is special."

"Good, because I may feel like touching you sometimes."

"And Emma is okay with all this?"

"Hard to believe, isn't it? But yes, we are Emma Green-approved. Because I am no longer your therapist. If we are in each other's lives, then we will never be patient and therapist. By the way, when Birgitte mentioned that you would be taking two people besides yourself and her to the museums—and Emma can't wait—and having two people over for lunch, what were you thinking?"

"Oh, I just thought that she meant Cora and Melanie would be visiting. Do you remember the couple that I told you I had made happy, because I had told Cora to be honest about her feelings?"

"Yes, I do. And they are still together?"

"Yes! Cora is doing her PhD in History. I convinced her to work with Bradley—"

"—Magda's husband, and the man that lusted after you when you first got to Munich?"

"Yes, that Bradley. But Cora still comes to visit me all the time and works on her thesis with me. I just don't tell him. We see Magda and Bradley almost daily. They have a boy the same age as Roberta and he goes to the daycare, like our kids, at the university. Anyway, Melanie is working for some firm that manufactures prostheses, so they will not have to live in the United States.

Melanie's parents have basically excommunicated her from the family for being a lesbian."

"So, you just assumed they were the couple that was coming this week."

"I never would have guessed it would be you. And I never expected to see you tonight because we had made that agreement about no contact after you came to hear me play Chopin at the Conservatory."

"My famous conditions." They both laughed.

"So, Astrid, will you be in my life from now on?"

"Yes, Francesca. Yes, I will."

"Can I ask *you* a difficult question now?"

"But I can choose not to answer it." The two women laughed again. *We have so many inside jokes.*

"So, do you always have to get everything Emma Green-approved before you can act?"

"Good question. I'll tell you a little secret. If I think that my 'expert' will probably say no to me, I tell her after the fact."

"Astrid!"

"Well, she's not in my room with me, and I have to make decisions very quickly. She talks to me in my head, of course. Sometimes I listen. Sometimes I don't. But if there is time, I ask before the fact. But more and more, she is supporting me in my unusual way of doing things. But when it came to you, after it was apparent to me that the two of you were going to have a relationship, I avoided discussions about you. Unless...unless...she figured out that something was making me very unhappy. She's my wife. Sometimes I just need her to be my wife, not my expert. Do you understand?"

"Of course I do. I live with a musical expert. And I mostly do what she suggests. She makes sense to me. I also just know what she wants from the way she plays. I guess music can be much more intuitive."

"But I do my job rather intuitively...I think."

"Astrid?"

"Yes?"

"I think your intuitions, your instincts, are always right. I know you have tons of knowledge, and you have studied so much, too, but all of that intellectual stuff just becomes part of your intuition. Your mind considers that stuff without you consciously having to ask the books in your head to give you their answer."

"Well, that may be the case."

"So, your wife doesn't admonish you when you go ahead and do something untraditional?"

"It doesn't mean I'm not scared of her sometimes."

"Scared of your wife?"

"Scared that she will admonish me."

"Does she?"

"No, Francesca, she is amazing and wonderful to me. She always says that she doesn't advise me. She just loves me."

"Astrid, I may have to revise that number of how many people I love."

"Are you falling in love with my wife?"

"You are so adorable, Astrid." She started to laugh.

"Now you? Marisa calls me that all the time. I'm fifty-two years old. There is no way in hell I am adorable! I'm a mature, wise psychoanalyst." But at this point, she was laughing, too.

"Francesca, I notice you're wearing a wedding ring on your ring finger."

"Yes, after my *nonno* died, my mother rented a big sprawling house on a lake in the Laurentians, near to where my *nonna* lived with her parents when they first arrived in Quebec. Ghita's parents came, too. My mother and Stefano had decided to get married there, and since my *nonna* had figured out about me and Ghita all on her own, my mother suggested that we also get married. The guy from the Quebec government was coming out anyway to marry them. So, with baby Marcello in my arms—he was two months old—Ghita and I exchanged rings again. I guess I thought it would stop men in the future from coming on to me."

"Did it work?"

"Not really."

Chapter Fifty-Four

<u>Francesca and Emma</u>

Francesca and Emma were out on the big balcony that stretched the width of Stefano's big apartment on the top of an eight-storey structure. The incredible lunch, prepared by Francesca and '*nonna*', who lived in Italy with Francesca's parents now, was over. During the course of the meal, Roberta had asked Astrid, or Asti as Emma had told them to call her, what kind of doctor she was, and Francesca had said a 'mind doctor'. "Just like Zio Alfredo and Zia Margherita." Stefano then explained to Astrid and Emma that his son was a psychiatrist who ran a detox hospital for addicts in the countryside outside of Florence, and his daughter and her husband were child psychologists who had a practice in Lugano, Switzerland, where her mother was from, and to which she had returned after the divorce. The funniest thing that had happened was that Roberta had asked Emma if she was a mind doctor, too, and Emma had answered that she taught in the same university as their 'Mamma' and taught others how to be mind doctors. "Oh, so you're the boss." Astrid and Francesca couldn't stop laughing after that at Emma's expense, and then Astrid said, "I prefer to call her the 'expert'."

At this moment, Francesca and Emma were looking over the roofs of Florence and admiring the view. Then they turned away and looked through the glass doors at what the family was doing. Astrid was on the floor with the two kids, drawing and talking with them. At some point she sat up with her legs crossed and Marcello crawled into the space between her legs. He leaned backwards against her body and Astrid put her arms around him. She kissed the top of his head. She and Roberta were having an intense conversation.

"Look at my son. He is just so comfortable with Astrid. How unusual. And Astrid is probably using that voice of hers to bewitch my daughter."

"I call it the voice that could melt icebergs."

"She certainly got a lot of practice using it with me. Why, Emma, you're crying."

"I usually tell people that it's menopause, but it's not. I sweat and Asti cries. But she is crying a lot less these days. She is much surer of herself as an analyst." Emma sighed and wiped her eyes with the back of her hand.

"Look what Marcello is doing now. He just turned around, laid his head on her shoulder, and put his arms around her. He's going to fall asleep."

"My beautiful, wonderful wife. I love her so much, Francesca. And you have to know that I'm a selfish bitch when it comes to her. I have deprived her of the one thing she so rightfully deserved."

"What are you talking about? Not everyone can have children. I always thought that it was a case of not being able to bear children."

"The truth is I was afraid to have children."

"Emma Green, afraid? But you...you...you're married to the woman who could have been the best mother imaginable. She's so giving and understanding and...and...patient. Just what one needs to be a mother."

"Okay. Okay, Francesca. I know all that. Oh, God. I'm watching her with your kids and I'm crying. I made a terrible mistake."

"But, why? Didn't she want kids?"

"Of course, and I was unwilling. And Astrid, being Astrid, would never have done anything that she could have imagined would hurt me. She always puts others first, especially me. I took advantage of her naturally altruistic nature."

"Does she resent you?"

"Not at all, Francesca. Not at all. She did what she thought was right for me. She continues to love me, and she never shows any antagonism towards me. She once asked me if she was so maternal with her patients, you especially, because you did not have a good mother, because we never had a child."

"What did you tell her?"

"I told her the truth. Not even having ten children would have impeded her maternal nature with her patients."

"Do you feel guilty?"

"Not usually. But today, watching her with your children, I do."

"So why, Emma? Was it just the fear of being a parent? Oh, look, Emma. Now she's carrying Marcello to his crib. He's going to have a nap, and your wife is presumably going to sing him to sleep. This never happens."

"Let's sit down and face the other way, or else I'm going to cause a flood."

They sat down. "Okay, I am going to tell you the ugly truth." For a moment, Emma placed her head in her hands. Finally, she raised her head and spoke. "I can't share, Francesca. I can't share her. When I first met her, I fell in love instantly. It's been twenty-five years and I'm still in love, the same way I was then."

"I still love Birgitte like that, too."

"But when she told you she wanted a child, what happened?"

"I...I...knew it would make her happy and there was no way that I could say no. I love her too much."

"You're a much better person than I am."

"Didn't you discuss it with her?"

"*Ad infinitum.* But she finally made the decision to please me, to love me in the way that I needed. And she did. And now it is with your children that she is being the mother she was meant to be. I'm not a good person, Francesca."

"No, Emma, that's not true. I can understand how she could love you that much. You are so lovable. The night that she came to see me after the concert and she hugged me, she was a little worried because I have difficulty when it comes to being touched, but I wanted desperately to be in her arms. I told her that besides my children, I only loved two people—Birgitte and her. And later, I said that I may be revising that number, because I was beginning to love you, too."

"Oh, Francesca, you are going to make me cry some more."

"If she doesn't resent you, I wouldn't worry. She's so happy with you. You can tell how much she loves you. And she can spend as much time as she wants with my kids."

Emma laughed. "I'm sure she would love that. And now we should go in there because Asti wants to have a *tête-a-tête* with you. I shouldn't be hogging you. And she's coming out of the bedroom. I think your little boy must have been very tired."

"What does she want to talk to me about?"

"Actually, she didn't say."

The two women returned to the living room, and when Astrid shut the bedroom door, Roberta ran over to her and asked if she would play some game with her. Emma went over to them and asked Roberta if she could play that game with her instead, since Asti wanted to talk to her mamma. Astrid looked up at Francesca and Francesca nodded to her. She indicated the balcony from which she and Emma had just emerged.

Chapter Fifty-Five

<u>Francesca and Astrid</u>

"It seems I have fallen in love with your children."

"It seems they have fallen in love with you. Marcello never goes to strangers like that. He just knew you were the most comfortable person in the room to hang onto."

"But he loves your mother."

"Yes, my mother is an excellent *nonna*."

"I noticed your children, Roberta especially, are completely bilingual."

"Yes, they speak Italian here and with me, and with Birgitte in English, and when we are all together, we speak English. Sometimes, without thinking, Birgitte speaks to them in German, and they understand. In daycare, they learn German for an hour a day. They will have to speak German. And Roberta loves going to spend the night with Birgitte's parents. They are teaching her Danish."

"I told her that I speak Dutch to my mother, and English to my father, and German a lot of the time, and she thought that was totally normal."

"Because for her it is."

"Who's the musical one, or are they both musical?"

"I think it's going to be Marcello. He copies me at the piano. I will play some notes, and in another octave, he will play the same notes. Roberta is much more interested in words and stories..." Francesca stopped and took a deep breath. "Has it been okay to be around my mother? You seemed fine with her."

"Yes, it's been fine. She talks about her women's shelters very passionately. I can see why people are drawn to her and think she's an inspiration."

"Yeah, but you know the truth."

"Yes, I know the truth. Don't worry, Francesca, I don't hate your mother. I may have hated your father—"

"—Really?"

"Yes, because I know the truth."

"I couldn't tell that you felt that strongly about him."

"Thank God there were some things you didn't know."

"You are one of the most amazing people in the whole world, Astrid."

"Francesca! Enough! I was just your analyst."

"No, Astrid, you were much more than that, and you know it."

"Let's sit down. You explain yourself." They sat and looked at the roofs of Florence.

"You saved me, Astrid, so that I could have all this. I don't think I could have survived without you. I would have made a mess of my relationship with Ghita. I was so demanding. She was amazing with me, but people have their limits."

"You're right about how extraordinary a partner you have. I felt like we were working together without even having to talk."

"Do I deserve her, Astrid?"

Astrid put her hand on Francesca's hands, which were resting on her lap. *How many times have I wanted to do this, but couldn't? This relationship is right for us now.*

"Francesca, there are so many things that I have told you over the years that did not get through to you. But now, I am going to do my best to convince you that you deserve each other. You are a wonderful team, and all of your past trauma, which you spent a great deal of time very bravely divulging to me, has made you both stronger now."

"Because I divulged it to you?"

"Yes, because you did. Because you decided to be a person that examines her life, not a person who runs away from it."

"I don't think I could have divulged it to anyone else."

"Well, we know that no one else would have reacted as I did. But I know now that I did the right thing. You have made me so much more confident."

"I did that?"

"Do you know what I am doing now, at Em's request?"

"What?"

"I am teaching a seminar for graduate students in her department, because, as she says, I do it. I do the work. She used to teach it, but she felt like a fraud, because she no longer practices. But I am a practicing analyst—"

"—With a very unique way of working. Do you tell these students that you can get down on the floor with your patients if they want to hide under your desk?"

"No, I haven't yet. And it was only you. But I have let them know that I believe it's okay to do things like that."

"And they don't ask for examples?"

"Well, I told them I had a patient who refused to lie down, and that when she finally did lie down after many years, I knew that she was going to leave me."

"Did you feel as if I was leaving you?"

"Of course, I did. Because you *were* leaving me. I felt abandoned."

"I abandoned you?"

"No, you grew up and I helped you. That's just the way it felt."

"What did Emma do?"

Astrid started to laugh. "She bought me a car."

"She what?"

"Francesca, it's a long story. And there is something we have to talk about before Emma and I leave you to your family. I know you have planned a very long day for us tomorrow, one in which we have to climb around five hundred steps to get to the top of the cupola of the Duomo."

"For you it will be a piece of cake...Okay, so tell me Astrid, what do you want to talk to me about?"

"We have to talk about Chopin, my dear. There is no getting around it."

Francesca nodded. "I know. I know."

Why do you look so sad? I will help you. I think I can.

"Astrid, I accepted to play a solo piano recital in Paris in six months, and I am going to have to play Chopin's second piano sonata and probably his scherzo no. 3. In the first half I am going to play Bach, an English Suite, a few Partitas. In the second half, probably those two pieces by Chopin. The second sonata has the famous Funeral March in it. Can you believe it! It's Bronzino all over again. Am I worthy? Benoit has already arranged it. The date's been set."

"Wow! Francesca, that's amazing!"

"But what if I can't get on that stage? Do I play Chopin at the beginning and get it over with? Do I play him at the end? What if...what if...? What if you can't come? What if you're not there?"

"Surely you now know that you are worthy of playing Chopin."

"Knowing something with your head does not mean feeling it."

"I accept that. And let us assume that I can't come, although I have no idea what will be happening in six months. Presumably I will be working. We have to solve this. Of course, over the course of the next six months, you can always talk to me about how you are feeling, but we have to decide something for the day itself. I know that you could probably play these pieces now. Am I right?"

Francesca nodded.

"Could you perform them in your house, let's say, a month before, for a few friends?"

"You included?"

"I'm not sure if that's the wisest choice, but we will have to see."

"Why not?"

"Because I'm the element that will have to be excluded on the night of that performance. Perhaps you should get used to that before."

"Unfortunately, that makes sense. Although I could just call Benoit and cancel the concert."

"Francesca, you will not do that. We are going to work this out."

"How? I almost couldn't play in Rome until Ghita came down off her podium to tell me that you were in the audience—"

"—And that I love you."

"Then she threatened to hit me over the head with her stick if I didn't play the goddam piano."

Astrid laughed. "What a woman!"

"I know it."

"I want to tell you something now about why over the years you could not have destroyed your relationship with her."

"I'm listening."

"And you should believe me—because I was there through it all. Right?"

Francesca nodded.

"Unfortunately, you don't always believe me."

"But eventually, I do."

"Tell me how it was that you came to see me in the first place. What brought you to therapy? "

"Really? You really want to know that now?"

"I wouldn't have asked if I didn't want to know."

"You're sounding a lot like Dr. Paul right now."

Astrid shrugged. "This is me. This is what you get."

"On the first day that I arrived in Munich, and Birgitte brought me to what was then her house and is now ours, I was stunned at how much I was feeling. I couldn't get over the fact that I was with her after all that time apart. When we entered the house and shut the door, we kissed for the first time. I had never experienced anything like that. I had never enjoyed kissing a man. Anyway, that's not important. This is not going to be a conversation about sex. Then we went upstairs, and since I had just spent seven hours on an airplane, I wanted to take a shower. So we took a shower together and washed each other. I was overcome with wonder. I had never felt that way about a body before. And then we made love, and it was such an emotional experience. When it was over, I could not contain myself. I began to sob. You know what it's like when I cry."

"I do."

"I don't know if Birgitte was shocked, but she knew exactly what to do. She wrapped herself around me and held all those tears. I had never felt love before. I had never been loved like that before. The love that was inside of me came from me towards her, and it came from her towards me. And then I told her everything. I held nothing back."

"And so Birgitte suggested you go into therapy, and she asked her therapist to suggest someone who spoke English."

"Basically, yes. And within two weeks I was spilling my story to you. Maybe not everything right away, but you got the gist of it immediately."

"And over time, did you ever hold anything back from Birgitte?"

Francesca shook her head. "No. I told her whatever she wanted to know. I told you, too, whatever you wanted to know."

"Tell me about the time you told me that you loved me. Why did you tell me that?"

"I don't know. It was inside me. And it came out. It overflowed out of me."

"Do you remember what Birgitte said to you on the phone?"

"Of course. She said that you loved me because you wanted to know whether Birgitte would be home when I got there. You didn't want me to be alone."

"Did you ever think that that was true?"

"What? That you loved me?"

"Did you ever feel that? Or you only found out when Birgitte told you to play the goddam piano?"

"I felt something, something special coming from you. It was a wonderful feeling. I didn't really know what it was. And then you were on the floor with me. And then you touched me."

"Francesca, could you tell me a little bit now about Simon and Richard? Why do you think it didn't work out between them?"

"Simon was dishonest. He dissembled love. He chose second-best, but Richard didn't know until I got there. It was a relationship built on pretense. And he hurt Richard. It was a horrible thing to do, and I haven't spoken to him since."

"Why do you think I believe you could never have destroyed your relationship with Birgitte, no matter how complicated and hurt and damaged you were by your history?"

Francesca took a deep breath. "Because I was honest. Because I could never dissemble anything, not with you, not with her. Because I felt so much, and it just gushed out of me. And Birgitte never rejected me. Neither did you, for that matter. I guess it's easy to tell when I'm filled with love."

"I love that we are having this conversation and neither of us is crying...Now, let's talk about Chopin. Will Birgitte go with you to Paris?"

"I couldn't go alone."

"Will your parents go?"

"I'm pretty sure they will."

"What about Birgitte's parents?"

"I can't be sure. They may have to stay with the kids. But if they want to come, maybe the kids could go home with Magda and Bradley after daycare, and stay the night there. I'm not sure. I hope it won't be a problem."

"Well, Em could pick them up from daycare, too. And if they still like us then, maybe they could stay the night with us, and Em could take them in the morning back to daycare."

"Really?"

"It's a possibility. I haven't discussed it with my wife, but I think I could persuade her. Now let's talk about you and Chopin."

"Okay."

"As I said, during the next six months, you can call me and talk to me when you feel it is necessary. Remember, this time there was no communication between us since your *nonno* Marcello died. You didn't feel sure about me. Now you can feel sure about me. I will not abandon you. You got that?"

"Yes. I got that."

"On the night of the concert—this is very important, Francesca—about an hour before, you call me and talk to me about what you're feeling. Okay?"

"Okay."

"But I get the last word. You have to leave me time to talk to you. I want the last thing you hear before you walk on that stage to be my voice. I want you to feel that I am with you even though I am not physically there. I will know what to say."

"You always know what to say in that voice of yours that Emma says could melt icebergs."

Astrid laughed. And then Francesca joined in.

"Oh, Astrid, I wish I could be like Marcello, crawl into your body, and be taken care of."

"Francesca, you will never do that while your mother is around. Got it? No touching, even, while she's around."

"Got it."

Chapter Fifty-Six

<u>Astrid and Veronica</u>

After all the goodbyes, and telling Roberta that they actually lived in Munich, so they could see each other whenever she wanted, Astrid and Emma went to the door with Veronica. Francesca didn't come because she had sworn that she would not show affection for Astrid when her mother was around. Emma went ahead and waited in the corridor in front of the elevator, since it was apparent that Veronica wished to say something in private to Astrid.

"Astrid, I know you were my daughter's 'mind doctor'." They both laughed at the appellation chosen by her grandchildren. "You have done an excellent job where I have failed." Veronica took time to compose herself and swallowed. "I did a terrible job. I screwed my daughter up, despite having the best parents in the world. Thank God for those two wonderful people in my life, and in hers."

Okay, where is this going? I promised Francesca I didn't hate her mother. But I don't know if I have it in me to forgive.

"So I am thanking you from the bottom of my heart."

Really?

"She's a different person now, so much more open, so much freer. And you did that."

"I think Birgitte has had a lot to do with that transformation as well."

"Yes, they are a beautiful couple."

What are you trying to tell me, Veronica? Is this a simple message of appreciation for my skill and hard work? Why don't I believe you? Come on, Astrid. Francesca said I have enough compassion in me to feel compassionate about her mother.

"Those were terrible years—for both of us. Owen was the kind of man I had never known before. First his business acumen, and maybe even his ruthlessness attracted me."

Are we getting an excuse now? There is no excuse. She does feel guilty. No question.

"I guess I needed a mind doctor, too."

That *is an excuse. I have nothing to offer you, Veronica. Wait a moment, that isn't guilt on her face. That's shame. She feels shame. And she says she needed a therapist?!*

"Yes, your ex-husband was a monster. We have all understood that. Perhaps a therapist now might be in order, for you?"

Veronica smiled weakly. "Yes. Stefano is trying to convince me."

"Let him, Veronica. Of course, I am prejudiced when it comes to the value of therapy."

"But you probably know best. I am so glad to have met you, Astrid."

"Me, too, Veronica."

Chapter Fifty-Seven

<u>Astrid and Emma</u>

In the elevator, Emma burst out with: "Asti, something's wrong. What's the matter? Tell me."

"Not now, Em. When we get back to the apartment."

"It's a half-hour walk, Asti. You have to tell me now."

"No, I need the walk. I need to calm down."

Emma sighed. "Okay, but as soon as we get inside the apartment."

Astrid nodded.

Chapter Fifty-Eight

<u>In Munich</u>
<u>Five years before</u>
<u>Francesca in the Office</u>
"You know, one time my father hit me so hard. He slapped me across the face, and I fell to the floor. Then he kicked me."

"Oh, Francesca. What did you do?"

"What do you think I did?"

"You crawled to your desk and hid underneath it."

"And I cried and cried. Then I heard him open the door and leave the room. My mother was coming down the hall. The thud of me falling to the floor must have woken her. She said to my father, 'What happened, Owen?' And he said, 'Nothing, really. Francesca fell out of the bed. But she's back in bed now. Nothing to worry about. Come, you must get to sleep. You have an early morning and some big operation you have to be part of. You need your rest.'...Dr. Paul, is it possible she had an inkling of what was going on?"

"How can we ever know that? She was never in the room with the two of you. And her head, from what I've gathered, was always a million galaxies away."

"That's true. She just wasn't there. She was never there. She was somewhere else."

"Do you think you could ask her, Francesca?"

"Not in a million years!"

Chapter Fifty-Nine

<u>In Florence</u>
<u>Present time</u>
<u>Astrid and Emma</u>
The two women entered the rented apartment and removed their shoes. Astrid ran to the couch in the living room and sat down. She bent over and put her head in her hands.

"Talk to me, Asti." Emma sat down beside her and put her arm around her partner.

Astrid sat up and removed her hands. There were tears in her eyes.

"I promised Francesca today that I did not hate her mother."

"Okay, that's a good thing, not a bad thing."

"But, Em, I think I do."

"Why?"

"Because she knew!" wailed Astrid.

"What?! How could that be possible? What are you saying? How do *you* know?"

"I'm a psychologist, Em. I'm trained to read faces and the things that are said behind the words themselves."

"Yes, I get that, but the woman was actually never present at the horror going on between her husband and her daughter. Did she know? Or did she suspect?"

"Em, what's the difference? If you had suspected something like that going on, what would you have done?"

"Uh...I would have taken my daughter out of that house immediately, gone to live with my parents, called the police, got a restraining order, and then found the best child psychologist in the business—surely, her mother knew everyone in town."

"Em, I saw shame on her face—not just guilt. *Shame!* Because she suspected. And that would be enough for any mother to do what you have just described!"

"Asti, let's go sit on the balcony now and enjoy the waning of the day in this beautiful city. Come, take my hand. Let's sit together and breathe...And, Asti, you can never tell Francesca."

"It will never happen. I promise."

Astrid got up and together they went to sit on the balcony. They continued to hold hands as they sat in silence and faced the streets of Florence.

After about a half-hour, Emma turned to her wife and asked," What can I do for you now, my love?"

"Em, I've had enough of hate. Let's go to the bedroom and do some loving."

Chapter Sixty

Epilogue
Munich
Six months later

Astrid and Emma were home, sitting in the kitchen, finishing their evening meal. Astrid's phone rang. She got up and walked to the living room, where she had placed her phone on the coffee table before coming into the kitchen.

It was Francesca. "I did it, Asti. I did it!"

"I know. I got a text message from you at midnight saying, 'Success!'"

"I'm sorry, if I woke you. I couldn't contain myself."

"I was waiting for it, Francesca. I wanted to know."

"I couldn't have done it without you, Asti. I know now that you are always with me. Always. Every word you said to me on the phone last night went straight to my heart and my hands. My fingers flew over the keys, and I saw you. I saw your face, your beautiful face in front of me. I will never doubt myself anymore, because of you. I love you!"

"And I love you."

"You'll never guess what I played as an encore, Asti."

"Tell me."

"The most famous Chopin piece out there."

"The Polonaise?"

"Yes! I had no idea I was going to do that. I just sat down, and it came out of me. If I could write about that dwarf by Bronzino, I could play the Polonaise. I wasn't even thinking. I just did it. Who plays that old thing anymore?"

"Obviously, you do."

"And the audience went crazy. It was as if they were starved for it. They wouldn't let me go. Finally, I sat down and played a very quiet Nocturne...And by the way, I am writing a history book now;

not an art history book, a history book about dwarves at court in the Renaissance."

"Oh, Francesca, how I love that brain of yours."

"The CBC is going to do an interview with me in my office at the university next week. The interviewer will be in Canada, of course. And he said he was going to ask me about how I came to choose two professions."

"And you're going to tell him about your brain."

"Of course. I'm certainly not going to talk about my father."

"I hope to be able to see the interview."

"You will. I promise. And thank you for thinking of my children when I was going to be away. They really would have loved to come and be with you. They love you guys. But Birgitte's parents just came into town and lived here. It was simpler...I was wondering if you could come to us tomorrow evening for dinner. Besides the fact that the kids desperately want their Zia Asti and Zia Emma, Birgitte and I want to play a sonata for you. Would you like to come?"

"A sonata for violin and piano written by your ex-friend Simon?"

"Oh, Asti, you always know everything. Yes. We received it a few weeks ago and have been learning it. It's published, and right on the front, it says: 'Dedicated to my beloved friend, Francesca Oliver'. And it's really quite beautiful—melodious, jazzy, and sometimes tender."

"I guess he really loves you."

"I guess so."

"Francesca, do you think you could play the Polonaise for us as well? Or something else, if you prefer, by Chopin."

"Of course, I would play anything at all for you. Anything. Whenever you want. Always. Always. Oh, Roberta wants to talk to you. *Vieni, amore.*"

"Zia Asti?"

"Yes, my love."

"I wrote a story for you and Emma. Mommy typed it on the computer, and we printed it, so we could give it to you."

"Oh, that's wonderful. I want to read it right now."

"You'll have to wait until tomorrow."

"Okay, I'll wait."

"My brother is bugging me. *Certo, Marcello. Te lo do. Te lo do.* I'm just telling him that I'm going to give the phone to him. See you tomorrow."

"Yes, see you tomorrow."

"Ciao, Zia Asti."

"Ciao, Marcello."

"When you come, I'm also going to play something on the piano for you." Astrid could hear Francesca laughing softly in the background.

"Oh, Marcello, I can't wait."

Acknowledgements

A big thank-you to two of my reader/writers: Virginia Fisher Yaffe (*Butterfly in a Net: Memoir of a Maze* and *Carefully Taught*) and Katharine O'Flynn (*Coming Home* and *The Suffragette and the Soldier*) who read the manuscript, commented constructively, and encouraged me.

I would also like to thank the Italian psychoanalyst, Anna Maria Loiacono, who in all the years that I have known her and translated her work, has always taught me the ins and outs of this very difficult profession.